y this l
date.

C000215091

KILL OUR SINS

HIDDEN NORFOLK - BOOK 3

J M DALGLIESH

First published by Hamilton Press in 2019

EXCLUSIVE OFFER

KILL OUR SINS

PROLOGUE

A FAMILIAR FEELING, the tightness in the chest, returned as the car headlights illuminated the brick pillars set to either side of the driveway's entrance. The metal gates hung open. Granting them a cursory glance as she passed by, they looked like they hadn't been closed in years. One hung low, embedded in the ground with the vegetation growing through it. A sign, cable-tied to the bars, indicated danger and advised the public to keep out. It too had seen better days, no doubt put there years previously.

The drive wound its way up towards an imposing building, standing almost in silhouette as the first shafts of daylight threatened to crest the horizon at any moment. Bringing the car to a stop a hundred feet or so away from the building, she sat there, staring at it unblinking, her fingers flexing on the steering wheel as she sought to control her breathing. The only audible sounds came from the fans circulating warm air to the cabin along with the car's engine, quietly ticking over in the background.

Was she ready? She would never be ready.

No light was visible from the interior of the building. It was long since abandoned. The windows boarded up. The once well-tended gardens left to run wild. Parking the car before the main entrance, she switched the engine off and the cabin lit up. Getting out, she braced against the cold, shivering as the breeze blew across her. The overnight skies were clear and the slate grey of the pre-dawn light illuminated the heavy frost underfoot.

A solitary call from a crow broke the silence.

Opening the door to the rear seats, she retrieved her coat and pulled it on, hurrying to fasten it up. Pushing the door closed, it did so with a loud *thunk*, the sound carrying in the crisp air. She looked around. There was no need for concern. There was no one around to hear.

No one ever heard.

Set within three acres of grounds, the building was wholly encompassed by farmland, in its heyday its status unparalleled. A masterpiece of the Victorian Arts and Crafts movement. But that was a bygone age. Now it remained empty, bordering on derelict. Forgotten by the world, unwanted.

The sound of another car approaching came to ear and she turned. The beam from the headlights could be seen first, flickering through the hedgerow lining the main road before it slowed and took the turn onto the drive. Moments later, the car briefly came into view as it cleared the trees before the lights fell on her. The beams were dazzling and she raised a hand to shield her eyes. Glancing at her watch, she waited patiently. A strange feeling passed through her as the car came to a stop and the driver got out, nervous anticipation mixed with a sense of relief. A passing sense of self-doubt flashed through her mind and she dismissed it almost as soon as it manifested. This was the time.

It had to be.

CHAPTER ONE

Tom Janssen stooped and retrieved the frisbee, brushing the damp sand from the surface before turning back into the wind. The gusts were getting stronger, of that he was almost certain, and the sand whipping up into the air stung his face. There would be a degree of wind burn resulting from this little excursion. Not that this was any concern of Saffy's. She was a little way away now having caught the flight of the frisbee to coincide with a monumental gust of wind that carried her throw well clear of his outstretched arm and left him chasing it down the beach.

The little girl hopped excitedly from one foot to the other, flapping her arms above her head calling to him as she did so. Alice was nearby, her eyes and the bridge of her nose all that was visible from beneath her woollen hat and scarf wrapped tightly across her face. She would be smiling, he was almost certain. Possibly through gritted teeth. Taking a measure of the wind speed and direction, he angled his throw in order to gain height but to still reach his target. Saffy's yelp of excitement carried to him as he let fly. It passed quickly as the flight of the frisbee veered steeply off to the right and nowhere near either the little girl or her mother. Saffy chided him before setting off in pursuit, cutting an awkward running style in her wellingtons.

He picked up the pace and trotted over to where Alice stood, her back facing towards the wind coming in off the North Sea.

"Why on earth did she choose this?" Alice asked as he came to stand before her.

"She doesn't feel the cold."

"Nor the wind or the sand... or the rain either, apparently."

He looked to the sky and felt the early drops of rain on his face. It wasn't forecast but with weather like this you couldn't really bank on anything. Saffy appeared, brandishing the frisbee before her like an Olympic medal.

"Is it your throw or mine?" he asked her.

Saffy scrunched up her nose, seemingly deep in thought before shrugging.

"Nah. Let's build a sandcastle!"

She dived into the bag they'd brought with them, rummaging around for the spades and selecting which of the bucket designs she wanted to use first. Alice dropped to her haunches alongside her daughter, pulling the scarf away from her mouth as she did so.

"I think, young lady, it's time we headed home before the rain starts proper."

The suggestion was met with a howl of protest.

"But we've only just got here and we haven't built a single sand castle. Not a single one!" Saffy whined. "And that's not fair."

"What's not fair is working a twelve-hour shift and only getting two hours of sleep," Alice replied with a smile that belied her state of mind. He knew she wasn't serious. Saffy's needs came first with her mum. They always did. Sometimes he wondered about how savvy the decision to leave the GP surgery and return to working at the hospital was. The impact of the shift rota was playing havoc with her childcare arrangements but he understood the financial benefit was a necessity that must have outweighed everything else. Alice wasn't one to complain but life as a single parent, particularly one with a deadbeat ex-husband barely in tow, was a challenge.

"We've got time to build one, though, haven't we?" he argued, lowering himself to the same height as the other two.

"Just the one," Alice said with a smile accompanied by a wink.

Saffy recommitted herself to the search with added enthusiasm, withdrawing a red bucket with crenellations ringing the base and setting off towards the water's edge in search of damp sand and fewer stones. They both stood up, watching her go.

"How long do you give it?" he asked.

"Before she wants our assistance?"

He nodded.

"Three minutes... tops!"

"Then we'll get back to the boat before the rain hits. I'll cook. You can get your head down for a bit if you'd like?"

"I would love that," Alice said, looking skyward and allowing her jaw to drop for emphasis.

Bending down to put the frisbee in the bag, he caught sight of her watching him in the corner of his eye. She was focussed, thoughtful. He glanced up at her. "Is something on your mind?"

"What makes you ask?" she said, smiling in amusement.

"I'm a detective, remember."

"Oh yeah, that you are."

Her expression changed from a half-smile and broadened into a grin. He returned it with one of his own, standing and wrapping one arm around her waist, pulling her into him. Stroking her cheek with one hand, he kissed her.

"Stop it!" she protested playfully before responding in kind. Cupping his face with both her gloved palms, she smiled warmly as she met his eye.

"Now... tell me what's on your mind."

Alice was about to speak but a ringing phone caught his

attention before she could. Retrieving the handset from his pocket, he eyed the screen.

"It's Tamara," he said apologetically, withdrawing his arm from her waist.

"Hi Tamara," he said, turning his back and moving away from Alice.

"Tom, I'm sorry to call you on your day off."

"That's okay. What's up?"

"I have something I need you to take a look at. Where are you? I can hardly hear a word you're saying."

He turned sideways in a vain attempt to shield the mouthpiece from the wind.

"We're on the beach, building sandcastles?"

"Of course you are. Why wouldn't you be on such a glorious day"

He laughed.

"Parking isn't an issue," he said, smiling and casting a glance down the beach. Aside from a handful of people walking their dogs and an adventurous kite enthusiast they had the strip to themselves.

"Listen. I'm sorry I bothered you. I can probably deal with it myself and you can read over—"

"Hey. If you think I need to see it, I'll be there. Where are you anyway?"

The sound became muffled as Tamara angled the phone away from her mouth as she called to Eric Collet.

"Eric, where are we exactly?"

DCI Tamara Greave had only recently taken up her new position and her local knowledge, although improving, was still lacking when it came to the more remote parts of north Norfolk. Moments later she returned her attention to the call, her voice coming across loudly as she sought to be heard above the conditions.

"The old harbour at Thornham," she said. "You know it?"

"Old Thornham Harbour. Yes, of course."

"There's a solitary building alongside the moorings. That's where you'll find us."

"I know it. What is it you've found?"

"A body."

Her tone was flat.

"Or at least what's left of it."

"I'll be there as soon as I can."

He hung up on the call and turned back to Alice. She'd moved closer to her daughter and the two of them were erecting yet another fortification in the little girl's epic building project, the completion of which wasn't going to be quick. As he approached, Alice looked up and came over to meet him. The expression on his face conveyed the message and he saw the beginnings of a frown forming on hers but the moment passed before he reached her.

"Something's come up. They've found..." he paused, glancing at Saffy who was happily absorbed in packing more sand into a bucket, "something over at Thornham. It doesn't sound good."

Alice nodded.

"I understand."

"What was it you were about to say?"

She stood up, placed a gentle hand on his forearm and led them away from Saffy who paid them no heed. He slipped his arms around her waist, pulling her closer, as she turned her back to the wind.

"You, me... us," she said, pursing her lips and adopting that same thoughtful expression as before. "We never seem to be able to get anywhere. Either one of us is heading out to work or... Tamara's calling... We need to have these conversations, you know."

"Ah... the where are we heading, what is to become of us? That type of thing," he said, swaying them both gently from side to side. Alice didn't resist. Not that she could have stopped him, such was the difference in their stature. Tom Janssen pretty much towered above everyone he met.

"Yes, something like that. We should talk about it, don't you think?"

He released her from his grip but remained close with an arm still around her midriff.

"We do talk about it, though."

"Yes, but we never reach any conclusions, do we? Nothing really changes."

"Is there anything wrong with where we are right now?" he said. His expression must have involuntarily implied irritation at the question because he saw a shift in her demeanour.

"No. Nothing at all. It's fine," she said but he thought there was far more that remained unspoken behind those words.

"I sense a *but*."

"However…" she said with a smile.

"That's just an *educated* but," he said returning her smile with a grin of his own.

"If this was fifteen… hell, even ten years ago, then *fine* would be perfectly okay," she said, looking towards her daughter, "but it's not okay now. I've got responsibilities. Things I have to plan for. I can't just be playing around. Do you know what I mean?"

He followed her gaze towards Saffy, seven years old and already acting like a teenager on occasion. He understood.

"You're right. We should speak more about it," he said, tilting his head to one side as he made the concession. "I get it. Really, I do."

She leaned into him and angled her head up to meet his lips as he kissed her affectionately.

"That is disgusting!" Saffy shouted, destroying the tenderness of the moment and ensuring they both burst out laughing.

"And there's another reason we never get to finish these conversations," he said. "I'm sorry. I have to go. We will talk about this later. I promise."

"Tom, it's okay. It's what you do."

It was true he avoided talk about the future. The rekindling of their teenage romance was special to him but there was much that neither of them knew about the intervening years. He was in no rush to experience a repeat of what had brought him home.

Saffy stopped what she was doing as the realisation dawned on her what they were talking about.

"Does that mean you have to go?" the little girl called out, her voice drifting away on the wind.

"I'm afraid so," he said, crossing over to where she knelt and dropping to his haunches in front of her. Her face dropped. "But not before we finish the finest example of castle building that Holkham Beach has ever seen!"

Saffy's face lit up and she redoubled her efforts. He caught Alice smiling at him in the corner of his eye. Looking to her, he mouthed the word *sorry* once again. Alice shook her head slightly.

"You'll make this up to me later, Tom Janssen. Mark my words."

CHAPTER TWO

THE MAIN ROUTE heading west picked its way along the old coastal road of north Norfolk. Thornham was a quintessential Norfolk village, a picture postcard view of brick and flint buildings with an imposing thirteenth century church at its heart. Approaching Thornham, Janssen turned right. Staithe Lane bordered the village, a tree-lined road leading directly to the old harbour, well into the marshlands with its access to the tidal creeks, rivers and the coastal walking trail. The threat of rain had passed with the cloud cover breaking enough to allow glimpses of blue skies and some low autumn sunshine. The wind was still up and everything could rapidly change.

Where the lane ran clear of the wheat fields, situated to either side, the trees stopped and the vista opened up to reveal the flatlands leading out to the sea. The first of two small car parks came up on the left, a jumping-off point for those walking the coastal trail in the direction of Holme Dunes. There were a few hardy walkers wrapped up against the elements making ready to head out. A handful of people were standing near to the police cordon, their interest in the operation borne out of curiosity. Here, members of the public were barred from accessing the moorings and the second car park, the last point before the marshlands took over and became passable only by boat.

The constable standing at the edge of the cordon recognised Janssen on his approach, lifting the tape to allow him to drive under. He acknowledged the gesture with a wave and proceeded slowly, taking in the scene before him. The lane became more of a well-maintained track at this point. The old coal barn, a well-known local landmark, was up on the right with the river to the far side of it. This was where the moorings were to be found, the river curving away from the lane. The tide was out and therefore many of the smaller boats were currently grounded. The larger ones were moored to jetties which were further out towards the centre of the waterway, accessed by walkways, some of which had clearly seen better days.

To the left was an impromptu parking area, presumably where the owners of the various boats would stop to load or unload their vessels. Two CSI vans were parked here along with three liveried police cars. Tamara's Healey was nowhere to be seen but a CID car was positioned at the end of the run. Seeing as DC Eric Collet was also on duty, he assumed they would have arrived together. As if on cue, Eric appeared and Janssen pulled the car up alongside him.

"Morning, Eric."

"Morning. We're just past the end of the road, up on the right," Eric said with little hint of his usual puppyish exuberance. He waved his hand in the general direction, turning his gaze to accompany it. Janssen nodded, pulled his car in to the verge and got out.

The sunshine was pleasant but far from warming. The wind buffeted him as he pulled his coat about him and turned his collar up. The two men set off. Once past the end of the vehicular access the ground leading to the water's edge became compacted earth and grossly uneven. Beyond this the moorings continued and were reachable only on foot by crossing mud and grass.

Here they found Tamara Greave and the forensic officers who were already busy cataloguing the scene.

"Hi Tom," Tamara said, leading the greetings as she eyed his arrival. Dr Fiona Williams, a forensic medical examiner, was also present. They were both standing below the edge of the riverbank in the muddy water which reached up above the ankle height of their wellingtons.

The flash of a photographer's bulb drew his attention to the body. From where he stood, a metre or so above and several away from it, he couldn't make out much detail. The figure was fully clothed and part submerged in mud and silt. From the angle of the one arm he could see, he judged most of what he could see was the upper body. Although the head was caked in mud the hair was long and must have been shoulder length. The hair appeared to be light brown in colour but could easily have been blonde when the grime was taken into account. What immediately struck him was the coat the body was wearing. It looked remarkably light for the season, particularly when considering the location. Anyone rambling or being aboard one of the many boats passing in and out at this time of year would surely have been better prepared for the elements.

"Would I be right in assuming this is a woman?" he asked.

Dr Williams glanced up at him.

"Very astute guess, Inspector. You must be a professional."

"I do try, Fiona. What do we have?"

"Hard to tell until we get her out of the mud but my best guess at the moment is a woman in her mid-forties."

"Any suggestion how she came to be in the water?" he asked.

Both women exchanged glances and it was Tamara who spoke first.

"It's either a tragic accident or something very sinister," she said, gesturing for him to move along the bank a little. He did so, following her direction. This opened up his view of the woman which was far more horrific than he was expecting. Her face, along with much of one side of her head was largely missing.

Where her facial features should have been was now a pulped mass of flesh and bone. The hair, matted with as much blood as there was sediment, was draped across what remained in an ad hoc veil. Tamara anticipated his question. "We think she's been caught by a passing boat's propeller... or two."

Janssen let out a slow exhale of breath as he took in the scene, glancing out towards the horizon.

"How long do you think she's been in the water?"

Dr Williams thought about it. Her brow furrowing as she contemplated the answer.

"That's tough to say at this point. Minimum of three days. The problem is with the conditions. Any body that goes into a large expanse of water will sink but likewise will eventually bob back to the surface unless they're weighted down. It's the bacteria that causes them to do so. As it grows and multiplies the gases and chemicals given off by the putrefaction will cause it to rise. In cold water, such as what we have here, that time frame multiplies somewhat. Judging by how she is embedded in the sediment, she could have been here a while. Just as equally, it could be more recent."

"Do we have any missing person reports filed in the last few days, either locally or missing passengers from the North Sea ferries perhaps?"

Tamara shook her head.

"Negative on both counts. Eric put in a call to the border force just to check if any passengers boarding overseas were unaccounted for but nothing has come through on the wire."

Eric found his voice. To Janssen, the young detective constable looked a little green. Unsurprising, bearing in mind the bloated, mutilated remains they were standing over.

"Could it be a suicide?"

Almost immediately he must have felt the urge to justify the suggestion, although there was no need.

"I mean... she could have jumped from a ship or something. That might explain why no one has reported her missing."

"It's a thought," Janssen said, inclining his head slightly in Eric's direction. "Any ID?"

Tamara moved in his direction, struggling to free up her feet such was the draw of the riverbed. With difficulty, and using her outstretched arms to stabilise her movements, she made it to the water's edge offering up two transparent plastic evidence bags. He took them from her and then used his strength to help her clamber up to the bank alongside him.

"This is what we've found on her so far," Tamara explained as he took in the contents.

There was a remote key fob for a Ford car in one bag. At one end the casing was cracked and a chunk had been gouged out, possibly meeting the same fate as the unfortunate victim's face. In the other was a laminated business card. The plastic sheath was most likely what kept the card even remotely intact. Due to the mud coating the card, he couldn't quite make out what was written on it but there was an image of a landscape printed on the reverse.

"Is there a Ford parked up around here?" he asked, glancing back along the lane in the direction of the car park.

"No, we're not that lucky," she said, an air of resignation in her tone. "The business card is in the name of Abigail Thomas. You ever heard of her?"

Janssen shook his head.

"No. Should I?"

"She's an artist. Lives locally. Quite well regarded as I understand."

"New one on me," he said, looking to Eric. "Any idea?"

"I think she has a gallery over in Brancaster, if memory serves. I don't know her, mind you, but the name of the gallery rings a bell."

"Could this be her?" he asked.

Tamara nodded.

"Can't rule it out. We'll have to pay the gallery a visit. If Abigail Thomas is alive and well, she could be one of the few leads to finding out who our Jane Doe is, unless we turn an ID up in the meantime. No doubt we will be able to trace the vehicle from the serial number of the fob but that will take time."

"Any sign that the body has been weighted down at all?" he asked, glancing between Tamara and the FME.

"There is an indication of restraints having been placed around the wrists. Whether that has any correlation with why she's in the water I couldn't say but I'd suggest you look at it," Dr Williams said. "They don't appear to have still been there when she went into the water."

"Any idea about the nature of those?" Tamara asked, lowering herself back down and into the water before moving closer to see for herself.

"I'd rule out anything as proficient as cable ties due to the nature of the marks," Dr Williams said, leaning over and pointing towards an area of the left wrist with the pen she held in her hand. "You see here, the indentations are almost circular. That suggests a fabric of some sort but there isn't the grooved pattern you'd expect from…" she thought about it for a moment, "say, a nylon rope or similar."

"Meaning?" Tamara asked.

"I'm not a detective, obviously, but if her wrists were in some way bound around the time of death then I'd suggest it was with something close at hand, a scarf or other item of clothing perhaps."

"That'd suggest a lack of planning or an impulsive action," Janssen said. "If so, why remove it?"

"To make it look less like a murder," Tamara said.

"It could still be accidental," Eric said. "Could have been a sex game gone wrong."

All eyes turned to the young man, Janssen raising his eyebrows at the comment. Once again, Eric sought to elaborate.

"Happens all the time these days, doesn't it? People are well into this type of thing and… well… it happens."

Eric's eyes flitted between those assembled but no one spoke.

"It is popular, though," he said, seemingly quite self-conscious with much less confidence than before.

"It's a thought, Eric," Janssen said, clapping him on the shoulder. "Without a missing person's report, I'd tacitly suggest this isn't accidental. Either it's suicide, misadventure... or someone put her here."

Tamara looked around, scanning the area.

"This is tidal, right?"

Janssen nodded.

"So there's every possibility that she was brought in on the tide, not that she was necessarily dumped here."

"It's conceivable. The tide could have brought her in and a passing boat did the rest. If she was submerged there's every possibility that could happen," Janssen said. "But we also have to concede how remote the location is. A car's headlights are quite visible heading this way in the dead of night, which may draw someone's attention; but let's face it, birders will come down here at all times to catch sight of migrating wildlife. A car moving this way in the dead of night wouldn't be too unusual. As a location, this is a great spot for disposing of a body."

"Only one road in and out though," Tamara said. "It'll be worth arranging a door-to-door. Places like this... someone's always peeking out through the curtains."

"Yeah, well worth it. Despite the one road in, let's also face it, with a clear line of sight pretty much all the way back to the end of the tree line you'd have a lot of time to see someone coming. The risk of being caught in the act would be pretty slim," he said.

"And who would know that?"

"Local knowledge would be essential. You'd need to be aware or have at least scouted the location beforehand. That would put a question mark against the suggestion of spontaneity," he said.

Tamara thought about it for a moment before realising the forensic team were itching to get moving and she was in their way. The tide would begin its advance soon enough and they still had a lot to do.

"Eric, you stay here and oversee what's going on. Tom and I will pay Abigail Thomas's gallery a visit. We've got a lot of theory but not enough fact for my liking. Maybe she can put a name to our victim."

CHAPTER THREE

TAMARA GREAVE INCLINED her head a little and subtly observed Janssen while he was driving. He had said very little since they left Thornham which in itself couldn't be considered completely unusual. It was noticeable how much of an introspective man he was, incredibly analytical and self-aware. This was somehow different today, though. She couldn't put a finger on what was on his mind but he was certainly preoccupied with something. Perhaps it was the case, mulling over how the woman came to be where they found her. That would be understandable but she doubted it. For a moment she thought it might be a result of her calling him in but she dismissed the thought.

Deciding not to mention it, she figured she'd wait and be receptive if he raised it. Tom had helped her a great deal since she moved to the area, even though her acceptance of the promotion scuppered his chance of taking the role himself. Despite his protestations to the contrary, she still thought that rankled with him to a degree. On occasion, he seemed standoffish which was in stark contrast to how he'd been when she was there purely on secondment. Not that he struck her as the type to hold a grudge or to take offence. He was far more likely to plough on regardless of what circumstances befell him.

Her focus turned to the brochure that she held in her lap. Abigail Thomas couldn't be found at the gallery in Brancaster. A young woman was there when they arrived, welcoming and enthusiastically helpful. Abigail rarely spent time at the gallery apparently, preferring to leave the day-to-day running of the premises to the manager and her team. That consisted of the woman they met and two others, both of whom were part time. None of the staff matched the description of their victim.

The brochure was a four-page advert for the artist's work showcasing some of her most successful pieces. Landscapes appeared to be her niche, if that was how it could be defined. On the reverse was a paragraph offering a little background about Abigail herself with a professionally taken photograph above it. The lines of text offered little insight to her.

Abigail was a lifelong resident of Norfolk who had received much praise and critical acclaim for her showpiece works but beyond that there was little that she could glean about the woman herself. Studying the picture of her, she considered the likelihood of her being the deceased. It was possible. She appeared to be of a similar age, height and stature, as much as could be determined from a photograph at any rate. How recently the picture was taken could also change things.

The gallery manager stated she had spoken with Abigail a few days prior and nothing untoward came to mind during the conversation. Having been given her home address and some directions, the house being isolated and apparently easy to miss, they left the gallery behind and made the short journey to her house along the old coast road. Their directions highlighted a kink in the road where it narrowed before passing through a couple of bends. After this they would see a house on the left set back from the road amongst a clump of mature trees.

"Should be coming up on it at any moment," she said.

Janssen nodded and slowed the car. Once through the twisty section the road opened up and they almost missed the access to the driveway as it was shrouded by wild vegetation. The property was double storey and yet barely visible from the road. With farmland to either side and rolling fields opposite, it was the trees that stood out and caught the attention as described to them. Between the house and the highway were a number of centuries-old sycamore, oak and elm trees that masked the presence of what was a substantial property.

Janssen pulled the car up to the front of the house and they both looked around. Built from traditional construction materials for the area, brick and flint, Tamara judged it must have originally been part of a wider collection of agricultural buildings. Evidence of arches running along one side, now bricked up, suggested it was once a barn with hay storage above judging by the size of the windows to the second floor. It was possibly part used to accommodate livestock but she didn't really know.

She got out of the car and Janssen followed. Aside from the wind passing through the branches of the nearby trees there was nothing to hear. She looked for a car but couldn't see one. The curtains in the upstairs rooms were open as they were downstairs. There was little evidence of activity. A sign hung in the nearest window to the front door depicting an image of a dog, advising visitors to be wary. However, there was no sound of a dog barking at their arrival which she found unusual.

Approaching the front door, Janssen fell into step next to her. There was no button to press but a metal bell the size of a closed fist hung alongside the door with a clapper. She rang it forcefully. The accompanying sound caused Janssen to wince. She shrugged unapologetically. They waited but after a few minutes with no response, she looked to Janssen and inclined her head to indicate they should take a look around.

The access to the rear wasn't closed off. The only boundary the property had was the tree line that formed a natural barrier between the house and the farmland surrounding it. That is except for the rear. Once they passed around the house they could see a sweeping vista stretching out towards the coast.

"Nice view over Scolt Head," Janssen said as he caught her admiring the scene.

She questioned him with a flick of the eyebrow, encouraging him to elaborate.

"An island nature reserve. It's beautiful. You should check it out when you get the time."

"I will," she replied before breaking her gaze and moving off once more. "Once I have somewhere permanent to live, recruited a DS and people stop dying."

Janssen cut a wry grin. She was pleased. His expression had been stern since the moment he'd arrived on the scene.

"Can I help you?"

The voice came from somewhere off to their right and both stopped in their tracks to look around. A figure appeared from an outbuilding set apart from the main house. It was shrouded in vegetation and it took a moment to realise that it was actually in use. A figure stood in an open doorway. She wore an apron, randomly adorned with paint splashes, some fresh, others clearly built up over many years. Tamara recognised her from the brochure shot. The woman addressing them, wiping her hands on the foot of her apron, bore little resemblance to whom she was expecting to see. However, she was in no doubt this was Abigail Thomas but she looked much older, slimmer, bordering on skeletal, than she did in the glossy brochure.

"Abigail Thomas?" she asked, out of politeness rather than seeking confirmation.

"Yes. Can I help you with something?"

Her brow was furrowed, her expression not quite aggressive but she didn't have a welcoming demeanour.

"Mrs Thomas, we're from the police," she said, withdrawing her warrant card and approaching the artist. "DCI Greave and this is Detective Inspector Janssen," she said, gesturing to Tom.

"I see."

The air of hostility dissipated but the expression remained stern, unmoving.

"And what on earth do you want with me?"

"We're hoping you can help us with something," Tamara said.

Abigail shrugged.

"If I can. You'd best come in. I'm not one for standing around outside. Not in this weather at least. The cold seeps into my bones this time of year."

She turned and led them back into the building. Once inside, Tamara was pleasantly surprised. The creepers growing along the length of the building masked its true size. The interior was open to the rafters, every aspect painted white, and in a rectangular shape with the far gable end facing out towards the sea. This was fully glazed from the floor to the top of the roof line. This was a working art studio.

Several canvases were set upon easels in various stages of the process. One was sketched in pencil or charcoal, another had seen some paint applied but was very much a work in progress. More canvases lay against one wall, stacked side by side. Abigail noticed her interest and came to stand alongside her.

"Those didn't make the grade and are waiting to be reused," she explained.

"But this one is lovely," Tamara stated, eyeing the foremost painting.

Abigail retorted with something of a laugh that became a snort.

"Although art is very subjective… some pieces just aren't considered to be of a high enough standard. I hanker for the days when I could paint what I wanted just for me."

"You can't do that now?" Janssen asked over his shoulder, taking in some of the other works situated nearby.

"I was pigeon-holed some time ago, I'm afraid."

"That's a shame," Tamara said, meeting her eye.

"Don't feel sorry for me," Abigail said, smiling. "I've made a good living from it before I die, and that's not something that can be said for many of those with a more famous name than mine!"

"Fair point," she said.

"Now, what brings you to me?"

"I'm afraid it's not welcome news," Tamara explained. "We've found a body over in Thornham. A woman."

"That's dreadful," Abigail said, fingering her necklace.

"We haven't been able to identify her as yet but she had one of your business cards in her possession. We thought you might know her."

"That is awful news. Do you have any more information than that?"

"Very little, I'm afraid. She's a brunette. Shoulder-length hair. Our forensic officers have provisionally put her in the forty-to-fifty age range. Does that sound like anyone you might know?"

Abigail shook her head, her face a picture of concentration.

"I'm afraid that description could match half of the women I know."

"No one matching the description has been reported missing recently. Is there a friend of yours who you haven't seen recently and may have expected to?"

Abigail's brow furrowed as she considered the question but no name was forthcoming.

"I'm terribly sorry but I don't know what to say. She could just as easily have visited my gallery and picked the card up from there rather than be an acquaintance of mine, couldn't she?"

"We asked at your gallery. The description didn't ring a bell with your manager either."

"Aw... Carol, bless her. She's wonderful when it comes to attention to detail in the gallery but doesn't really have a memory for people. Art is her thing... and accounts. She's very good with money. Something I am eternally grateful for. If it was left to me I would most likely be in a mess."

"Do you live here alone?" Janssen asked from the other end of the studio. He was facing away, looking out of the glazed wall towards Scolt Head and the sea.

"I do, yes," Abigail said, shifting her focus to Janssen and moving to join him.

"I thought so," he said.

Coming to stand alongside, he glanced towards her with a welcoming smile.

"Why do you ask?"

"I'm a detective. Sorry, I didn't mean to pry. It just becomes second nature."

Abigail seemed genuinely intrigued.

"What brought you to that conclusion? You've not set foot in the house and we've barely spoken never mind met before."

"This is quite a remote place to live," he said. "Don't get me wrong, you're hardly in the back of beyond but there are no neighbours for some distance. Some people might find it a touch isolating to be here but I imagine you enjoy it. Is that correct?"

"You're not wrong, Inspector, but that could be equally so were I to live here with someone else. I'm sure you don't need to be an expert to notice I'm not wearing a wedding ring but in this day and age one would be a fool to read too much into that fact."

"No, that's right. It was more your paintings."

Tamara looked around, as did Abigail.

"How so?" Abigail asked.

"You're known for your landscapes, I understand. Much of what you have here depicts that."

The artist nodded.

"They are also... I don't think this is a technical term but I would describe them as emotional or moody depictions, judging by the colour range you use and the choice of lighting you recreate."

"I paint sunsets as well, not only storm fronts."

"And yet, all of the canvases you have discarded appear to be those set in spring or summer."

Abigail's face split a rueful smile.

"Are you suggesting a darkened mind is my predominant

mood and therefore I must live alone? A broken and bitter woman... with cats?"

"Something like that, yes," Janssen replied. "Although, not quite with your choice of wording... nor the cats."

Abigail fixed him with her gaze. Tamara found it hard to interpret whether she was likely to take offence. On the surface she didn't seem like a particularly laid-back individual. The impression given at their meeting was quite the opposite, rigid and cold. Then Abigail broke into laughter. It subsided quickly. How genuine it was only she could know.

"There could be something in that, Inspector," she said, breaking the eye contact.

Crossing to a multi-shelved unit, she pulled out a promotional leaflet, returning to pass it to Janssen. Tamara joined him and the two of them cast their eyes over it. It was dated from the previous year, entitled *The Human Soul Exhibition*.

"That is what I am known for, depicting the human soul in my landscapes. In your line of work I'll bet you can appreciate how the darkness of the human spirit is infinitely more appealing to the voyeur than the goodness."

Tamara looked up first, meeting Abigail's eye.

"To some, yes. Not necessarily the most rounded of individuals, though," she countered.

"And does the average member of the public remember the serial killer's name or that of their victims?" Abigail asked.

She had to concede that Abigail had a point.

"Which is why I paint darker landscapes. The weather, as much as most of us love the sunshine, when it turns nasty it draws your focus. You may hate the rain but we love to see the passion of the storm."

Tamara looked out through the glazing, noting it was the only source of natural light aside from a tiny window to the side that would offer little.

"I would have thought you would have more windows in here," she said, thinking aloud.

"What I have is perfect for painting. The gable faces north. Therefore the available light changes little throughout the changing seasons, maintaining an ambient light source. Perfect for an artist, less so for living," Abigail said.

"I see," Tamara replied with a bob of the head.

"I'm sorry I can't be more helpful with your case. I wish I could."

"That's okay, we appreciate your time," Tamara said. "Perhaps when we can put a name to the body we can come back. Maybe you'll be able to help then."

"Of course," Abigail said, smiling.

Tamara thanked her and then she and Janssen made their way back to the car parked at the front of the house. Neither of them spoke. Once they reached the car and Janssen unlocked it, she drew his eye as he opened the driver's door. She knew him well enough to be confident he was thinking similar to herself.

"Gut reaction. Lying?" she said, opening her own door.

"Undoubtedly," Janssen said with a flick of the eyebrows before sliding into his seat.

She got in and closed the door, reaching for her seatbelt as he pressed the ignition button.

"Question is," she said, "about what? And why the hell does she feel the need to... unless she has something to hide? I don't know what you think but she'll not be forthcoming until we have something to tie her to the victim."

"A bit of leverage wouldn't go amiss," Janssen said.

"A name of the deceased would be a good start. It's very easy to deny all knowledge when we have nothing to counter with."

"Agreed," Janssen said, engaging the car in first gear. "Early days, and I reckon she's withholding, but Abigail Thomas doesn't strike me as a killer."

She shook her head.

"Need not necessarily be one. People wind up dead for all manner of reasons and sometimes those connected to the victim would prefer it all to just go away."

"True enough. Often people choose to keep their own counsel," Janssen said.

Turning right onto the coast road, Janssen accelerated the car up to speed. She watched him in the corner of her eye and he dropped back into himself in the same way he had done on the way out. For a fleeting moment she considered whether it was her company but dismissed it soon after.

"Was that a comment about Abigail or yourself?" she asked, trying to sound casual and turning her gaze to the surrounding countryside flashing by her on her left. Janssen glanced across and she caught a glimpse of his more usual humour in the expression.

"Just thinking, that's all," he said, clearly aware of his mood.

"Anything you want to talk about?"

"No," he said, accompanied by a brief shake of the head. "Not right now anyway."

She let the matter drop. He would talk about it if he wanted to. If he changed his mind, she would be happy to listen.

CHAPTER FOUR

ABIGAIL THOMAS WALKED out with the two detectives but remained at the threshold to the studio as they stepped out. A light drizzle was steadily falling now. She bid them goodbye and watched as they walked around to the front of the house, disappearing from view. A moment later the sound of an engine starting carried to her. Soon after, she heard the car move off. Realising she had been holding her breath, she exhaled deeply. Removing the apron, she leaned back into the anteroom and hung it on a hook before stepping out and pulling the door closed behind her. The clouds parted, sending shafts of sunlight through the gently falling rain.

The wind cut through her linen blouse. The brief sunshine belied the reality of the autumn day but she barely noticed as she returned to the warmth and security of the house. Once inside the sound of a ticking clock, mounted on the kitchen wall, was all that broke the silence. Retrieving a mug from the shelf above the kettle, she set the latter to boil and left the kitchen walking through into the expansive living room.

Her eye was drawn, as was often the case, to the wall opposite the mantelpiece where her breakthrough piece hung. That painting propelled her fledgling career to a different level.

The first incarnation sold for several thousand pounds and set the tone for greater interest in everything that followed. She leaned against the arm of the sofa and folded her arms across her chest as she stared at it.

From the moment the two of them arrived and identified themselves as police officers all she could think about was this scene. The sky was stark, angry, black as night and casting an oppressive cloak over the body of the painting. Beneath the clouds, in the forefront of the scene, was an ageing, gnarled oak tree. Stripped back to its bare outline, the dominant figure was the barren tree rooted in situ overhanging the creek that trickled alongside it. The branches hung low over the water, reaching out across the glow of the fiery sunset slipping beyond the horizon.

There were several more versions of the piece but this one truly captured the raw emotion of that moment, searing the scene into memory as if that was ever needed.

That day started out much as this one, a cold autumn feel with the hint of sunshine and yet more than a threat of rain. The memory brought forth a surge of emotion, feelings she immediately sought to repress much as she had done many times over the years. The rumble of the kettle snapped her back to the present. Opening a jar of coffee, she found her right hand shaking and had to put it down before physically restraining the involuntary movement with her free hand. Abigail felt her chest tightening and she fought for calm in the face of rising panic.

This will pass. It always does.

Leaving the kitchen she tentatively made her way back into the living room, feeling light on her feet, her eye drawn once again to the same painting. Putting her palms together she drew her hands up and placed her fingers beneath the point of her nose, covering her mouth as she slowly exhaled, as if in thoughtful prayer. She closed her eyes and images came rushing to her mind's eye. The excitement, the energy... the anger and frustration. Opening her eyes to the image once more, those memories dissipated only to be replaced by a different emotion. The feeling she feared more than any other. Guilt.

This was the reason why she kept this particular painting so close to her. It wasn't vanity or a celebration of success. This was an ever-present reminder. The one constant that would ensure she remained grounded, knowledgeable about where she came from and what spurred her forward in life. Up until now this was a private memory, her concealed motivation hidden from everyone surrounding her.

The day would come when that wasn't the case. She knew it. Always had. As the years drifted past the focus shifted from assured certainty to a mere probability; and, if she was honest with herself, she hoped the likelihood would lessen over time. Now it would appear the end was rushing forward to meet her. Either the truth comes out or the past remains buried for eternity.

Which outcome would she genuinely prefer? She had no answer. A day of reckoning beckoned where she would be judged. Somehow, Abigail Thomas felt when it came she would be left wanting.

CHAPTER FIVE

"JUST GIVE me a moment and I'll bring up the file."

Tom Janssen glanced around the office of the hire-car company. It was nondescript, little more than a Portakabin in an enclosed yard. Eric appeared at the door and the assistant looked up to let the newcomer know he would be with him as soon as possible. Janssen's acknowledgement identified him as another policeman and the assistant returned to his database.

"I'm sorry," the man stated shortly afterwards, not taking his eyes off of the screen in front of him, "sometimes accessing this stuff can take a while. It'll come up in a minute." He glanced up and Janssen gestured for him not to worry.

Stepping away from the counter, Janssen raised an eyebrow in query to Eric who'd remained in the car to take a phone call.

"They managed to get us a set of fingerprints from the deceased," Eric said. He lowered his voice to ensure he wasn't overheard. Only the clerk was present and focussed on the task in hand, appearing to be paying little attention to them.

"It took a while because of the distortion of the skin due to the onset of decomposition and the length of time in the water."

"How long are they saying now?"

"Estimating a minimum of three days since she went into the water. They're trying to narrow down when the damage to the head and face came about."

"Before or after entering the water?" he asked.

"And, if so, how long she was submerged before the damage took place," Eric said. "It's still looking likely that she had an altercation with a passing propeller."

Janssen considered the information. Three days would put the day of death to be at some point over the weekend. If it was three then she would have gone into the water on Sunday night. If the records of the hire-car company could shed some light onto the movement of the victim then that time frame could be widened or narrowed accordingly.

"Have we run the prints?" he asked.

Eric nodded, looking across at the clerk again. He was ignoring them.

"Yes. Our victim is a woman by the name of Susan Cook. She is local to Norfolk. Forty-four years of age, married and her last known address is registered in Fakenham."

"And how is she known to us?"

"Ah... finally got in!" the assistant said loudly, beckoning them over.

They crossed to where the clerk stood, Janssen indicating to Eric that he could fill him in later.

"It's the right car?" Janssen asked, coming to stand before the counter.

"Yes, it matches," the man said, angling the screen so Janssen could see but there was far too much information for him to process in a glance. "It's a white Focus."

Janssen was happy. That matched the information the car manufacturer was able to provide from the serial number documented inside the key fob. With that they accessed the DVLA database to find the registered owner of the vehicle which brought them to the hire-car firm.

"When was it taken out?" he asked, happy to be making progress.

"It was picked up on Friday afternoon, this past week."

"And you can confirm it hasn't come back to you. You don't have any notes on file about accidents or any such like, contact from the driver?"

The man shook his head.

"No, it's been hired for a week and won't be overdue until... tomorrow. Yes, Friday."

"Who picked up the car?"

The man returned to his screen.

"Only the one person was authorised to be the driver and she picked it up. Barbara Keller."

Janssen exchanged glances with Eric before narrowing his gaze as he spied the cameras mounted on the wall behind the counter. They covered the entrance as well as the man's workspace.

"Do those work?" he asked. The clerk nodded. "I want to see the footage of who picked up the car as well as copies of the identification used to procure the vehicle."

"No problem," the clerk replied, turning away and opening a nearby filing cabinet. "I'll get the file out and while you're having a look at that I'll bring up the camera footage."

Janssen thanked him, gratefully accepting the paperwork that was subsequently passed to him. Eric joined him as he sat down at a coffee table in the waiting area, sweeping aside a number of information leaflets left out for casual reading and opening the file. Spreading the contents out before him, they cast an eye over what they had. The forms signed by the customer as well as the proof of identification and home address. The printed name and signature was for Barbara Keller. The home address was in Lincolnshire but he was unfamiliar with the area.

Turning his attention to the photocopies of identification used to hire the car, he saw a utility bill for the same residence in

Lincolnshire. Dated within the last two months, it was also in the name of a *Mrs B Keller*. Stapled to this was a copy of a photocard driving licence. A brief comparison of the two signatures, one on the licence and the other on the company form, appeared similar enough. Looking at the ingrained black and white image of the photocopy it was difficult to judge if it was a match for their victim. The woman's hair was collar length but straight rather than wavy. Looking at the date of issue he could see the photo was at least eight years old and styles could change.

"How old did you say Susan Cook was?"

"Forty-four," Eric said. "Why?"

"Babara Keller's date of birth has her a decade older than our victim."

"Is there a great deal of difference between forty and fifty?" Eric asked. "Old is old."

Janssen smiled at the blissful ignorance of youth.

"It comes up on you faster than you might think, Eric," he said.

"Are you thinking she used a fake ID?" Eric asked.

"We're about to find out," Janssen said, indicating towards the counter as the clerk returned with a laptop in hand.

Opening up the laptop he inserted a USB stick and set about accessing the recording. Once he was confident, he turned the machine around so that both Janssen and Eric could watch the footage. The time and date stamp indicated it was lunchtime of the previous Friday. The footage was split into three with one camera dominating half the screen and two others recording those entering the building. One was mounted outside while the second was mounted on the interior wall facing the entrance to the office.

Staff members were visible in the background outside, dealing with other customers either picking up or returning vehicles. A woman entered the shot approaching the Portakabin on foot. She moved into sharper focus as she came through the door and Janssen assessed her. She was slim with shoulder-length wavy hair, wearing a light-coloured overcoat that stretched just past the waist. Glancing at the entrance, he judged her to be around five foot nine. That was above average for a woman.

The footage was recorded in black and white but was good quality. He watched as she approached the counter, waiting patiently in line until someone was free to serve her. Two members of staff were on the counter that day but she only appeared to speak with one of them. They exchanged words and set about the paperwork process.

"It was a prearranged lease?" he asked.

"Yes, she booked a week ahead," the clerk confirmed.

"Not a spontaneous visit then?" The remainder of the recording consisted of the formalities of the hire before she was escorted outside to where the car was parked. There didn't appear to be anything irregular.

"The man who served her. Can we speak with him?"

The clerk shook his head.

"I'm afraid he's on holiday. He's out of the country and not due back until next week."

Janssen was disappointed. Sometimes the casual conversation that takes place between two unrelated people can offer significant insight into a person's movements, even if that goes unnoticed at the time.

"Okay, we'll come back. Can we keep a copy of this?"

"Sure, I've made up the USB stick for you to take with you."

"Tell me, how did Mrs Keller pay for the lease?"

"One moment," the clerk said, turning back to his computer. "She paid in… cash."

"Is that common?"

"No, not at all. I mean, it happens from time to time but a week's hire… that's like… almost five hundred quid. Card payments or paying online at the time of booking are more common."

"Would paying cash raise an eyebrow?"

"It might but to be fair, it would depend how busy we are. Fridays tend to be pretty full on, so I'm sure you can imagine it's usually about getting customers in and out as quickly as possible."

Janssen thanked him for his time and pocketed the USB stick. Stepping outside with Eric in tow, they made their way back to the car parked a short distance away at the edge of the compound.

"You never said how Susan Cook is known to us," he said, unlocking the car.

"She's the subject of a MisPer," Eric said.

Janssen released his grip on the car door handle, instead he leaned both his forearms on the roof and absently tapped the key fob in his right hand against the palm of his left.

"That's a possible explanation for using cash rather than card."

"You think she's one and the same person then, this Barbara Keller?" Eric asked.

"Stands to reason," he said. "Keller is a decade older. You can pull it off in this sort of place where they give your details little more than a cursory inspection. How much do they really scrutinise? As long as the paperwork checks out, it's pretty straightforward."

"Stolen identity?"

Janssen inclined his head.

"We'll have to find the real Keller and ask her. What else is there in the file about Susan Cook?"

Eric took out his pocket book, thumbing through to the most recent entry.

"Not a lot, I'm afraid. Her husband reported her missing nine years ago. It was considered unusual at the time, out of character for her. But then, there is a note from an investigating officer to suggest that there were some long-term mental health issues at play. There was no subsequent activity on her bank account or credit card following her disappearance and therefore not a great deal to go on. The file is still open."

Janssen thought on it.

"Any indication of foul play?"

"Sorry, I only got the headlines. Anything more will have to wait until we get back to the station."

CHAPTER SIX

TAMARA GREAVE SAT at her desk in ops reading through the file recently pulled from the archive. The documentation surrounding the disappearance of Susan Cook was interesting but it was her husband, Simon, who'd caught her attention. Without taking her eyes from the page she reached out to pick up the cup from the desk in front of her. Her fingers curled around the warm porcelain that held her green tea. She was so engrossed that she didn't register Janssen's arrival or Eric a few steps behind. She was startled when he came to stand alongside her, so much so that she spilt some of her tea as she sipped from the cup.

"Sorry," Janssen said. "I thought you'd heard us come in."

"No problem," she said, wiping her mouth with the back of her hand and replacing the cup on her desk. Checking the front of her blouse she brushed absently at the spillage hoping it wouldn't stain, shaking her head slightly. "How did you get on with the hire car?"

Janssen screwed up his face, rocking his head from side to side.

"No one we spoke with remembered her from when she picked up the car. The person who processed the hire is out of the country until next week. She's on CCTV though, picking up the car and signing the paperwork. It looks like she's wearing the same clothes as the body we pulled from the water. I'd venture the hair is the same length, colour and style. It shouldn't be too hard to confirm."

Tamara turned her chair slowly so that it faced out into ops. Sitting forward, she stretched both arms out before her and stifled a yawn.

"Tired?" Janssen asked.

"Life in the guest house isn't as peaceful out of season as one might think," she said. "Was she alone?"

"Yes. No one else was with her or appeared to be waiting outside. Not unless they were beyond the confines of the compound, out of sight of the cameras. What is interesting is the ID she used to place the hire. Susan used a driver's licence and utility bill under the name of Barbara Keller. Both are registered to an address in Lincolnshire. Has that name come up elsewhere?"

Tamara revisited the paperwork on her desk. She had pulled the investigation report from nine years ago when Susan Cook's husband walked into the police station to report her missing. Along with that was the case officer's investigation notes and summary of conclusions. Although the case was officially still open, the reality was that no one had revisited this file by way of furthering the investigation in the previous eight years. The file would remain dormant unless a flag was triggered in the system somewhere.

However, a request had been submitted by the High Court, a year ago, for all files pertaining to the case. The investigation into Susan's disappearance seemed reasonably thorough at first glance. However, the more she read the more the thought occurred to her that something had been missed. Not that a mistake had necessarily been made but there were questions she would have asked had she been in charge of the investigation that weren't and possible lines of inquiry that were either neglected or just flat out never considered. All of which bothered her greatly.

In her opinion, Simon Cook was someone who warranted more scrutiny than he got at the time and she felt he had been given a free pass at a relatively early stage. Scouring the names of known associates, friends and work colleagues drew a blank. There was no entry in the name of Barbara Keller. She looked back at Janssen with a brief shake of the head.

"No. That's not one that came up," she said. "Have you looked her up on the PNC?"

Janssen looked to Eric. It was his first task for when they got back.

"Yes, here she is," Eric said, glancing back at them over his shoulder with a look of excitement. "Barbara Keller. Fifty-six years of age, registered at the same address Susan Cook used to obtain the hire car. No priors. No convictions."

"And the address? What can you tell us about it?" Janssen asked.

"It's a farm," Eric said, opening a new window on his computer and bringing up a search engine. He typed the post code into the box on the screen and brought up a map of the area. "Here it is, looks like it's this side of Sleaford. It's probably less than a two-hour drive from here."

"We need to have a word with her. Somehow, I don't see Susan Cook as a pickpocket or rooting through bins for this stuff. I'd guess she's close to Keller. She may have taken them without her knowledge or did so with approval," Janssen said.

"Either way it stands to reason she can shed a little light on where Susan's been all this time," Tamara said. "We'll have a word with her tomorrow. In the meantime, Tom, I want you to come with me to see Simon Cook, Susan's husband. Local media are already sniffing around and sooner or later we're going to have to make a statement with more detail than we've released so far."

"Agreed," Janssen said. "This is a tight community and word

will already be getting around. It would be bad if it was reported before we break the news. Was it Simon who reported her missing?"

"Yes. Nine years ago," she said, glancing at the file in front of her although she didn't need to check. "He has a colourful past. I'll fill you in on the way."

Tamara stood and picked up her jumper from the back of the chair. Janssen fell into step alongside her as they headed out of ops. Tamara spoke to Eric over her shoulder as they left.

"Eric, while we're out I want you to revisit Susan's missing person's report. Double check every detail you can to see if it was recorded accurately."

The detective constable appeared confused.

"But why? We know she was actually missing and not dead. What am I expecting to find?"

"We still don't know why she left or where she's been," she said, pulling up as they reached the door. "Thousands of people go missing each year in this country and the vast majority reappear within the first twelve months. A very small number become victims of something sinister. Most just choose a different path to the one they are on and don't wish to come back. Susan vanished into thin air. I want to know why she left just as much as what brought her back."

"Right you are," Eric stated, turning back to his computer.

"You think the two are linked then?" Janssen asked her as they resumed walking, leaving ops. "The reason she left and what brought her back?"

"That's what I'm thinking, yes," she said. By the look on Janssen's face, he was less than convinced. "You disagree?"

Janssen appeared hesitant.

"Not necessarily disagree but I'm open to it."

"Think about it. Susan disappears without apparently telling a soul. There's no record of her existing after that moment. Her bank account and credit card remain untouched, family and friends are ghosted. She was married with a son and yet she vanishes. What would that normally suggest to you?"

"Suicide would be my presumption. Everyone leaves a trail, however small," Janssen said. "Once we get drawn into it things become clearer. Contrary to popular belief it isn't that easy to disappear in the digital age. Not without help."

"Exactly my thinking," she said. "Susan Cook went to an awful lot of trouble to make sure no one could find her and she pulled it off. Everyone, including us, figured it was a suicide. I'd like to know how she managed it. Let's face it, by the look of her she's not been living on the streets and eating out of bins for nine years. Someone knows where she's been. Maybe this Keller woman can tell us what's been going on?"

"And now she returns. A shot out of the blue, just as before," Janssen said, descending the stairs to the ground floor, his shoes echoing on the polished steps.

"Only this time, she winds up dead before anyone gets wind of her presence."

"As far as we know," Janssen corrected her.

"Right. When did she pick up the car?"

"Friday afternoon."

Tamara thought about it for a moment.

"The pathologist has her preliminary death recorded as on or around the following Sunday. She will try and narrow it down for us but that's what we are working with at the moment."

She really wanted to have some idea of Susan's movements from Friday and across the weekend. What she really wanted was to find the car. The details had been circulated and she was confident it would only be a matter of time before it would be found. If the car was abandoned somewhere then it would stand out. Ironically, if it was parked in a large car park in an urban setting then it may take longer to locate.

"Do the hire company have trackers on their vehicles or service agreements with the manufacturer?" she asked, irritated not to have considered it sooner.

Janssen shook his head.

"Wouldn't life be easier if they did," he said. "I asked that very question. They only do that with the higher-value marques."

"Shame."

"What do we know about this guy we're going to visit? Her husband, Simon, isn't it?"

"Something of a chancer by the look of his record."

"Known to us?"

"Not recently but certainly in the past," she said, glancing sideways at him as they walked. They were leaving the station and once outside they were struck by the cold breeze carrying inland from the coast. Tamara was dressed in a thick woollen jumper but it offered scant protection against the wind. Janssen noticed her shiver and looked about to offer her his coat. She could do without such gallantry. Her absentmindedness was something she'd repeatedly decided to work on without achieving any measurable level of success.

"Here, have my—"

"No," she said firmly without looking in his direction. In the corner of her eye she saw a micro reaction from him. She had been curt, it was true. "I have a coat in the car if needed." She didn't. She had left it at home, draped over the armchair in front of the fireplace of her bedroom.

"Okay. Do you want to drive or shall I?"

"We'll take yours," she said. "Then I can fill you in on Simon Cook's chequered past as we go."

They reached the car and Janssen unlocked it. The two of them got in and as soon as the engine started up she was reaching for the heated seat controls and setting them to the maximum. If Janssen noticed, he didn't comment.

"You said he was known to us," Janssen asked as he put the car in gear and set off. Fakenham was roughly a half-hour drive at this time of the day, more in the height of the tourist season.

"Multiple arrests on his file. He was convicted of affray on one occasion and given a suspended sentence which, fortunately for him, expired before his next arrest. That was for assault but the case never made it to court as the witness withdrew their statement."

"So he's a warm and cuddly guy then?" Janssen said with an accompanying smile.

"Likes a good time as well by all accounts," she said, tilting her head to one side and returning the smile. "He has cautions for possession and was arrested on suspicion of intent to supply too. Did a short stretch for burglary as well."

"I can see a few reasons why Susan might not choose to stick around."

"Yeah. Quite a catch," she said.

Conversation dropped and Tamara spent the time contemplating Susan's motivation to leave. She wouldn't be the first to think that getting away would offer her a better future. She couldn't be too judgemental bearing in mind her own situation. Richard, her fiancé until very recently, didn't take too kindly to her decision to leave. And she was up front and honest with him, to a point anyway. She couldn't see herself as the mummy type, marrying a man whom she loved... in a way... but not enough to honestly commit herself to spending the rest of her life with and certainly not if it meant bringing a child into the world.

The expectation that she would give up her career was enough to set the alarm bells ringing. She should have realised sooner, acted faster. That was certainly true. Somehow she'd allowed herself to be railroaded into a future that she didn't see as hers. It was Richard's. It was his family's, not hers. She was determined not to be so passive in the future. Most nights she still thought about what she'd done, how she had hurt him. Every now and then a doubt would creep in before she caught herself and discarded it.

Looking across at Janssen, his expression was stern. He had something on his mind as well. In many ways they were very similar. Neither of them was particularly good at articulating their thoughts when it came down to a personal level.

Perhaps she had judged Tom's offer of a coat in the context of what was happening in her wider personal life. It was an overreaction on her part to what was a genuine act of kindness.

"Thanks for the offer of the coat," she said quietly, glancing towards him. He looked over and she smiled.

"You are welcome," he said, returning the smile. "But to be honest, I'm pleased you knocked me back."

"Why?"

"Because I'm cold."

CHAPTER SEVEN

THE ADDRESS they held on record for Simon Cook was a campsite in the vicinity of Fakenham, the largest market town in north Norfolk. Barely ten miles from the coast it was popular with both tourists and locals alike. As he drove them, Janssen's thoughts were dominated by Alice and Saffy. Although they never got to finish their conversation, he was well aware of what Alice had been referring to. Occasionally she would drop lines into conversation while they were on a day out or over dinner when it was just the two of them, on the days when Saffy's father was interested enough to spend time with his daughter. He would almost always angle the conversation away and onto a different subject or contribute as little as possible, thereby stifling the conversation.

Thinking about it, this could easily be perceived as him being uncaring or detached. He wasn't. Far from it. He did understand that the time for being so casual about the future was coming to an end. He could see it clearly. The question he had in his mind was what should he do about it? The thought of both of them no longer present in his life was a vision he couldn't contemplate. However, the alternative was almost as frightening to him.

"Tom! That was it, wasn't it?" Tamara said, looking over her shoulder at the turning they'd just passed.

He swore under his breath, slowing the car and indicating to pull off the road and into a lay-by ahead. The traffic behind passed them and he quickly turned the car around and set off back in the other direction.

"Sorry. I was miles away then."

Tamara didn't comment but he felt her gaze upon him as he took the right turn through the gates and onto the campsite. The infrastructure was modest but organised. There was a line of buildings arranged in a horseshoe configuration. The first of which was an office. By the look of it the others were a mixture of utility facilities, a small on-site convenience store alongside a launderette and a detached shower block nearby.

Posters were displayed in the shop window listing available entertainments alongside scheduled activities for various age groups. Despite the autumn chill there still appeared to be a number of pitches in use. The way markers were clearly denoted and as Janssen stepped out of the car he cast an eye over the surrounding area.

Much of the site was closed off now. The fields, still laid to grass and used as pitches were well maintained which was necessary in light of how much traffic would come their way in peak season. The comings and goings of vehicles and their caravans would churn the ground up if it wasn't suitably prepared. A few unattended tents could be seen in one of the fields that wasn't gated off – hardy travellers in his estimation. The days and nights spent on the boat at this time of year could be cold until he got the stove going and, even then, it wasn't exactly comfortable. The prospect of spending time under canvas in the autumn wasn't appealing.

There was no one around who looked like a site employee. Presumably the campsite was operated by a skeleton crew during the quieter periods of the year with seasonal workers pitching in when trade picked up in spring and summer.

"The office looks closed," Tamara said.

He looked across. The interior was shrouded in darkness.

"I'll check."

Making his way over, he tried the door. It was locked and he peered through the window but nothing moved inside. Looking to his left, he indicated the nearby buildings and Tamara nodded and moved to join him. The next building was a self-service launderette and the sound of machines running inside came to ear. As they entered a lady appeared from a back room, smiling as she caught sight of them.

"Hello," Tamara said. "We're looking for Simon Cook. Is he around?"

"Simon, yes. You'll find him cleaning the shower block next door," she replied, eyeing them warily as the smile faded slightly. "Is everything all right?"

"Yes, I'm sure. We just need to speak with him," Tamara said.

Janssen turned and Tamara followed him out. The lady continued on with what she was doing but she kept an eye on them as they left.

"Can you take the lead with him?" Tamara asked once they were out of earshot.

"Yes, of course. Why?"

"I just want to watch."

He figured there would be logic behind her decision. She had already been through Simon's file and maybe didn't want her preconception to cloud the direction of the conversation. The shower block was distinct from the launderette. It was purpose built, split with the male block to the left. A collapsible sign was set up at the entrance to the female block advising of cleaning in progress. Walking in, they found a man running a mop across the floor.

"Simon Cook?" Janssen asked.

He glanced up from his activity, his eyes narrowing. Janssen took out his warrant card.

"Yeah. What can I do for you?"

"We would like a word, Mr Cook. Is there somewhere that we can talk?"

Simon Cook put the mop back into the bucket and wheeled it across to the wall, resting the handle against it so it didn't topple over. He ran the back of his hand across the base of his nose, sniffing loudly as he did so.

"Sounds important," Cook said, glancing between them.

"I'm afraid it is, Mr Cook. It's about your wife, Susan."

His face dropped momentarily, his mouth cracking open. Whatever he expected them to say, evidently they'd caught him by surprise.

"Susan?" he asked quietly, regaining a little composure but still looking lost. "What about her?"

"Is there somewhere we can talk in private?" Tamara reiterated.

Cook appeared confused before shrugging and gesturing for them to head back the way they'd come.

"We can go to my place. It's just across the way," he said, pointing beyond them as if they were capable of seeing through a brick wall.

Back outside they were met by the lady from the launderette, a concerned expression etched on her face.

"Is everything okay, Simon?"

"Er... it'll be fine, Margaret. Don't worry," he replied as they walked past her. "They're with the police. I'll not be long."

They crossed a path and he led them in the direction of some static caravans. Most of the units had a raised deck around the exterior, some with barbecues or patio furniture outside. Cook stopped at the second one they came to, climbing the steps to the door. It was unlocked. Pulling the door open, he ushered them inside, nervously glancing back towards the shower block where the ever-watchful Margaret was observing them.

"You'll have to excuse the mess," Cook said, as they followed him inside. Gathering together a number of items of clothing scattered across the sofa, he walked past them, depositing the collection on one of the chairs at the dining table.

Janssen looked around. They were in a living space that consisted of a kitchenette and a dining area at one end with a corner sofa arranged around a television at the other. Further into the caravan was a narrow corridor with three doors off it, presumably granting access to two bedrooms and a bathroom. To some this would be considered cramped but when compared with his own living area on the boat it was ample.

After another swift intervention to make the caravan more presentable, Simon Cook slowed and glanced between them. They were both standing in the middle of the caravan, waiting for him. Cook offered them a seat and they chose to sit on the sofa. He remained standing, folding his arms across his chest and leaning against the kitchen counter.

"Do you live here all year round?" Janssen asked.

"I do, yeah. It comes with the job."

"What is it you do?" Tamara asked.

"A bit of everything to be fair," he said. "General maintenance, groundworks... whatever. It's steady money and as I say, we get to live here as part of the deal."

"We?" Janssen asked.

"Me and my son, Connor," Cook said, flitting his attention between them and the floor before taking a deep breath and looking to Janssen. "You said this was about Susan? I thought you had already handed the files over to the court. That's what they told me anyway."

Janssen exchanged a glance with Tamara and she nodded.

"That's what you're here for isn't it," Cook said, looking surprised. "The declaration of death application? Look, I know I'm behind but with work and everything it's been manic. I didn't think you'd be chasing me up."

"We're here about your wife, but not in relation to the court application," Janssen said. "There's no easy way to say this but we found a body and we believe it to be that of your wife, Susan."

Janssen watched closely for a reaction. Simon Cook stood stock still, his face expressionless, eyes staring straight ahead. It was as if the words hadn't registered.

"I... don't understand. You've found her... after all this time? Are you sure?"

"Her fingerprints are on file and we are reasonably certain, yes."

Simon frowned, his brow burrowing deeply as he looked to the floor once more, closing his eyes and shaking his head in what appeared to be an involuntary action. Freeing one hand, he scratched at the side of his scalp, his eyes narrowed but his expression remaining unchanged.

"I... but... where was she? Where did you find her?" Simon said eventually, meeting his eye.

"Two fishermen found her at Thornham, yesterday, when they returned from a night-time sea trip."

"In the water? That's where they found her?" Janssen nodded.

"How did she end up there?"

"We're still trying to figure that out," Janssen said.

"Susan was frightened of water, always had been ever since I knew her. She would steer well clear of it. Couldn't swim. Absolutely terrified, she was. I don't know why she'd go near it."

"As I said, we're still trying to figure it out," Janssen said. "Can we ask you a few questions about when your wife disappeared?"

Simon appeared to snap back into the present. His eyes became more attentive as he dropped the faraway look he'd carried for the past few minutes.

"Again? Don't you already have it down in your files?"

Janssen shrugged.

"All written down a long time ago. Sometimes it pays to hear it first-hand."

Simon Cook blew out his cheeks.

"If you like. What do you want to know?"

"What was she like, Susan, as a person?"

"She was lovely. A great mum and wife. Must admit, I didn't appreciate that at the time. I wasn't exactly the best husband a woman could hope for, you know."

"Why not?"

"Oh, you know. I was thirty going on seventeen, still trying to live the same life I did back in the day. I was a crap husband and a piss-poor father. It took me a lot of years to come to terms with that... same as it did to accept she wasn't coming back."

Janssen thought about his next question. He looked to Tamara but she still didn't seem inclined to ask anything, so he went with his instinct.

"Susan's car was found out near the cliffs at Sheringham, wasn't it? What did you think when our colleagues told you that?"

Simon shook his head, absently rubbing at the back of his neck and staring out of the nearest window before answering.

"I didn't believe what everyone else kept telling me."

"Which was?" Janssen asked.

"That she'd topped herself. She'd prefer to make me suffer rather than check out."

"That's an odd response, if you don't mind me saying so," Tamara said. "What makes you say that?"

Cook looked over to her and snorted with derision.

"Look... I'm the first to admit I could be a bit of an arse, you know. But she was something else. Don't get me wrong. I said she was lovely and she was. But there were two Susans. That one and the other... attention seeking, manipulative... always moaning or crying about something or other. She was up and down all the time and I was the one who got it. Is it any wonder I used to go off on a bender having to put up with that day after day? Not that she wasn't capable of faking something... for the attention, I mean."

"For example?" Janssen asked.

"The whole leaving the car near to the cliffs thing. It wouldn't have been the first time she made it look like she was trying to do herself harm. She'd had a half-hearted go at it twice before. Both times I found her just as I was supposed to. The first she was sitting in the bath with a razor blade and a bottle of vodka. She was hammered, making threats. The water was stone cold. Must have been sitting there waiting for me to get home. The last time I caught her having downed a bottle of pills."

"There's no record of these events in the file or anything to say she was admitted to hospital," Tamara said.

"Wouldn't go, would she!" Cook replied, his tone turning aggressive or, Janssen considered, echoing his frustration at the memory. "She puked shortly after. The pills made her sick and it looked like a lot of them hadn't been digested yet. I did an internet search and what she took wasn't going to kill her. She was taking them for her acne and in the end she was just ill for a couple of days. She could have downed twice as many and it wouldn't have had any long-term effect... but they did make her ill, that's for sure. I never really knew if she was really serious but... when it comes down to it, if you really want to do yourself in, you will won't you. She never did."

"Did she have a history of depression?" Janssen asked.

"Oh, yeah. I'd say so. Who wouldn't with her background? Abandoned as a kid, no family, growing up in care. I know it doesn't mean you can't do all right in life but she was behind from the start. She got dealt a crappy hand. More so when she met me, let's be honest about it."

Janssen looked around.

"You're working, doing okay. You're raising a son."

"Susan leaving made me wake up. I had to deal with it. I couldn't carry on living the way I was... the drinking, the drugs... I had a kid to think about... along with everything else."

Simon turned away from them and momentarily stared out

of the window before glancing at the clock on the wall. He shook his head.

"Connor will be home from school soon. I don't know how he will take this. The boy doesn't remember much about his mum. He was only six when she left..." He let the words drift away, shaking his head. "You know, died, whatever. It was years before I could accept she was gone." He turned back to face them, his eyes watering as he spoke. "I told friends she'd be back, that she just needed some space but they said I had to move on. I mean, they were right. Living with me was a bit rough but I always thought she would walk back in some day. That is until a couple of years after she went. Then, somehow, I realised everyone was right all along and she was dead. I could feel it."

Simon placed a closed fist on his chest for emphasis.

"I knew it in here."

"I don't think you understand," Janssen said.

"No, I don't," Simon interrupted him. "All this time she was so close and we didn't find her. How did she wind up out in Thornham when her car was left over in Sheringham?"

"We believe that Susan died at some point over this past weekend."

Simon looked at him with a blank expression. He was no stranger to the police, so he may have an idea how to act a part and be deceptive but his response seemed genuine enough.

"She was alive... all this time?" Simon said, his expression shifting. "Where? Where has she been?"

He looked between the two of them, seeking an answer.

"We don't know yet. To your knowledge, did Susan have any friends or relatives living in the Lincolnshire area?"

"No. I told you. She didn't have any family."

"What about friends?"

"No! Not anyone of any note. She had a couple of friends around here she used to talk about. Sarah was one."

"Sarah?" Janssen asked.

"Caseley. I never spent any real time with her but Sooz used to talk about her quite often. They went back a bit."

"And the other?"

"Tara... something or other. Like I said, I don't really know either of them. Apart from that, Sooz kept to herself. She wasn't really the sociable type, you know. Certainly didn't know anyone outside of the county. I don't remember her ever leaving Norfolk, let alone Lincolnshire."

Janssen made a note. A moment passed and there was a visible shift in Cook's demeanour. Up until now he was calm and helpful if a little bemused by events but the news appeared to be sinking in now and he was developing questions of his own.

"So, she's been alive all this time!" Simon repeated, a statement rather than a question, sounding incredulous. "That..." he didn't finish the comment about her, catching himself in time but from his tone and the accompanying glare in his expression it was unlikely to be a positive statement. His anger was rising, thinly veiled. "Do you have any idea what we went through... me and Connor... believing she was dead? I've had a nightmare."

"I can imagine," Janssen said.

"Really. Can you? The bloody bank wouldn't let me have access to her account... I couldn't cancel direct debits, pay the rent or anything. The bastards evicted us. The council were bloody useless. We were living in a bedsit for a year!" His fists were clenched, pressing down on the worktop in the kitchen.

"I know it can be tough in those circumstances," Janssen said.

"Tough? I was bloody ruined. Don't get me wrong, we didn't have a lot at the time but we've got even less now. My credit is so screwed I can't even rent a place for us to live in. Why do you think we live here? Do you think I like scrubbing toilets? That selfish cow. She loved Connor. Me... maybe not so much. I probably deserved that but the boy... she doted on him. I figured if she had had enough... couldn't take any more and... but to just abandon him like that. *Like mother like daughter*, eh?"

Janssen couldn't help but think this was a reflection of the man Simon used to be coming back. You could make a justifiable case for the reaction under the circumstances.

"They told me that if I believed she had killed herself I could do something to have her declared dead, but as much as I thought she was, I couldn't do it to our boy. How do you tell a six-year-old kid that you think his mum's dead if you're not absolutely certain? I left it as long as I could..." Simon looked between the two of them. "But in the end I started proceedings through the court. It's time for us to move on, draw a line under it all. I mean, don't get me wrong, I still didn't want to do it even now. And then you rock up here, after all we've been through to tell us that she was alive the whole time!"

He raised his fist and pounded it onto the worktop several times. No matter how angry he was, that action had to hurt. He glared at Janssen, tears brimming.

"How could she do that to me? To Connor?"

At that moment the door to the caravan opened and a boy in school uniform entered. He was mid-teens, quite tall for his age with a mass of floppy, permed hair that was the current fashion among teenagers. He looked shell shocked seeing his father's expression. Glancing at both him and Tamara, he focussed on Simon.

"Dad, what's going on?"

Simon looked away, raising a hand to his face and using thumb and forefinger to wipe his eyes. Janssen didn't think it was his place to say anything. This was a conversation that father and son needed to have alone.

"These... are police officers, Connor," Simon explained, stepping over and placing a reassuring hand on the boy's shoulder as he lowered his backpack to the floor. "They've come about your mum."

"What is it? Do they know where she is?"

Simon nodded slowly.

"Yes, they found her."

Connor's mouth fell open, eyes wide. His father didn't need to say the words, his expression relayed the truth.

"I'm sorry, son," Simon said, pulling Connor into his chest. The teenager's face was buried from view and Janssen knew he was already crying. He looked to Tamara and raised an eyebrow. She nodded in response to the unasked question.

"We'll give you both some space," he said to Simon. Taking out one of his contact cards, he laid it on the worktop next to Simon who was fiercely embracing his son. "We will need to speak with you further. In the meantime, if you have any questions for us then you can reach me on that number."

He gestured to the contact card, tapping it with his forefinger. Simon Cook didn't acknowledge the card or their leaving. He gently rocked his son from side to side making soothing sounds to the sobbing boy. Connor wept for the mother he didn't remember and now would never know. Janssen followed Tamara outside, stepping down from the caravan and shaking his head. He was determined to find out how Susan came to meet her end.

CHAPTER EIGHT

"THAT WAS HARSH FOR THE BOY," Tamara said as they made their way back to the car. "What did you make of him?"

"Simon? Not what I was expecting, I have to say," Janssen replied. "Looks like he cleaned up his act."

"Yes, that is what it looks like."

Something in her tone piqued his curiosity.

"You're not convinced?"

Tamara clearly thought about it before answering, glancing over her shoulder back in the direction of the caravan. No one was visible within it.

"I know some people can change... but more often than not, they rarely do. Susan ran away. She was scared enough to stay away for the better part of a decade and then something brought her back."

"And now she's dead."

"I wouldn't mind knowing where Simon was over the weekend but now isn't the time."

"You think she would come back after all this time and his first response was to kill her?"

"Not necessarily his first response. There's a lot of repressed anger in that man. Even if that reaction back there was just a show for our benefit, he's got it inside of him. By his own admission he was a terrible husband. Now, years later, financially crippled and full of resentment..." She stopped, drawing a deep breath. "I've known people kill for much less."

"The preliminary autopsy report should come in today. Then at least we should know if we can treat it as a murder inquiry," Janssen said approaching the car and unlocking it. Tamara went around to the passenger side, pausing as she grasped the handle.

"It would be tremendous misfortune to return home after nine years only for a tragic accident to befall you," she said with a wry grin and got into the car.

SIMON COOK EASED his son away from him, keeping a reassuring hold on both Connor's upper arms. He lowered his head, encouraging his son to lift his own in order to meet his eye. The teenager's cheeks were tear-stained and he looked ready to crumble once again at any moment. Raising a palm and gently placing it against his son's face, Simon cupped his cheek and forced a weak smile.

"We will get through this. I promise you. We've been through tough times before and come out the other side. This is no different."

Connor nodded, fighting back the tears. Simon pulled him back in to his chest and wrapped his arms tightly around his son. Angling his head to one side, he looked out of the window and watched the retreating figures of the two detectives. Casting a glance towards the card left on the worktop he contemplated the conversation. With the experience of his past involvement with the police, he knew not to have faith in them. Reading between the lines they were approaching Susan's death as something other than accidental. Neither of them suggested anything to the contrary. They would be formulating a list of suspects, much as they did before. He was on that list. Probably near to, if not at the top of it. *Just like before.*

Nine years ago they expended a great deal of time and resources on trying to link her disappearance to him. They failed. They would fail again this time.

Tracking their progress back to the car park, he saw the woman stop, looking back in his direction. Could she see him watching her? The guy was what he'd expect, questioning, doubting. She, on the other hand, spent her time watching him. It was obvious. Regretting his angry reaction, his concern grew. If they were looking for a killer, as he assumed, then they would look at him.

Not for the first time he silently cursed his wife. *Why did she have to come back? Of all times, why now?*

Connor withdrew from him, wiping his cheeks with the palms of his hands. The boy seemed embarrassed, ashamed even. Mustering a smile, he ran a hand through the boy's hair, pulling his head forward and kissing him on the forehead.

"It'll be fine, Connor. You'll see," he said as confidently as he could. Connor seemed less so but he nodded. "Hey, why don't you get changed out of your uniform and while you're doing that I'll pop over and have a word with Margaret about finishing early. Under the circumstances I'll bet she won't mind. Then you and I can go and play some football or something. I'll show you how the old man still has a trick or two. What do you reckon?"

"Okay," Connor replied. Not a ringing endorsement but the teenager set off to his room.

Once he heard the latch of the door click, he opened a cupboard above the sink. Reaching to the back he took out a small bottle of gin. Glancing over his shoulder towards Connor's room he unscrewed the cap and took a swig. Sucking air through his teeth as the aftertaste bit, he took a deep breath before downing another mouthful and telling himself it was just to take the edge off. Putting the cap back on, he secreted it back in the cupboard, moving a pack of dried pasta to obscure the bottle from view.

Taking a packet of chewing gum out of his pocket, he unwrapped a strip and put it into his mouth. Picking up the police contact card, he slipped it into his back pocket and left the caravan, heading for the utility block where he expected to find Margaret. The police car was gone. He would need to watch his step in the coming days because he was absolutely certain the police would be paying attention. They'd be back and he would need to be ready.

CHAPTER NINE

ERIC COLLET BOUNDED across the ops room to greet them the moment they returned. Janssen was still hanging up his coat as Eric began running through what he'd already found. Reviewing the case files surrounding Susan Cook's disappearance nine years ago, he was keen to share what he'd learnt. Initially the task seemed like something of a waste of his time and effort. After all, it was a case file detailing the search for a missing person who turned out to not have been missing at all.

The more he read of the investigative reports, the more the sense grew that there was more than just an unhappy person seeking to change their life by starting over.

"I can see why the general consensus was that she committed suicide," he explained as Tamara pulled up a chair and sat down. Janssen leaned himself against the edge of a desk, folding his arms across his chest. "Susan Cook's car was left near to Sheringham cliffs and the weather that particular weekend was brutal. There was a storm hammering the east coast at the time, everyone on watch for a predicted tidal surge. When no sign of a body could be found and nothing washed up in subsequent days it wasn't considered unusual bearing in mind those conditions."

"Subsequent to her disappearance there were no hits on her

bank account or credit card and her mobile never flashed up on the network. If she'd thrown the latter away or sold it... whatever... it should have pinged a cell tower at some point. Total silence. It was like she vanished that night."

"Did she give any hint to friends or family?" Janssen asked.

"Her husband said she didn't have any family. Is that correct, Eric?" Tamara asked.

"That's true," Eric said, glancing at his notes to make sure he got the detail right. Both his senior officers were hot on detail and he didn't want to be slack or lazy. "At least, none that she was in contact with as far as we know. She was taken into care as a child. Social services judged her mother was abusive and neglectful, citing alcoholism and a diagnosis of Munchausen Syndrome as justification for Susan being made a ward of the court at the age of six."

"Did she harm her, the mother I mean?" Tamara asked, leaning forward and placing her elbow on the table, resting her chin on her hand.

"No, not that it states here. Not directly, at any rate. The family court decided she was in an unstable mental condition, recommending she undergo treatment before any application for her daughter's return could be heard."

"And did she?" Tamara asked.

Eric shook his head.

"There's no evidence she did. Tiffany Cole dropped off the radar. There's no record of her coming back into Susan's life and a permanent care order was passed three years later," Eric said, nodding to himself as he reread the detail. "Susan remained under the care of social services after that. Unfortunately, I'm not sure things got much better for her. She bounced around between foster parents for that period. I have a social services record here, released to me because she's deceased, that outlines what one counsellor referred to as her *disruptive nature*. He references multiple incidents of behavioural issues that led to her being removed from several placings. She also has a medical history that makes for a shocking read. A diagnosis of a bi-polar disorder, dyslexia and suffering from emotional trauma, most likely brought about by the upheaval of her early life."

"What about adoption?" Janssen asked. "Was that pursued at all?"

"It was, yes. Once the state took responsibility for her on a permanent basis she was added to the lists. She was adopted by a family in Norwich but the placement failed and she was returned within the first year."

"Returned," Tamara said softly. "Poor kid. What was she then, nine or ten?"

Eric nodded.

"Apparently she attacked one of the other children in the family. It was nasty but I'm afraid I don't have all the details. After that, she was moved to a specialist children's home where she remained until released from the system."

Eric sat back in his chair, confident he'd supplied a concise and accurate picture of Susan Cook's childhood. He found both Tamara and Janssen eyeing him expectantly. The confidence dissipated. It was Tamara who spoke.

"Suicide or not? You were saying," she raised an eyebrow in query.

"Oh yes, that's why most people figured it was a suicide," Eric said, sitting forward and pointing with both forefingers in front of him as if they were pistols. "But, and here's the kicker, in the run up to her disappearance there were multiple cash withdrawals from her bank account. Each was for a similar amount, not enough that would draw attention from... say a husband... but enough to begin mounting up to a substantial figure."

"The husband had a drug problem," Janssen said in a mildly dismissive tone. "That could easily be him feeding his habit."

"True," he agreed, "but there are others that are more random. This was the same two days every month for the previous twelve, prior to her vanishing act. I did a bit of checking through the financials and it was always the same day as when her pay went into the account as well as the day before."

"What do you take from that?" Tamara asked.

"That she took a proportion of her wages on the day she was paid and then waited until the end of the month before clearing out the excess. The second withdrawal of the month was always a random amount."

"Was it a joint account?" Janssen asked.

Eric shook his head.

"Simon wasn't listed on the account, it was only Susan who could make withdrawals."

Tamara's mobile rang and she stepped away from them to answer it, crossing to the other side of the room.

"She was building up a cash nest egg," Eric said. "It's a likely conclusion. She could have kept it in the account if she didn't want her husband to spend it but he may have seen her statements. I guess she could have been spending the cash on something but in light of her Houdini act it stands to reason she was getting together some travelling money."

"To go where, though?" Janssen asked.

Eric shrugged.

"I don't know about that."

Tamara Greave finished on the phone, thanking the caller as she returned to them.

"That was Dr Bellington, the pathologist," she said, retrieving her bag and withdrawing her laptop from inside. "He's completed his autopsy and emailed me through a summary of his preliminary findings. I reckon it's going to be enlightening."

They waited as she started up the machine and accessed her email. Whilst waiting for the details she relayed the conversation.

"As we suspected, in all likelihood the damage to her face and body was caused by the propeller of a passing boat. There was oxygen trapped in her lungs which would have helped it rise from the water but not enough to bring her to the surface. The degradation of the tissue and subsequent bacterial growth would have caused that to happen. When coupled with a low tide, it would have been enough to bring her up eventually."

After a few moments, she brought up the report and began reading through it.

"This is the part that settles things," she said, pointing to a line with the tip of her finger and reading aloud. "Fluid was found in the *paranasal sinuses and had ground-glass opacity within the lungs.* There was also evidence of a frothy fluid within the airways that strongly indicates—"

"That she was alive when she went into the water," Janssen interrupted.

"And there is also suggestive evidence of an increase in peripheral airway resistance and decreased lung compliance. Both of which indicate a vagal reflex as she inhaled water. The body dropped the heart rate and shut off the oxygen and she would have lost consciousness," Tamara said. "What is striking, however, is he describes another wound to the head that he believes was unlikely to be the result of a propeller or a collision with the hull of a boat. He says there is a *focussed impact point* at the back of the skull directly on the posterior fontanelle, where the three parts of the skull knit together."

"It is a weak point and the nature of the blow caused the parietal bones to fold inwardly against the brain and embedded splinters in the tissue. The damage is far too localised to have resulted from a glancing blow against the hull of a boat for example."

"*Localised.* Is he suggesting it might be the result of a weapon?" Janssen asked. "Maybe a hammer?"

"Quite possibly, yes. However, at that point of the skull it wouldn't take much to do the damage. A five-year old with a small hammer could do some damage. You wouldn't need to apply much force, so it could have been the result of a fall as much as an assault. It's fair to assume someone wanted to make sure she wouldn't live by dumping her in the water."

"Even if someone hadn't done so there is every chance she would have died anyway. Below the impact point is where the brain meets the spinal cord, veins and arteries. The autopsy provided evidence of a massive bleed on the brain. The bodily reactions to hitting the water could easily have been involuntary. Dr Bellington believes she wouldn't have known anything about being submerged."

"That settles it, then," Eric said aloud, echoing what they were all thinking. "Whatever led to it, Susan Cook was murdered."

"Any indication of a sexual assault?" Janssen asked.

"No. The report states there is no evidence of trauma to the body indicative of that."

"That most likely rules out a sexual motive for the attack."

"Although sex attacks are about power and not erotic stimulation," Tamara said. Janssen nodded his agreement. "What's also of note is that Susan was living with advanced cancer."

"How advanced?" Janssen said.

"Multiple tumours were present in her stomach, liver and bowel. The size and spread of the tumour growths were *aggressive and indicative of a cessation of treatment*. Going back to the files, Eric, who do they list as being close to Susan? Who did they look at when they thought she was dead?"

Eric turned to his notes. He had looked into that as the suicide was the final unsaid conclusion due to lack of evidence. It was a circumstantial outcome that most people leaned towards after the facts had been investigated but not the only theory.

"Initially, the investigating officer interviewed her work colleagues but none of them offered up anything insightful. She worked two jobs. One was a part-time affair in the bar of a local golf club. She was popular with staff and customers but everyone who was spoken to struggled to offer up any details of her life. They all thought she was quite shy and quiet," Eric said, reading from his notebook.

"The other jobs she did were full time. She worked in a succession of retail jobs, moving between different shops and businesses. At the time of her disappearance she had a junior supervisory role but again, she didn't really mix with anyone outside of work. That was considered unusual because the staff tended to work and socialise together. I imagine, not unlike us, because of the hours they work they are likely to face the same curbs on their social time."

"Fair enough," Tamara said.

"As I think you know, they took a look at the husband," Eric said. "Drug offences, assault and a six-month stint inside for burglary. His solicitor asked for twelve other counts to be taken into consideration."

"Breaking into houses in order to feed his habit," Tamara said absently.

Eric nodded.

"Looks that way. Being so close to her made him the primary suspect but he had a cast-iron alibi for the night of Susan's disappearance. He'd taken their son with him to a friend's house and, despite those present being habitual drug users, they all said he was there and didn't leave. There was nothing at the time to tie him to it."

"Anyone else?" Janssen asked.

"Not as a suspect, no. She had a couple of local friends who were spoken to. Apparently, she was tight with a woman by the name of Sarah Caseley. They were good friends from childhood."

"Simon mentioned her as well as another, Tara someone," Janssen said.

Eric checked his notes. "That would be Tara Byrons. She works at a local school, I believe."

"Believe or know?" Janssen asked. He was curt raising an eyebrow from Tamara.

"I'll check on that as soon as possible," Eric said, appearing deflated.

"What did the friends make of it?" Tamara asked.

"There's nothing of note in the file to say they had any knowledge of her disappearance or plans to do so."

"Is the other one still around. Caseley, was it?" Tamara asked.

Eric hesitated, his eyes darting to Janssen.

"I'll check," he replied, making a note.

"We'll need to revisit these people, see if a few years have given them any clarity of thought," Tamara said. "Someone didn't take kindly to Susan's return. Maybe one of them was the reason she left in the first place.

CHAPTER TEN

The town of Sleaford was situated at the edge of the fens, a wide expanse of land that prior to drainage across three centuries was predominantly marshland and prone to flooding. Consequently the surrounding landscape they encountered as they left Norfolk and headed into southern Lincolnshire was largely agricultural with few distinguishing features as landmarks. Tom Janssen was preoccupied as he drove himself and Tamara Greave to Barbara Keller's registered address. Although the case was a welcome distraction from his personal life, albeit a dark one, he still found his thoughts drifting back to Alice and Saffy. He knew what Alice wanted. At least, he thought he did. He found himself questioning whether he was ready to make the step she was angling for. But was it readiness that perturbed him or self-doubt?

"It's a bit flat around here, isn't it?" Tamara said, bringing his attention back to the present.

"What's that?" he said, realising he'd switched off and wondering where the last few miles had gone.

"The area. It's a bit flat. I know about the fens but I've not really spent much time here. We could be in the Netherlands."

Janssen grinned at the mention of his ancestral homeland. As a child he'd paid many visits to Friesland, in the north of the country where his grandfather came from. Despite his strong family ties, his language skills were far from polished and getting by was about all he was capable of. Carrying the family name was still his greatest contribution. She was right, though. If the road signs weren't visible, then the fens could easily pass for rural Dutch.

"They brought a Dutchman in to mastermind the draining of the fens, you know. A beautiful part of the country."

"If you say so," Tamara said, glancing across at him. "A bit quiet for my tastes."

"Coming from the woman who has just moved to north Norfolk," he said playfully.

"There's more to it. The coastline. The beaches."

"Lincolnshire has beaches."

"The fens have damp fog and marshes," she said, putting her head back and bringing her knees up to her chest before stretching and placing her feet on the dash in front of her.

This wasn't the first time she'd done this in his car. At least this time she took her shoes off first and he still marvelled at her ability to do so. His size made a big car a necessity but even so, there was no way he could contemplate adopting that position.

"Are you going to tell me what's going on with you?" she said without looking over to him. "I didn't plan on asking but let's face it, I'm nosy. Comes with the warrant card."

He glanced across.

"How do you mean?"

"Come on, Tom. I know you well enough to know something is bothering you and it's not the case. You were a bit short with Eric yesterday."

He shrugged almost imperceptibly.

"Maybe I was," he said, his brow furrowing. "We're probably laying too much on him in the absence of having a DS. He's doing a great job. I hadn't realised. Where are we with getting a sergeant?"

"Nice attempt at deflection there, Thomas. Tell me to mind my own business if you like," she said. "If I had a self-esteem problem I might think it was me."

"You? Why would I have a problem with you?"

"I don't know," she said quietly. He sensed her reticence, thinking she must have been considering this already. "Taking the promotion maybe. I heard after the fact that you were in line for it."

He shook his head. The decision to offer her the DCI role was not an issue for him. She was worthy of it, arguably a better candidate than him.

"I never pushed for the position. Coming back here was never about my career," he said, not taking his eyes from the road. In his head he figured the former was one reason he may have been passed over for it.

"Then why did you come back?" she asked.

Again, he shrugged.

"Ah… I don't know… a quieter life perhaps."

He glanced across at her and could tell the answer was unsatisfactory.

"Sometimes life throws things at you and it's good to take a step back, re-evaluate things. You know what I mean?"

She was watching him intently. He was unsure if she understood or whether she felt he was brushing her off with the comment. If she did then she was as astute as he thought because he was. Her gaze lingered on him for a moment longer before she turned to look out of the window at the passing landscape. They were coming up on Sleaford and he knew they had to turn off the A17.

"This is us, I think," he said as the dual carriageway came to an end at a five-exit roundabout.

"Yeah. Head towards Lincoln and then the turn should come up soon on the right," she said, dropping her feet down and sitting upright.

They arrived at the turn-off sooner than he anticipated.

Pulling across the oncoming traffic he found the road immediately narrowing, consistent with the fact it was only used for farm access. The tarred road came to an end at a set of gates that were sitting open. A sign hung from the right-hand gate, it was old and tired but the name was still readable, *Bluebelle Farm*.

Passing through it, they moved onto a gravel-lined access road. The wheat fields set off to their left and right had already been harvested, leaving stubble interspersed with bales awaiting collection. As they approached Janssen found himself wondering if this was still a working landholding or if it had been swallowed up by a larger landowner as so many other smallholdings had been in recent years.

The track dipped and passed around a copse of trees before the buildings came into view. The original farmhouse dominated but as they drew closer it was apparent that the ancillary buildings were very much in use. Another gate barred their way from entering a large courtyard which was encompassed by what would once have been barns used for storage, produce and livestock. They were now being utilised as living space. Each section of converted building had a naming plaque mounted alongside the front door, brass lettering fixed to a wooden background.

Switching off the engine they both got out of the car. The day was overcast with gentle rain falling on a stiff breeze. This time Tamara had brought her coat, an all-weather hiking jacket that she retrieved from the rear seat. Putting it on as she came alongside him, they both looked around. There were cars in the courtyard and despite the farm appearing to have been converted into living space, there were still agricultural vehicles in view. They were still working the land to some degree.

"Can I help you?" a voice called to them from their left. Janssen turned to see a woman standing on the other side of the perimeter wall running adjacent to where they were. She was dressed for the season in a knee-length waxed jacket and wellingtons. A golden Labrador stood alongside her, mouth open with its tongue lolling to one side. Tamara took out her warrant card as she stepped across to speak with her.

"Police," she said, holding up her identification. "We're looking for Barbara Keller. Is she here?"

The woman eyed Tamara's identification closely before glancing to Janssen. He felt like she was gauging him.

"Yes. I dare say she is. I'll get the gate for you. You can park your car over by the main house," she said, indicating the largest building. "You can't leave your car there blocking everyone who wants to come and go."

"How many people live here?" Tamara asked, mirroring the woman's route from this side of the wall as she came across to open the gate.

"A few," she replied. Janssen thought it a guarded response to an informal question and more than a little rude. He got back into the car and started the engine, waiting for the gate to pull clear before passing through.

Parking the car on the far side of the courtyard, he got out just as another figure appeared from a shed to his right, quickly disappearing from view having granted the newcomers a cursory glance. He was sure that he also saw a net curtain twitch in the nearest property but couldn't see anyone behind it. The movement could just as easily have been the result of a draught but nonetheless, he felt eyes upon them as they walked.

The lady who opened the gate led them along a path running down the side of the main house and underneath a brick arch that was covered in ivy. She stoically rebutted any advance of conversation, content to be their guide but seemingly unwilling to engage with them in any meaningful way. They entered the house via a door at the rear, taking them into what would have been the old scullery and then on into the kitchen. Voices were deep in conversation when they came to the kitchen. All fell silent when they appeared.

They were an average-looking group, perhaps eight to ten in total. All were adult, male and female and a variety of ages. They were sitting around a large rectangular table eating lunch together. By the looks of the pans on the stove along with the sweet smell that hung in the air the offering was a mixture of soup, freshly baked bread and at the centre of the table lay a platter of cheeses. After the initial reaction to their presence, a couple of people began helping themselves to food and conversation resumed, albeit a little quieter. Janssen didn't need intuition to know they were intruding.

Their guide left them, crossing the kitchen to join the group. A couple of people continued in conversation whereas most eyed the newcomers warily.

"They're the police, Gretta," the lady said coming to stand alongside a white-haired woman who Janssen judged to be in her seventies. She wore a long black dress with a white collar, adorned with a beaded necklace hanging to the centre of her chest. "They are asking after Barbara."

A couple of people exchanged glances but no one spoke. Gretta looked between the two of them, smiling warmly. With assistance from another, she pushed back her chair and excused herself from the table. Although to the casual eye she didn't appear to be infirm, Gretta stood with difficulty. Indicating for the others to continue with their lunch, she gestured for the two detectives to join her and headed out of the kitchen. The group resumed their lunch, conversations starting up as if there had been no interruption.

Janssen found it unnerving. He was used to the reaction of some people to the presence of the police, usually interpreting it as a result of a guilty conscience, but on this occasion it was more than that.

"You must forgive them," Gretta said over her shoulder as she guided them into the adjoining room. By the look of it, it was something of a formal drawing room. There were at least a dozen chairs stacked at one end with an oblong table set at the other, draped in a white cloth. "We tend not to receive visitors very often."

"That makes this sound like an island community of sorts," he said.

Gretta stopped, placing a hand on the door and allowing them to pass by her. She then closed it, offering them a seat by the open fireplace.

"That's exactly what we are," she said with another smile. It seemed genuine, far removed from the reaction of everyone else to their presence. "As I said, we don't tend to encourage visitors. Please don't think of it as a gesture of rudeness. It is merely that we only break bread with our own."

"And how would that be defined?" Tamara asked, her eyes scanning the walls around them, taking in the various paintings.

"We are not an open assembly," Gretta said. "We only welcome like-minded souls. It is our way and has been for generations."

"You are Brethren?" Janssen asked, ensuring his tone could not be considered dismissive.

"Quite right..." Gretta said in such a way as to seek introductions.

"I'm sorry," Tamara replied. "Detectives Greave and Janssen. We have this address registered for Barbara Keller. Is she here today? It is her that we really need to speak with."

"I'm afraid that will be impossible."

Before either of them could advise that their guide stated she was here, Gretta put a hand up to stop them.

"Barbara passed away last year. She suffered with illness for quite some time. She's buried here, in our chapel grounds."

"I see," Tamara said, glancing at Janssen.

"What did you want to see Barbara about?" Gretta asked. "I will help if I can."

"A woman using Barbara's identification hired a car recently in Norfolk, at the end of last week."

"How peculiar. I'm afraid you'll understand that this can't have been Barbara," Gretta said, appearing shocked at the notion.

"Apparently not," Tamara said. "Does the name Susan Cook mean anything to you?"

Gretta's eyes narrowed and to Janssen, the reaction to the mention of Susan's name was not well received.

"Yes. Susan is a past member of the community. She left recently."

"Can you tell us the nature of how she came to leave? By your reaction it sounds… abnormal. Is that fair?"

Gretta drew herself upright in her chair, taking a deep breath. Janssen had the impression she was formulating her response carefully. He couldn't help but wonder why.

"Susan was a troubled soul. She came to us many years ago. I never did understand what brought her on the path to us but she threw herself into the community much as any other. I had my doubts at the time… and in subsequent years that her path was not truly ours. I should have trusted my instincts as well as God's instruction. There was always something about her that was… different."

"What caused her to leave?"

"She had to," Gretta said flatly.

"What makes you say that?"

"Susan was close with Barbara, nursed her when she was unable to care for herself. I believe Barbara's illness shook Susan's faith, highlighting the genuine weakness of her beliefs. Of everyone within the community, they were the only two not in a union. Aside from the children, of course."

"You mean marriage?" Janssen clarified.

Gretta nodded.

"Did you know Susan was married?" Tamara asked.

Gretta appeared taken aback.

"No! And I must admit to being surprised. If so, she hid it well. What is all of this about? Has Susan been involved in an accident or something?"

"I'm afraid to have to tell you that Susan passed away. She was murdered this past weekend."

Gretta let out a gasp, momentarily losing her control.

"My word. That's dreadful. Who on earth would commit such evil?"

"How recently did she leave the community?" he asked. Gretta inclined her head to one side.

"A little while ago."

"Did she leave anything here? Any of her possessions," he asked, glancing around.

"I believe so, yes. We haven't reallocated her living space to anyone else, so I think everything will be as it was when she left us."

"May we see it?" he asked. Gretta eyed him for a moment, assessing the request. Tamara intervened.

"We can always return with a search warrant for the whole site," she said, smiling. Gretta fixed her with a gaze.

"There is no need for the implied threat, young lady. I'll have someone escort you to Susan's residence and you can do as you please."

"Thank you," Janssen said, smiling warmly. However, Tamara remained impassive.

CHAPTER ELEVEN

GRETTA ROSE FROM HER SEAT. Janssen offered her his arm for support and she accepted the offer graciously. Gently patting him on the forearm once she was upright, she headed for the door and guided them back into the kitchen. The lunchtime meal was at an end and the group were in the process of clearing away. It was a hive of activity and everyone was playing a role. No one paid them any attention as they entered the room. A marked difference from when they arrived. Gretta stepped into the throng, gently placing a hand on a man's shoulder and gently steering him away from the others.

"This is Martin," she said, with a warm hand still resting on his shoulder.

He smiled but it seemed to be a forced expression, quickly averting his eyes from Janssen's, seemingly happier to meet those of Tamara Greave. He was a slight man, balding and with a receding hairline that was kept long on top, hanging down across his forehead to hide the fact. His brown hair was straight and thin and certainly likely to catch the wind if he were outside. Martin was also not very tall, which Janssen found to be the case with people much of the time but, even so, he was arguably shorter than average.

"Martin handles all of our administration, both here in the community as well as the business," Gretta said. "He will show you to where Susan lived and is best placed to clarify anything you may wish to know. It has been a pleasure to receive you, albeit under such terrible circumstances."

Before either of them could reply, Gretta gestured for Martin to take the lead and he immediately ushered them towards the door. She turned and walked away, overseeing the last of the clear up. Janssen was surprised at how polite and yet offhand she could be.

Martin's voice was unexpectedly strong. His stature and demeanour suggested he would be quite weak and softer in tone.

"If you will please come with me," Martin said, setting off without looking back to see if they were following. Janssen looked to Tamara who raised an eyebrow in response but said nothing.

Once outside, the cold breeze buffeted them and caught Martin's hair as anticipated. He led the way across the courtyard to the last property in a double-storey brick terrace. These were positioned beyond the largest of the barn complex and Janssen figured they were originally cottages built for the farm's labourers. They were old, the brickwork at the base of the walls was crumbling with evidence of some prior remedial work. Approaching the last property in the terrace, Martin reached for the door handle and opened it before stepping aside and allowing them to enter first. Janssen was surprised the house was open.

The door opened into one of two downstairs rooms and Janssen looked around. A small sofa was set against one wall with an occasional table alongside it. Upon that, were a couple of books and a magazine. A loud clock was ticking and alongside that hung a barometer whose needle was firmly lodged in the zone marked *changeable*. There was a picture on the adjacent wall depicting a harvest scene. The room had an open fireplace and, by the look of it, it was still very much in use. The smell of soot and blackening around the grate was evidence of this.

A radiator was set beneath the one forward-facing window, pipes running along the wall and up, disappearing into the ceiling. Despite the apparent heating the house felt cold and there was a large patch of black mould in one corner, growing at the base of where two walls met. He was struck by how spartan the accommodation was. No television. No method for playing music.

"You say this hasn't been cleared out?"

Martin shook his head.

"It is as Susan left it," Martin said. "I take care of all the administration for the community. That includes residences, maintenance, work rosters... I'm effectively the company and community human resources manager. Whatever you can think of, I'm probably the one to know."

"Gretta mentioned the company as well. What is it that you do here?"

"We have an ethical food production facility. We grow our own produce as well but the bulk of what we package and trade is sourced through our network."

"A network of the Brethren, other... what do you call them... Gospel Halls, is it?"

Martin laughed.

"No, we are certainly not so exclusive. We source from ethical suppliers."

"She wasn't one for collecting things?" Tamara asked, scanning the room. "Did you spend much time here with her to know if anything has been taken?"

"Much of what was here has always been so. Susan didn't want for material items."

Martin stepped past them in what was a narrow passage through the room and into the kitchen beyond. They followed. This was very basic. Half a dozen cabinets were set against two walls, all of which were clad in pine and painted white. Above the sink was a window and Janssen crossed to look out of it. The view stretched across open farmland. There was no garden, no individual space available for any of the properties as far as he could tell.

"This is very much collective living, am I right?" he asked.

Martin inclined his head, sporting an expression that considered it a daft statement.

"Yes, of course. A life beyond our community is one of single-mindedness, driven by ego and desire. Here, we act as one."

The answer felt scripted, as if it had been delivered many times in the same matter-of-fact way. Martin, still not meeting his eye, gestured with an open hand towards the stairs leading off the kitchen. Janssen took the lead. The stairs were incredibly narrow, even for someone less broad than himself. His shoulders almost scraped the walls to either side as he mounted the stairs. The landing was small giving access to one bedroom, a bathroom and another tiny room that was only fit for storage.

Opening the door to the box room, he poked his head in. There were removal boxes inside along with an old lamp and some pictures. By the look of them they had been there for some time, such was the level of dust that had built up. Retreating from the room, he joined Tamara and Martin in the bedroom. She was casting an eye over the wardrobe. Stepping back from it, she allowed him to see inside. Clothes hung on hangers or were folded neatly on shelves. He turned to Martin.

"Gretta said that Susan had left the community."

"Yes, she left at the end of last week. I'm expecting her back soon."

He exchanged a quick glance with Tamara, who narrowed her gaze. Gretta was far less specific.

"Gretta gave us the impression Susan wasn't expected to return," Janssen said.

Martin seemed confused.

"No, not at all. I'm sure she will be back. That's what she told me."

Something in Janssen's expression must have alerted Martin because his expression changed.

"What is it? Why are you so interested in Susan anyway? Is she okay?"

"I'm sorry, Martin," Janssen said, keeping his tone neutral. "I'm afraid Susan passed away."

The man's jaw dropped and he stared at Janssen, expressionless.

"But... that can't be... she was here on Friday morning..." he stammered, appearing to wobble on his feet. "She said she had to... then she would be back."

His tone elevated in pitch and the words tumbled out of him, so much so that he appeared unable to take a breath as he struggled to form a sentence. Janssen stepped across and only just managed to catch him as Martin's legs went weak. With a firm grip on his arm, Janssen helped him sit down at the foot of the bed. Moments passed and the man's breathing settled, becoming less ragged.

Looking closely at him, Martin appeared broken. He sat staring straight ahead, his hands clasped together in his lap. The image was like that of a lost little boy unsure of where to put himself. Tamara must have thought similarly as she came before Martin, dropping to her haunches and placing a supportive hand on top of his.

"I'm sorry this has come as such a shock to you," she said, reassuring him warmly. Martin met her eye. Janssen could see tears in them.

"I... I don't understand. What happened? An accident?"

"Susan was murdered," she said. "I'm very sorry."

Any measure of control departed and Martin broke down. His head sagged and he wept openly. Tamara glanced up at him and Janssen bit his lower lip, inclining his head to one side.

"You were obviously close to Susan," he said. "Is there anything you can tell us about where she was headed when she left here last week?"

Tears fell, landing on the back of Martin's hands without reply. He looked up and held Janssen's gaze for the first time.

"Susan was special… different to the others."

"Different how?" he asked.

Martin wiped his eyes with the back of his hand.

"I'm so sorry. Awfully embarrassing," Martin said, staring at the floor.

"Not at all," Tamara replied, sitting down next to him. He smiled at her weakly, bobbing his head in gratitude for the sentiment. "It must be a shock. What were Susan's plans?"

"She said she had to go home for a time," Martin said. "There were things that needed to be settled."

"What things?" Janssen asked, once again focussed on the subject at hand.

"Susan didn't speak much about her life prior to coming to us. I know she was troubled. For a time she barely spoke, not just to me but to anyone. There were those who said she shouldn't be here… but Gretta saw something in her they didn't. That is her gift. Gretta's, I mean. She has a wonderful ability to see through the barriers we construct around us right through to the person we are trying to hide. Gretta saw something in Susan, as she has done with all of us."

"She sounds like a formidable woman," Janssen said.

"Oh, she is. Mark my words," Martin agreed, nodding enthusiastically.

"But you grew close with her, with Susan?" Tamara pressed. Martin looked at her, his eyes flitting between Janssen and the door. It seemed as if he was fearful of being overheard. "Didn't you?" Tamara's tone was soft, gently probing for the information both of them knew was in there.

"Yes. We have become close," Martin said, barely above a whisper. His hands remained interlocked and he was absently fiddling with something. Janssen took a half step to his left to enable a better view and realised Martin was turning his wedding ring with thumb and index finger, apparently staring at it. He chose his next words carefully.

"Susan was special to you."

It was a statement. Martin glanced up at him and then away.

"How long has it been going on between the two of you?"

"I don't know what you mean!" Martin said, pulling his hands apart and glaring up at him with the look of a guilty teenager.

"The affair. How long has it been going on?" Janssen persisted. Martin's resistance crumbled in a matter of seconds and his head sagged once more.

"I know that this is painful, Martin, but we need to understand what was happening in Susan's life in order to find out who killed her," Tamara said, angling her head low to ensure she dropped into his peripheral vision. He looked across at her, nodding almost imperceptibly.

"A while," he said. "You must understand, neither of us planned it… it just happened. I can't explain it. We both have… had… something missing in our lives. I can't believe I'm never going to… see her smile, feel the warmth of her arms around me…"

The words tailed off as he fought back another wave of emotion that threatened to overwhelm him. Janssen felt a stab of emotion in his chest. Empathy for the man's plight brought Alice to the forefront of his mind. He tried to sweep the image away but the guilt remained. He'd pushed her aside too much recently.

Here was a man desperately trying to comprehend never seeing the woman he loved ever again. It resonated with him. The realisation struck him hard. He caught Tamara watching him with a look of concern. Her eyes narrowed and he waved a hand gently to signal he was focussed again.

"Watch and pray that you may not enter into temptation. The spirit indeed is willing, *but the flesh is weak*," Martin whispered, raising his head and meeting Tamara's eye. "Matthew, twenty-six, verse forty-one. He spoke wisely… but a life of devotion and prayer has not prepared me to resist as I thought it would. I am a wicked, *wicked man*."

"You are a man," Tamara said but Martin appeared not to have heard the comment. If he did then he didn't react to it. Ensuring that Martin wouldn't notice, Janssen mouthed the words *thank you* towards her. The gleam in her eye told him she'd seen it.

Martin sniffed loudly and he looked across the room to the bedside table.

"Susan asked for my help," he said, looking back to Tamara beside him. "She said she needed to go home but for now no one could know she was headed that way. No one here in the community nor anyone from her former life in Norfolk."

"Did she say why?" Tamara asked.

Martin shook his head.

"Not really. She said it was dangerous. I wanted to know why of course, but she wouldn't tell me. She said she would come back, once it was all over. That we... that we could leave. Start again."

"What did she ask you for?"

Martin looked at the floor again.

"She needed to hire a car. As I said, I have access to the community paperwork."

"Barbara Keller," Janssen said. Martin looked up and nodded.

"I didn't see the harm. I mean, Barbara isn't going to mind... and she was close with Susan up until the end. If Sooz confided in anyone it would have been her."

"Sooz? Was that a nickname?" Tamara asked.

Martin smiled.

"She held that back for those of us who she loved... or maybe who she felt loved her."

"Did she ask you for anything else?"

"No, not really. We tried to come up with a plausible reason for why she needed to leave the community for a while...

without raising suspicions. I wasn't much use with that, I'm afraid. I'm not great when it comes to deception."

Janssen found himself thinking the opposite was true. He'd managed to keep an affair secret amongst a close-knit community for quite some time. He was arguably better at it than he thought.

"What did she come up with?" Janssen asked.

Martin shook his head.

"I don't know. There was something else though," Martin said, returning his gaze to the bedside table. "She said that if anything ever happened to her then all the answers would be in her diary. I found it an odd thing to say at the time but now... maybe... maybe that's what you need to see."

Janssen moved to the side of the bed. Donning a pair of latex gloves that he kept in his jacket pocket for occasions such as this, he bent over and eased the drawer open. It was empty. Reaching to the back of the drawer, he fumbled around in case it was secreted inside but there was nothing there. Checking to see if anything had fallen down the back of the interior or behind the cabinet, he was disappointed to find nothing. Glancing at Tamara, he shook his head. Lowering himself to the floor, he looked under the bed but there was nothing visible. Kneeling, he looked to the two of them and shrugged.

"Nothing."

"I don't understand," Martin said, coming over to see for himself.

"We would rather you didn't touch anything. Just in case," Janssen said, holding up a restraining hand in front of Martin, who frowned.

"Did she say what was in it?" Tamara asked.

"No. Only that it would explain everything."

"Who else would know about it?" Janssen asked.

Martin shrugged.

"No one as far as I know. This is so strange. I don't understand."

"The house was unlocked when we came over to it. Is that always the case?" Janssen asked.

"Yes, of course. Why would we need to lock doors within our community?"

"In order to keep a secret," Janssen said, the irony not escaping him at all.

CHAPTER TWELVE

LEAVING THE HOUSE, Janssen saw Gretta near to where their car was parked. She was chatting to another woman whom he hadn't seen before, examining the plants growing at the edge of the path running alongside the main house. She saw them approaching as Martin closed the door behind them and he couldn't help but think she'd been lingering there, waiting for them to appear.

"Are you okay?" Tamara asked him. "You zoned out for a moment back there."

He shrugged off the question.

"Just something I'm working through."

He could feel her eyes upon him but he pretended not to notice her interest.

"Did you find what you were looking for?" Gretta asked when they were within earshot.

Janssen glanced at Tamara who smiled.

"Yes, thank you. Martin was very helpful," Tamara said. "We appreciate your time today."

"Always happy to assist the police," Gretta replied. "It really is awful what has happened to Susan. I trust you will apprehend the person responsible soon enough."

"We will do our very best," Tamara replied. "Tell me, you said that Susan had left a while ago and you didn't think she was coming back. That's a little vague."

Gretta's expression became fixed, thoughtful, although she did take a half glance towards Martin, walking in their direction.

"Did I say that? I don't really remember. When I last spoke with her, I had the sense of finality around the conversation. I'm afraid I can't remember the exact words. Why? Is it significant?"

"Oh… I had the impression from Martin that her departure was more of a temporary situation."

"Really? There must be some confusion. People hear what they want to so much of the time, don't they? Is it relevant?"

"Just trying to build a picture. What about when she first arrived here nine years ago, can you tell us how that came to pass?"

"I'm afraid not, young lady. People find their faith walking all manner of different paths. Our door is always open to believers."

"I see," Tamara said, disappointed at the somewhat vague answer. "Well, thanks again for your help. If we need anything else, we'll be sure to get in touch."

The two of them got into the car. Martin went to stand alongside Gretta and, again, he didn't appear able to look at them as Janssen started the engine, putting the car into reverse in order to turn around.

"Whatever Susan saw in that man, I will never know," Janssen said under his breath, careful to ensure no one would be able to understand him. Gretta was watching them intently.

"You're right. He comes up short on personality but maybe they were two unhappy souls who found one another."

"An opportune collision? Yeah, maybe," Janssen agreed as he steered the car back onto the approach road. "What do you make of the diary?"

"Perhaps Susan took it with her. Or someone else got to it before we could," she said. "If it's the latter, I would like to know who. If the contents are as explosive as Martin suggests then that someone is sitting on it for a reason. Do you remember Simon Cook saying how closed off she was? Martin said similar, but only in different words. Susan strikes me as cagey. I'm wondering why."

"Do you think she was adept at keeping secrets?"

"I think this place has its fair share of secrets. I'm not buying Gretta's recollection of the timeframe leading to Susan's departure."

"Why would she lie?"

"I don't know. To confuse things maybe... and before you ask, I don't know why she'd want to do that either. Whatever secret Susan was keeping, it was probably what led to her murder. She's kept everyone around her in the dark, that's for certain."

"So we can probably rule out the random stranger," he said.

"Far too coincidental for her to stumble across someone setting out to kill. Susan Cook returned to Norfolk for a reason but went to a lot of trouble to make sure no one knew she was coming. At least, no one she didn't wish to. To meet her death at the weekend, so soon after arriving... she must have made contact with her killer. In all likelihood, she not only knew them but I'd also suggest she trusted them as well."

"Trusted them enough to turn her back to them when close enough to kill her," he said, thinking aloud. "We need to get amongst those she was close to nine years ago. Try to find out who she would feel able to go to on her return."

"Then we'll find out who killed her."

"Makes you think about Abigail Thomas again, doesn't it?" he said.

Tamara bobbed her head.

Their conversation was interrupted by a phone call coming through on the in-car system. Janssen answered as Eric's name flashed up on the display.

"How is it going with Barbara Keller?" Eric asked.

"She's dead but it's been far from a waste of time. We'll fill you in when we get back. We're just leaving."

"Great. I thought you would want to know straight away. Uniform have found Susan Cook's hire car."

"Where?" Tamara asked, her eyes lighting up.

"Abandoned in a lane, a little way east of Ringstead."

"Condition?" Janssen asked.

"I'm just on my way out there now but uniform said it's fine. A local farmer reported it early this morning. He says it's been there for the last couple of days, thought it strange and called us."

"Send us the location and we'll meet you there," Janssen said.

GRETTA WATCHED the car moving back along the access road, Martin standing next to her in silence. Without breaking her gaze on the departing police officers, she took in a sharp breath.

"What was it they wanted to know?"

Martin chewed on his lower lip for a moment before replying.

"How Susan came to be here…what she was like. That sort of thing."

"I trust you were able to offer them your unique insight?" she asked, fixing him with a stare. He averted his eyes from hers, shifting his weight nervously between his feet.

"I… I… yes. I told them what I could, which wasn't much. I don't think I was particularly helpful."

"No. I don't suppose you could be. After all, you didn't really know Susan very well, did you?"

Martin nodded. He seemed anxious. More so than usual.

"I can't believe she's gone," he said. His tone clearly reflected the deep sorrow he felt. "Who could do such a wicked thing to her?"

"The guilty shall be judged, Martin. In the end that is one

reckoning that we shall all face. God bless her soul and may she find the peace in heaven that escaped her in life."

Without another word, Gretta left him and headed back inside. Passing through the kitchen, now clean and tidy with everything cleared away, she made her way to the room at the front of the house she utilised as an office. A blast of warm air greeted her as she entered. First checking no one was following her, she closed the door. The glowing embers of the fire flickered with the occasional lick of flame. Placing a hand on the edge of her desk to steady herself, Gretta eased herself down onto one knee and added another log to the fire. Within moments the flames danced around the freshly added fuel.

Letting out a groan as she righted herself, she moved to the other side of her desk. Sitting down and pushing aside some papers she opened a drawer and withdrew a small notebook from the back. Turning it over in her palm, she glanced out of the window and caught her breath. The city of Lincoln lay on the horizon, its mighty cathedral visible atop the hill even from this distance. The exertion of the short walk and her efforts to revive the fire had taken its toll.

The notebook was nothing special, little more than a lined pad. Casually flipping through the pages she didn't stop to read anything in particular, occasionally noting the handwritten dates at the top of each page, the entries were not meticulously made. Some days, even weeks, passed without mention only for there to follow sudden bursts of information in consecutive days.

Slowing as she neared the most recent entries, the focus shifted onto thoughts and feelings of the past. On more than one occasion Gretta found that reading the words sparked anger, frustration and, above all, a great deal of shame. Martin would be mortified by the limit of his mentions. He was a tool, used for the advancement of a separate goal. A reality he would be unable to comprehend should he ever get to learn about it. That wouldn't happen. Not if she had her way.

Closing the makeshift diary, Gretta stood up and returned the short distance to the fireplace. Holding the diary firmly in her left hand, she stroked the cover gently with the fingers of her right. For a moment she remained there, staring at it intently before leaning over and carefully placing it onto the fire. The flames seized upon the new addition, rapidly enveloping the book.

"Goodbye, Susan. You will always remain in my prayers."

CHAPTER THIRTEEN

ERIC FLAGGED them down as they approached a bend in the road. There was no need. The surrounding land undulated slightly but was all well-maintained agricultural land and they had seen the liveried police cars parked on the verge well before the constable noticed their approach. Janssen pulled off the road, barely wide enough to support two cars side by side and came to a stop. Getting out, he looked around. The nearest occupied property within view was a farmhouse but that was at least a quarter of a mile away as the crow flies. The fields were bordered by hedgerows and bushes but they offered scant cover for someone looking to be unobserved. The benefit of the location was its remoteness. You would consider yourself unlucky to be seen abandoning a car even though it was such a wide-open area. The choice puzzled him.

"SOCO have found something interesting," Eric announced in lieu of a greeting. He was evidently excited by the find, gesturing for them to follow him.

Janssen was pleased to see the confidence exhibited from the young detective constable. Eric was growing in stature but Janssen was looking for him to make the next step up in performance.

"Blood in the boot of the car."

The white Ford was parked off the road on an access track to the adjoining field, neatly, in line with the hedge and clear of the carriageway. It was reminiscent of the many vehicles parked by the side of the road by ramblers setting off across the network of paths and bridleways. The boot lid was open, raised to its full height with a forensics officer, clad in blue coveralls, taking photographs of the interior. As they came nearer, Janssen caught his eye and he indicated he was done, stepping clear to make room. The floor of the boot had two markers placed on it. One pointed to a dark patch on the carpet liner roughly the size of a small plate. The other to a brown smear on the lip of the car, most likely a scuff caused when loading or unloading. Janssen crouched for a better view and he echoed Eric's thoughts. It was dried blood.

"We'll have to compare it to confirm but it stands to reason that it's Susan Cook's. That would have been left when she was dragged out of the boot," Eric said. "Unconscious people are heavy, even a slightly-built woman like Susan would become something of a dead weight. Sorry. I didn't mean for that to sound like it did."

"That's okay, Eric," he said, glancing up at him. "You're right. Although it does beg the question as to how big her attacker was. An unresponsive person is difficult to manhandle but someone of my size could deal with Susan relatively easily compared with someone like you."

Eric nodded. The comment was not derogatory. Eric was a touch over five foot six in height. He was athletic and no doubt physically capable but the point still stood. Turning his thoughts back to the location, it still struck him as odd. Why would the car be dumped here of all places? It would be found soon enough. These roads didn't carry a lot of traffic and the car was in plain view. It was almost as if dumping the car was an afterthought, chosen without much consideration. Unless they weren't bothered by its potential discovery. If the latter, they would be unlikely to get much useful information from it. He half expected it to be wiped clean.

Stepping back, he looked into the interior of the cabin. No attempt had been made to further damage the vehicle, to mask its ownership or destroy forensic trace evidence. It was almost as if the vehicle had been treated with the respect of an owner rather than a killer hiding evidence which reinforced his view.

The clouds parted to reveal the late autumn sun, rapidly descending towards the horizon. Taking his bearings, he figured the old harbour at Thornham was just a short drive north of here. The temptation to look for premeditation, a structured plan of how the killer intended to get away with the crime was appealing. However, something about all of this struck him as amateurish. The location of the dump site for the body. The odd feeling he had surrounding the vehicle. On the face of it, random, in reality it was haphazard. The killer transported the body to Thornham, removing any means of identification before dropping her into the water but failed to take the key fob. It was an oversight. It was a modern car with a keyless start system. The fob need only be present in the car for the engine to start. Once it was running, the engine would continue until switched off. The killer didn't realise this or failed to notice, driving the car back here and abandoning it.

An experienced criminal would understand the investigation process. The longer the police were frustrated in building a time line in the first few days, the colder the trail became. Leaving the fob behind led them to the hire-car firm and on to Lincolnshire. *But why here?* It was so obscure, so apparently random. Random is how accidental murderers behaved. Their decision-making skills affected by coursing adrenalin, fear, leading to chaotic decision making that appears rushed and unfocussed after the event.

This didn't strike him as the case here though. The way the car was parked. The dumping of the body. This was evidence of someone acting with a clarity of purpose, not reckless haste and yet, he couldn't shake the sense of this being perpetrated by a first timer. The conclusion niggled him.

"Was anything useful left inside?" Janssen heard Tamara ask. He kept half an ear on the conversation but continued with his own analysis.

"No, it was clear," Eric replied. "Were you hoping for something in particular?"

"A diary or similar," Tamara said. "Hers is missing from where she was living."

"No. Aside from the blood and the paperwork from the hire company left in the glove box there was nothing. She can't have had the car very long. There isn't even a fuel receipt."

"That's a thought," Janssen said, moving to the offside door. It was open and he looked to the CSI tech for approval, putting on a pair of forensic gloves.

"Yes, we've processed much of the interior already," the tech replied, signalling it was okay for him to enter. "We've recovered prints for comparison and taken photographs. We still need to sweep the carpets and upholstery for fibres."

"That's okay. I don't need to get in," he said. "Eric, did you bring the fob?"

Eric came around to his side of the car and handed him a plastic bag with the fob inside. Mentally crossing his fingers that the unit was watertight, Janssen held the bag close enough for the car to pick up the signal. Reaching in he pressed the ignition button and was pleased to see the dashboard light up. The needles on the dials moved. The car had three-quarters of a tank of petrol. It was a family hatchback and he did a rough mental calculation as to how many miles Susan probably covered. If she picked the car up with a full tank on Friday, which was customary, then she hadn't done many miles in the car. That is assuming she hadn't needed to refuel in the subsequent time. He spied the mileage recorded on the dash. Leaning back out of the cabin, he looked around catching Tamara's eye. She came alongside him.

"What are you thinking?" she asked.

"From memory, the mileage on the car when Susan picked it up is not dissimilar to now. She didn't cover much distance. At a guess I'd say she died on Friday night. Saturday at the latest."

"Why?"

"We haven't found anyone using her name or Barbara Keller's checking into any local accommodation so far. From the looks of it, she hasn't been sleeping in the car. Wherever she went on Friday or whoever met her probably killed her then. Dumping the body and then the car here soon after."

Tamara surveyed the area, using the flat of her hand to shield her eyes from the setting sun clinging to the horizon.

"This is an odd place to leave the car," she said.

"I'm thinking the same," he agreed, scanning the surrounding landscape. "What is going through the killer's mind? Usually, they are looking to put as much distance between themselves and the body as quickly as possible. That way, any person between them and the victim becomes a suspect before they do."

"Yes, but that's more common with a stranger-on-stranger killing, wouldn't you say?" Tamara countered.

"True. We already think they knew each other, which means we are probably dealing with a local."

"Go on."

"When it comes to local knowledge, the killer has the advantage of knowing where to dispose of the remains as well as where they are less likely to be seen in doing so. But being local can also be something of a hindrance," he said, thinking hard. "For instance, the geography. Areas that you know extremely well make up your activity space, that is where your daily routines take place, school runs, commute to work, shopping and so on. Step outside of this space and you become less certain, less comfortable. You still know the area but not as well, which affects your confidence. Logically, you are less inclined to be bold. It is something of a natural barrier."

"Yeah, I see where you're going," Tamara said. "Factor in the geographic barriers that nature and man provide—"

"Exactly, the main roads, rivers, the coastline and we have a much smaller area to focus on. This can all happen on a subconscious level rather than necessarily an active consideration. If we're going with a local person then our killer most likely lives within the activity space which makes the dumping of the car here as well as where we found Susan's body significant. I don't think leaving the car here is as random as it seems."

He looked around them, Tamara following his lead.

"The A149 runs to our west and north along the coast. We've got Docking to the south. These roads around us are interlinked but they don't make for an easy access or egress. The car has been left here not because it was convenient or clever but more likely they had to."

"Doesn't answer why, though."

Janssen was momentarily perplexed. There had to be a reason. A thought came to mind and he returned to the interior of the vehicle. The car was still sitting in standby mode. Looking at the display panel, he noted the navigation system remained active. Pressing the tab, it moved to full screen.

"The sat nav was programmed," he said, selecting the destination tab. The screen changed to a bird's-eye view map of the area. He selected the address tab and hit go. The request was processed and then the map zoomed in highlighting their current position and a red-lined route that would take them to the destination. Taking out his mobile phone, he took a photograph of the screen before signalling for the CSI technician to come and document it.

"Where did it take her?" Tamara asked.

He looked towards the south west.

"I've just got the post code but looking at the route, I reckon it's about a mile that way," he said, pointing. "Towards Sedgeford."

"What do you think? Susan was killed, her body transported to Thornham in her own car before being dumped here."

"If acting alone the killer would need to pick up their own vehicle. A mile isn't too far to walk unobserved. Certainly not at night."

"And if local, they'd potentially know the route. Let's check it out," Tamara said, turning and heading back to the car. "Eric, stay here and oversee the recovery of the car."

"And when you're done, I want you to build a list of everyone who moved within Susan Cook's circle prior to her disappearance. Friends, family, colleagues... associates, ex boyfriends... whatever you can find," Janssen said before moving to join Tamara.

"Going back how far?" Eric asked.

"Until you run out of names," he said over his shoulder. He didn't see Eric look back at the hire car, then at his watch as he blew out his cheeks.

CHAPTER FOURTEEN

IN THE ABSENCE of a full address the post code programmed into Susan Cook's satellite navigation system took them on to a little used link road running through open fields. The sun had dropped below the horizon now and the darkness was enveloping the landscape, forcing them to look for a potential destination with the aid of the car's headlights. Tom Janssen slowed the car. There were no obvious signs of habitation nearby. Nothing for them to navigate to, which brought frustration along with even more questions. Why was Susan all the way out here in the middle of nowhere?

"Hold on," Tamara told him. "What's that we just passed?"

He braked hard. Whatever it was he had missed it. The road was narrow and the verges to either side were high and he didn't fancy making a turn, so he put the car into reverse. Backing up, they came to what Tamara had spotted. To the left were two pillars and a set of open gates, almost completely shrouded from view by the growth of vegetation among and around them.

"What does that sign say?"

"Keep out, I think," Tamara said. The access was also overgrown, mainly by grass and weeds but some wild wheat was also growing, seeds carried on the breeze from the nearby fields. Backing up a little further to enable him to turn onto the drive, he lit up the entrance to the gates. The track beyond bent away behind the trees and out of view.

"What's down there?"

He shook his head. The gates marked something.

"No idea. Let's take a look," he said, putting the car in gear and setting off.

The access road was poorly maintained and he found he had to carefully pick his way along it to avoid scraping the bottom of the car at several points. Once clear of the public highway, a building came into view. The sky was clear and the waxing moon cast some light upon it as they approached. It was substantial. A rather grand and imposing silhouette against the backdrop of the starlit sky. In front of the building they arrived at a parking area. It was gravel lined and resisting the advance of nature but vegetation grew through it nonetheless. Here the ground appeared to bear the weight of the car better than the approach track, feeling solid.

Getting out, Janssen scanned the exterior of the building. In its heyday it must have made quite a statement for the owners. An architectural style such as this must have cost a small fortune to commission, let alone maintain, which would probably go some way to explaining why it appeared to have been abandoned in recent years. The windows were boarded over, presumably to keep the building secure and free from squatters or vandals, neither of which he imagined would be a prevalent issue in these parts. Even in the limited light he could read the name plate, mounted alongside the porch. It read *Wellesley Manor*. Another warning sign was visible alongside the name, advising people to keep out. Old buildings such as this, if not maintained properly, rapidly fell into a state of disrepair.

Tamara approached the main entrance, pausing at the threshold.

"Well, someone's been inside recently," she said, activating the light on her mobile phone and using it as a torch to illuminate the door. Janssen looked. "And I don't think they had a key."

The door frame had been jimmied at the midpoint of the latch plate. The pale hue of the splintered wood meant it hadn't been exposed to the elements for very long. Janssen trotted back to the car and retrieved a torch from the boot along with fresh sets of forensic gloves, anticipating the need for them. Returning to the door, he handed one set of gloves to Tamara who put them in her pocket. He didn't put his on either but he held them in his hand when he pushed against the door, ensuring he didn't leave his own fingerprints. The door cracked open a fraction but the hinges protested. He needed to apply more pressure to create a gap for them to fit through.

Angling the torch into the interior, they eyed the hallway. It was in a terrible state of repair and the smell of damp and mould carried to them. Looking to Tamara, he inclined his head and she nodded. He stepped through and she followed. In contrast to the exterior, there was now no natural light source. All they could see was illuminated by torchlight. The building may have had a grand exterior but the interior had the feeling of having been sanitised. As they moved through they found the features one might expect to find inside were still present but often cut through with the installation of new stud walls when the space had been reconfigured at some point in the past.

"This must have been an old-people's home or something," Tamara said.

"Modelled on Colditz Castle, I should imagine," Janssen said quietly, angling the beam up the staircase to the landing above. The stairs themselves looked in a poor state and he had no intention of testing their ability to withstand his weight. Tamara sensed his hesitation.

"I'll go up. You carry on down here. Give me a shout if you find anything interesting."

"Go easy," he said.

She activated the light on her mobile again and set off up the curved staircase, keeping close to the wall. Turning his attention to the ground floor, there were three routes off the hallway. One led into a front room which looked like it was once an office. Next to that was a doorway which opened into a larger room. Standing at the threshold, he cast the beam of the torch around. On the far wall was a massive open fireplace. Once there would have been an ornate surround, probably fashioned from marble or granite, but this was gone, revealing the old laths in the wall where it would once have stood. Sections of the ceiling had collapsed bringing plaster and wood to the floor beneath. Illuminating the ceiling, he could see much of it was bowing and he decided it was too dangerous to proceed and returned to explore the alternative path.

The corridor led him deeper into the building. Anything of use seemed to have been stripped prior to it being abandoned. Any room he came to had nothing of note. In places, the floor coverings were lifting. The walls were peeling, regardless of whether the covering was paper or paint. The general impression was one of advanced decay. The building had been forgotten, left to rot. He found himself pondering Susan Cook's association with it. It had the air of a state institution. Tamara was probably on the right track with a care home. Susan's association implied it was most likely during her time spent in the care system. Each room he came to was nondescript, soulless with no discernible function.

At one point the corridor split, with one direction heading towards the centre of the building and the other terminating at a window probably overlooking the grounds but currently boarded over with all of the others. Here he found another pile of rubble made up of fallen plaster from the ceiling above. The debris spanned the width of the corridor and he took great care passing it. Something caught his eye, lit up in the periphery of the torch beam as he stepped over, causing him to stop. Dropping to his haunches he looked more closely, shining the light directly in front of him. There was a footprint in the dust. It looked fresh, the tread pattern showing through to the floor covering beneath.

Scanning the immediate area, he couldn't see anything of note. The direction of travel was off to his right, deeper into the building. Directing the torch that way highlighted a door at the end of the corridor, barely four metres away.

Coming to the door, a heavy four-panel Victorian original, he tried the handle and found it unlocked. Gently easing it open made an inordinately loud noise that seemed to carry. Casting the torchlight around the interior, he followed the beam around the room. Whoever left the footprint was coming here but he had no clue as to why. Stepping forward, he navigated yet more debris taking great care where he placed his feet. The room had only the one door with no windows and felt claustrophobic. The smell of damp along with mould growth visible on the walls left a strong earthy smell hanging in the air. A creaking sound came from above and pointing the beam of the torch upwards he was momentarily concerned that more of the ceiling was about to come down, but it didn't.

Bringing the light back down he turned his attention to a large cupboard unit built into the recess in one corner of the room between wall and chimney stack. Moving closer, he noted one of the doors was missing and the other swayed back and forth in the draught he'd introduced by entering. On the internal face of the door he found some markings. At first, he thought they were random lines before he realised they were actually letters. Scratched into the paintwork at the midpoint of the door, they were only visible to the naked eye if it was open and, even then, probably only if you were looking for them. He noticed them because he was looking for anything out of the ordinary. It was quite conceivable they would go unnoticed nine times out of ten. Many of the letters were set out in pairs and crudely fashioned making them hard to read.

Bringing the torch close up, he studied them. He connected a

K and a *D*. There was also an *S* and what he thought might be the letter *D* but he couldn't be sure. Beneath these were more letters but due to the artificial light and the crudeness of the carving they were too hard to decipher. Above all of the letters he found the only words. A simple sentence, *I was here*. The significance was unclear but the idea that the pairings were initials he found compelling. For some reason he guessed it might be relevant and took out his mobile. Illuminating them from different angles, he took several pictures.

Intrigued by the effort taken into making the inscriptions he leaned into the cupboard, arcing the torch around the interior but couldn't see anything else of note. On a hunch, he resorted to touch, systematically working his way around the interior edges of the cupboard and finding his fingers brush against something metallic, cold and smooth to the touch. Withdrawing it, he had a small butter knife in his hand. It had been wedged between the top of the cabinet and the frame. Holding it against the lettering, the flat of the blade roughly matched the width of the impressions.

"What's that you've got there?"

Tamara's voice startled him and he reacted by standing up quickly, catching his head on the edge of the cupboard.

"Strewth!" he muttered.

"Sorry," Tamara said. "Anything interesting?"

"Curious... but I don't know about interesting," he said, rubbing at his head.

"This is though," she said, pointing to the floor at her feet. He looked across and was surprised to see he'd missed it. The light from her mobile was cast down in front of where she stood at the threshold to the door. A dark circular patch, almost spanning the width of two of the aged floorboards, was visible to the naked eye. Crossing over to within a couple of feet, he knelt down and examined it closer. Both of them had visited enough crime scenes to recognise dried blood when they saw it.

"What do you reckon?" she asked.

"I think we've found where Susan Cook was attacked. Let's get the scenes of crime guys down here as soon as possible," he said, glancing up and meeting Tamara's eye. She scanned the room.

"What on earth brought her here?"

CHAPTER FIFTEEN

ERIC COLLET STOOD before the white boards, mounted in the ops room, checking and re-checking the information he had written up. The first board held the information documented by the scenes of crime officers from Susan's abandoned hire car. The car was pretty clean from a forensic point of view when it came to the interior. A quick telephone call to the hire company confirmed his initial thoughts. The car underwent a full valet prior to it being passed to Susan Cook.

The thoroughness of the clean was a bonus to the investigation. The steering wheel, handles and instruments of the interior were all wiped down leaving them with a number of distinct prints that could only have been left since Susan picked it up. By their very nature, hire cars would see a high turnover of different drivers and passengers. The sheer volume of these could have left them with multiple prints that were difficult to decipher from one another, let alone match to a person who was by now either located many miles away or perhaps abroad. One grouping could be confirmed as Susan's. The majority of those lifted corresponded to hers, however there still remained others yet to be identified. Of these, it was logical to assume some belonged to the staff at the hire firm who would have driven the car around the company lot. The hope was that the remaining prints were left by the killer. So far, the records hadn't provided a match. Tomorrow, he would drive to the hire firm and take the prints of all members of staff who had access to the car and try to rule them out.

The samples taken from the floor of the boot, as well as the smear on the tailgate, had been sent to the forensics laboratory in Norwich for a detailed analysis. He was confident that a profile matching Susan's would come back. Similarly, the car was also to undergo a rigorous inspection in search of other possible trace evidence that might help identify who had been in the vehicle. Hair or skin samples located deep in the carpet fibres were his best hope but soil or organic detritus could indicate where the passengers had been recently. Even the most innocuous of clues could provide a breakthrough. Pleased with his efforts, he put the file down on his desk and moved to the next board.

Scanning the information taken from the original investigation into Susan's disappearance, the missing person file, he double checked the names and dates. Tom Janssen was a stickler for detail, thorough and methodical. Not that the DCI was any different but Tamara Greave seemed to go with her instincts much more. This was his impression since she'd arrived. The more time he spent working for her, the more he liked her leadership style. She wasn't casual but neither did she micromanage. There was a calmness to her approach and she seemed quite adept at reading people, remaining quiet and respectful before revealing her thoughts. So far, they were right on the money.

When Simon Cook came to report his wife's disappearance, the report was made and assigned to a CID detective who didn't record anything for several days. That wasn't surprising to Eric. Thousands of people walk away from their lives annually and without any firm reason to believe any harm had come to her, the police response was likely to be lukewarm. The discovery of the car near to Sheringham cliffs was a turning point. The keys were left in the ignition, the car unlocked. A search was carried out along the coast, both on land and at sea but no body was recovered. At the same time, the investigation looked into those people closely associated to her. That included talking to friends, work colleagues, and a more detailed look at her husband, Simon Cook.

Tamara entered the ops room deep in conversation with Tom Janssen.

"Where are you with going over the old files?" she asked.

"Just running through it now," he said, indicating the three white boards with a flick of his head. "I've got forensics from the hire car plus the relevant data from the MisPer alongside all those who Susan interacted with prior to her disappearance."

Janssen hung his coat on the back of his chair, folding his arms across his chest as he scanned the information on the boards.

"What about Susan Cook's past? Have you been able to pull anything together?" Janssen asked.

Eric was slightly irritated by that. He'd been working around the clock for days now and was supposed to be meeting Becca for dinner, an attempt at making up for cancelling their date at such short notice upon the discovery of Susan Cook's body. It was a foolish commitment to make under the circumstances. He should never have agreed. A point Becca made to him when he called her to postpone... half an hour before he was due to arrive. The suggestion that her friend and work colleague, Keiron, would no doubt step in and keep her company if he couldn't make it did not sit well with him at all. Whether she was trying to make him jealous or not he wasn't sure, but a little recognition from his boss for his efforts would go some way to easing his frustration.

"Aside from the missing person report the only records we have of her were those kept by her social worker," he said, trying his best to mask his irritation. Janssen lowered his gaze on to him. "I haven't had a chance to go through it but it's here along with everything I could find on Wellesley Manor, just as you asked."

Eric crossed to his desk and sifted through the array of files. Pulling a manila file, he stacked it on top of another and passed it to Janssen who nodded his thanks. The irritation flared again. The inspector had been in a foul mood all week. He found himself wondering what he'd done to deserve such treatment. With an almost imperceptible shake of the head, he turned back to the boards to find Tamara watching him intently. He smiled sheepishly, worrying about how long she'd been looking at him. She returned his smile with one of her own. Clearing his throat, he pointed to the middle board detailing the missing person investigation.

"The investigating officer spent a bit of time looking at Simon, her husband. Apart from what we already knew there was also an occasion where we were called out to a domestic incident. A neighbour reported an argument to us fearing his partner was in danger."

Tamara looked up at the board as if searching for more information beyond what was written there.

"It was prior to his relationship with Susan," he advised her.

"Any arrests made?"

Eric shook his head.

"The attending officers judged the situation calm enough that an arrest wasn't deemed necessary. It was never picked up during the investigation into Susan's disappearance."

"We spoke with Simon," Tamara said. "He was pretty open with us about his inadequacies as a husband and father in the past... seemed genuinely shocked to find his missing wife had died recently. With that said, I still want us to take another look at him. What were his movements at the end of last week and over the course of the weekend? Who does he associate with these days? There was a lot of pent-up frustration and rage on show when we spoke with him. Usually people are more reluctant to show their emotions around us when we're asking questions. If that's how he is in front of us I wonder what he's like in private. What about friends? He told us Susan had a couple she mixed with."

"Only one significant name that was spoken to at the time. Sarah Caseley," Eric said, glancing at his notes and then up at the board. "I don't know the link between the two of them though."

"I'll bet I do," Janssen said, reading from the file in his hands without glancing up. "They were both resident in the same children's home."

"Wellesley Manor, by any chance?" Tamara asked.

"The very same," Janssen replied. "Wellesley was run as a children's home between 1984 and 2002, when it closed its doors. Prior to that it was a private residence. There's a report here written by Susan's case worker from when she was resident there. Susan was involved in an altercation with another child and claimed to have been defending a friend by the name of Sarah. Sarah West was the friend but that would be her maiden name. She was thirteen at the time."

"Was it state owned?" Tamara asked.

"Charitable foundation," Janssen said, returning to the document. "Eric. Do you have an address for Sarah Caseley?"

"Yes. She lives near Burnham Market."

"Caseley. Why is that name familiar?" Janssen asked.

"I'm not surprised it is. The Caseleys are big landowners around here. They have a mix of working land and tenant farmers."

Janssen looked up at the clock on the wall and then across to Tamara.

"I think we should pay Sarah a visit tonight. We might get to find out what drew Susan back to Wellesley," Janssen said. "Eric, maybe you could have a word with Simon Cook and see if Susan ever mentioned her time there to him. He didn't speak about it with us but perhaps he didn't realise the significance. If we all head off now, we can be back—"

"Or," Tamara said, interrupting him, "we could call it a day now and start fresh tomorrow. Didn't you say you had plans tonight, Eric?"

Eric was surprised. He hadn't mentioned it or, at least, he didn't remember doing so.

"I did, yes... but shouldn't we—"

"Remember that we have lives too, Eric. Yes, we should," she said. "Get yourself off home."

"Right, yes."

He didn't need to be told twice. Scooping up his coat from the back of his chair, Eric hot footed it across the ops room, spinning on his heel when he reached the threshold of the door and taking a step back. Tamara threw him the car keys he'd left on his desk and Eric caught them deftly with one hand.

"Brilliant. Thanks."

Barely two steps out into the corridor, he was rooting around in his pocket for his mobile. Resisting the temptation to break into a run, he tapped the shortcut on his home screen to call Becca. If he was quick, he'd only be a little later than agreed. With luck, Keiron wouldn't get a look in.

CHAPTER SIXTEEN

"We could have left this until tomorrow," Tamara said absently as Janssen negotiated the narrowing of the road. Leaving the coast road and cutting inland towards Burnham Market they came to a patch of roadworks. One lane was closed with temporary traffic lights managing the three-way flow of vehicles through a junction. He muttered a protest under his breath. "I said, we could have left this until the morning. Sarah Caseley will still be here then."

"I know," he replied, clearing the lights and accelerating. The address was located on the outskirts of the village and he began scanning the approaching properties in search of their destination. "But it would be good to get ahead though, right?" he said, glancing across at her.

It was dark, approaching seven o'clock and he couldn't make out her expression in the reflective ambiance of the passing headlights.

"You're always committed, Tom. No one could ever doubt you there," she said. "But are you sure that's the reason?"

"What do you mean?"

"It would be good to remember we have lives beyond the job."

The comment irritated him. He tried hard not to show it.

"Look, I didn't know Eric had plans. He didn't mention them to me."

"Nor me," she said, looking straight ahead. "I just heard him chuntering to himself when he thought no one could hear."

He felt guilty then. Eric always put in the hours without complaint. Maybe he hadn't been paying enough attention.

"Besides," she said, "I wasn't talking about Eric."

"Anyway, what about you?" he said, ignoring her reference and consciously attempting to switch the conversation.

"What about me?"

"When are you moving into your own place?"

Tamara appeared to turn her attention to whatever they were passing, looking out of the passenger window. He could see her reflection in it.

"I don't know. I'll see how it goes. The hotel is fine for now."

"Heard from Richard lately?"

The silence hung in the air for a few moments, so much so that he wondered if she'd heard the question. Tamara shook her head.

"It didn't go well... the last time we spoke," she said, focussing on the passing landscape. "I must admit I've not wanted to pick up the phone since."

He was surprised they were still in contact at all. Since Tamara called off the wedding and accepted a new job, moving her away from her former fiancé, it seemed clear their future was apart from one another. Far easier to cut ties in his opinion. Then again, where lives become so interlinked it can often be more complicated than that. Maybe they still had issues to resolve. He thought Tamara was that type. Someone who liked to talk her way to a resolution. Analytical. Empathetic. Qualities that he admired. Traits he wished he could see in himself.

"I think this is it," he said, slowing the car as they came upon a rather grand detached Georgian house visible through the trees. Access to the driveway was barred by a high double gate.

Janssen pulled the car up close to an intercom, lowering the window and pressing the button. They waited patiently until the speaker crackled into life with a woman's voice. "Detective Inspector Janssen from Norfolk Police. I'm looking to speak with Mrs Sarah Caseley, if she's home?"

There was a pause. Janssen's eyes drifted to the camera mounted above the gate aimed directly at him. A buzzer was audible through the speaker and moments later the sound of a mechanism could be heard as the gates began to move. He edged the car forward. The driveway was lined with lights guiding them up to the house. No sooner had he pulled up outside the house, the front door opened. They were met by a woman who greeted them with a warm smile and an expectant expression as her eyes flitted between the two of them, hovering behind the semi-open door.

She was in her early forties, Janssen guessed. Although it was difficult to determine. She was immaculately presented in her attire, hair and make-up. By this point in the day, he could usually feel his eyes hanging off him but she came across buoyant, fresh and alert.

"Mrs Caseley?" he asked. Her smile broadened, attempting to mask nervousness.

"Yes. What can I do for you, Inspector... Janssen, did you say?"

"Tom Janssen," he said, taking out his warrant card and showing it to her. She leaned forward and inspected his identification before opening the door wider still and coming out from behind it. "This is Detective Chief Inspector Greave." He gestured to Tamara who also smiled.

"Please do come in," Sarah Caseley said, stepping aside and making room for them to pass. She need not have. The door was wide and the reception space of the hall it opened onto was easily twice as generous compared with what most houses offered. "I'm intrigued to know what I can do for you this evening. Is everything okay? Nothing has happened to James, has it?" Her smile faded as she spoke, as if suddenly considering the visit could be the result of something terrible.

"James is...?" he asked as she closed the door behind them.

"My husband."

"I'm sure he's fine," Janssen said. "We are here about your relationship with Susan Cook."

"Susan? My... that's going back," she said, leading them through into a large open-plan kitchen and dining room. They were in a single-storey contemporary extension. The rear wall was a curtain of glass overlooking the back garden, which was well lit revealing a landscaped garden and an al fresco seating area adjacent to a swimming pool.

"You were friends... back before she went missing, weren't you?" he asked as she offered them seats.

She nodded enthusiastically. "Yes, I knew her. Although, it seems like another life now."

Janssen caught Tamara scanning the room and wondered what was going through her mind.

"I'm afraid we have some bad news for you. We found Susan's body earlier this week," he said.

Sarah's shoulders sagged and she sat back in her seat. "Oh my, that's awful," she said. "Poor Susan. Is this anything to do with the body found over in Thornham?"

"I'm afraid so," he said.

"Dreadful. Is it true what people are saying?"

"What are people saying?"

"That she was... murdered?" Sarah lowered her voice, as if fearful of being overheard.

"We are still investigating the circumstances of how it happened. At this point we are keeping an open mind," he said, flicking a glance up at Tamara.

"I see. How is it I can help? I haven't seen Susan in nearly a decade."

Tamara came to sit at the table with them, taking up a seat to Sarah's right where Janssen was seated opposite. He caught

Sarah casting a glance at her as she sat down. Her eyes narrowed; it was a fleeting micro expression but enough to pique his curiosity before her smile returned.

"We are more interested in going back a bit further to when you first met her," Tamara said. "It was at Wellesley Manor, wasn't it?"

Sarah's lips parted as if she was about to speak but no words followed. Silence hung in the air. Sarah appeared to be taken aback, staring at some far away point in the distance.

"Mrs Caseley?" he said, trying to grab her attention. She shook her head, snapping herself from her reverie.

"I'm sorry. What was that, Wellesley? Yes... yes, we were both there at the same time," she said, her face taking on a stern look. "But that was all a long time ago. How is it relevant?"

"We believe Susan may have returned there recently and are trying to understand why she would do that. Have you any idea why she might go there?"

Sarah shook her head. "I'm afraid I've no idea why she would do that. How could I?"

Janssen failed to mask his surprise. "We were under the impression that the two of you were good friends. That you were one of the few friends she had."

"Well... maybe our friendship was overplayed a little. I couldn't really say. I don't think I was able to help much with why she left back then, nor now, I'm afraid."

She glanced up at the wall to her left. He followed her gaze up to the clock mounted there. She sounded defensive, fiddling with her hands as they spoke.

"You see, Susan and I were at Wellesley together but our paths only briefly crossed... for a few months."

"Susan spent much of her teenage years there," he said.

"You didn't?"

"No. I was adopted when I was nearly fourteen," she said. "They were a wonderful couple who already had two boys and wanted a girl. They were older, so a teenager suited them. I guess I was one of the lucky ones."

"Lucky how?"

"I got to leave. Don't get me wrong, it wasn't all terrible. I mean, children thrust together in those circumstances is never going to be heaven but some of them were quite nice."

"And the others?" he asked, seizing on the unsaid implication. She met his eye.

"Some of the children there were quite troubled, Inspector."

"Susan?"

"Not particularly that I recall, no."

"Did she ever mention anyone else to you, Abigail Thomas perhaps?"

At the mention of the artist, Sarah inclined her head to one side.

"Abigail?" she said.

"You know her?" Tamara asked.

"Yes, of course I do," she said, her eyes moving between the two of them. "Doesn't everyone? No, I don't recall Susan ever mentioning her to me."

The sound of someone entering through the front door carried to them. Sarah glanced at the clock again. Her expression turned pensive.

"I'm terribly sorry that I can't be more helpful."

"Sarah! Where are you?" a well-spoken voice asked from the hall.

"In here, darling," she replied. Her tone lightened as she spoke. Looking to Janssen, she smiled. "That's my husband, James."

Further conversation was interrupted by James Caseley's entrance. He was more than a few years older than his wife, closer to sixty, Janssen figured. A barrel-chested man, rosy-cheeked with greying hair, he entered the kitchen and immediately cast a quizzical eye across the visitors.

"I wondered why the gates were open and whose car that

was blocking the drive," he said to his wife before meeting Janssen's eye and seemingly taking his measure. "I didn't realise we were expecting guests."

"They are with the police, darling," Sarah said, standing and crossing to greet him with a kiss on the cheek. He appeared not to notice.

"The police?" he said with a frown. "Which police?"

"*The* police," Janssen replied, standing and offering his hand. "DI Tom Janssen."

James Caseley politely took it.

"What brings you here? Not one of my wife's fanciful goose chases again, I hope."

"It's nothing, darling. I think they were just about to leave."

"I've told you repeatedly, no one is watching the house. We have it lit up like a Christmas tree everyday now. I upgraded the gates and the camera system for you."

He was building up a head of steam now, seemingly unstoppable despite his wife's best attempts to do so.

"Honestly, you can't be wasting police time with these fantastical stories of yours—"

"We're here on a completely unrelated matter," Janssen said, cutting him off. He glanced to Tamara who nodded. Sarah certainly seemed keen to bring the conversation to a close. James Caseley appeared less inclined for them to do so.

"What are you doing here then?" James asked.

It was his wife who answered before either detective had a chance to.

"They are asking about Susan Cook. You remember Susan, darling?"

"Oh... her again. It's been years. Why on earth are you coming back here with that?" James said, his brow furrowing.

"Unfortunately, she's died. After all these years of not knowing. It's awful. These officers are trying to figure out what happened to her."

James raised his eyebrows. He didn't seem too bothered to learn of Susan's death.

"Oh, right. Well, I still don't understand how we're supposed to know what our cleaner gets up to, especially after so many years. What the staff do in their private life has nothing to do with us. Not unless they bring it to our door."

The last was said pointedly in Janssen's direction.

"Your cleaner?" James nodded.

"Yes. To this day, I still think she was stealing from us. Did you mention that?" he asked, looking to his wife before turning back to Janssen and gesturing with his forefinger. "You should make a note of that."

"Oh James, for heaven's sake," Sarah said, rolling her eyes but keeping one arm around her husband's waist and the other resting casually on his chest.

"What?" James protested innocently. "She dressed well enough and never seemed short of money."

"Susan worked hard, darling."

"Not that I could see, she didn't, always drinking a cup of tea whenever I saw her. She'd up sticks and shoot off the moment I arrived. Suspicious. Something to hide, I reckon."

"Please ignore my husband's critique, Inspector. He barely knew Susan, despite what he says."

"Just my impression," James countered, freeing himself from his wife's loose grip. "Anyway, it's a good job you're just off. We need to get ready. I've been running late all day and it wouldn't pay to be tardy. We need to leave by eight," he said, tilting his head forward and tapping his watch. "If you'll excuse me?"

The last comment was made directly to Janssen, who smiled as James Caseley turned to leave the room. He made a show of indicating the clock to his wife. Once he was out of earshot, Sarah turned to face them. She was tense, the wringing of her hands returned as they both waited expectantly for the explanation.

"I'm sorry," Sarah said, lowering her voice. "Please try to

understand, my husband doesn't know about my time at Wellesley. I've never told him about that part of my childhood. After my time at the home, I didn't see Susan for a long time and then, one day, I bumped into her purely by chance and we got talking. She was having a bit of trouble at the time, with her husband I think. Anyway, I invited her back here for a chat. She came by a few times after that. James returned home unexpectedly one day and I had to think of something. Her being our cleaner was the first thing that came to mind. Sooz played along. She was good like that."

"Like what?" he asked.

"You know, keeping a confidence."

"And what about when she went missing?" Janssen asked.

Sarah glanced nervously in the direction of the hall, fearful that her husband might reappear at any moment.

"When the policeman came by it was a bit awkward," she said, "but James is here so little... Anyway, I'd rather not dig up that period of my life. James is a good man, a caring man... once you get beyond the bluster but... social status is important within his family. I don't know if you can understand what I mean."

"We understand," Tamara said, coming alongside her and placing a reassuring hand on Sarah's forearm. "Can I ask what your husband meant with regard to the security?"

Sarah seemed embarrassed but answered tentatively. "As I say, my husband is very busy and he is away from the house for much of the week. He often stays in London, we have a flat in Chelsea, and I am here alone. I'm not one for keeping dogs, so... probably foolish, I know, but..."

"Quite understandable. Thank you for your time, Mrs Caseley," Tamara said.

Sarah escorted them out. They bid her goodnight and they heard the door close after them before Janssen had even reached for his keys. Spying another camera mounted on the wall and trained directly onto the entrance of the house, he looked around. The view of the grounds surrounding the house was unobstructed all the way to the entrance gates and the trees bordering the property. He opened the driver's door and got in.

"What do you make of her?" Tamara asked as he closed his door and reached for his seatbelt. He looked back at the house as he started the car.

"Plausible."

"In what way?" she pressed. He looked at her, she seemed intrigued by his comment.

"Everything about her is plausible. Her limited relationship with Susan... not having seen her for years, occasional meetings which leave her none the wiser regarding Susan's motivations... plausible," he said with a casual shrug. "The reason for keeping her husband in the dark about her background... plausible. As for the reasoning behind all of these lights and security—"

"Plausible," Tamara finished for him.

He laughed.

"And did you notice how she reacted when Abigail Thomas's name came up? Yes, she's a well-known artist but..."

"She's lying through her teeth."

"Damn right she is," he agreed. "Anyone who can deceive her husband about where she was for the first half of her life, as well as keeping him in the dark when the police come calling, is pretty adept at masking the truth. It'll be worth going through the Wellesley records and seeing if Abigail is linked."

"I'm wondering about Sarah herself. The fastidious presentation, not only the hair, clothes and make-up but how she was with us."

"Always trying to put us at ease with a ready smile?" he asked.

"Exactly that. It's almost as if she's not only hiding her past but she's hiding herself, putting a barrier between herself and the Sarah she wants the world to see."

"Or she likes to look good," Janssen countered. "Some people are vain."

Tamara shrugged. "Those people have issues with insecurity, self-esteem or anxiety. Sometimes all three to a degree."

"Is that why you don't make an effort?" Janssen teased playfully.

She shot him a look and he grinned.

"Quite right," she replied, smiling.

"I'll be a bit late in tomorrow, if that's okay," Janssen said.

"Sure, no problem. I'll take Eric along and have a chat with Tara Byrons. Everything all right with you?"

"Yeah. I just have an errand to run. That preoccupation we were talking about."

"Oh, right. The one I was talking about and you keep ducking?"

"Yeah. That's the one," he said.

Putting the car into gear, he moved the car off. The gates automatically opened as they approached and he wondered whether they were controlled by a sensor or if someone inside the house was watching them the entire time.

CHAPTER SEVENTEEN

THE DOOR CLOSED and Sarah Caseley leaned against the wall, turning her face to the ceiling. Taking a deep breath, she attempted to settle herself. Holding her hands out in front of her, they were shaking and no matter how hard she tried she couldn't stop them from doing so.

"Is that them leaving, Sarah?" James called from the upstairs landing. "You'd better get a move on. We need to be away soon."

She stepped away from the wall, coming to stand before the mirror mounted on its surface. Staring at her reflection, she barely recognised the person she saw anymore. She would head upstairs, shower and change. The end result would be much the same as what she was seeing here. Sarah smiled, a conscious effort to choose her mood. That was what her therapist taught her. The ability to shape her emotions by choice rather than be led by the external environment.

"Sarah," James called. This time with more than a hint of aggression. The unspoken demand was there. She didn't really have a choice. Making her way up the stairs, she saw her husband in their bedroom adjusting a tie in the ham-fisted way he usually did. Hurrying across, she brushed his hands away and took the corrective action.

"There you go," she said, sliding away. He checked his appearance in the full-height dress mirror. Pleased with the presentation, he stepped into their en suite bathroom. Pushing the door to, she heard a tap start to run as he set about washing his hands. Perching on the edge of the bed, she placed her hands in her lap. They were no longer shaking. James reappeared, looking at her with a frown.

"You'd better hurry. I want us to leave in a quarter of an hour."

"I... I'm not feeling well," she said, pursing her lips. "I thought... maybe I would give it a miss tonight. Get an early night."

James fixed her with a stare, putting his hands into the pockets of his trousers. He rolled his tongue across the top of his lower lip, his gaze intensifying.

"I don't think that would be appropriate," he said, breaking his gaze and crossing the room to retrieve his blazer hanging from the face of the wardrobe. Slipping the jacket on, he checked his appearance in the mirror once again. Angling his head one way and then the other, he gently touched the hair to both sides of his head ensuring it was presented as desired. Once happy, he flexed his upper body and with one last affirmative response to his reflection he made to leave the room. Upon reaching the threshold, he rested one hand on the door jamb and looked over his shoulder towards her. Raising both eyebrows, he tilted his head forward and met her eye. "Fifteen minutes, Sarah. I'll expect you downstairs. Cleaned up."

James left without another word. She didn't object. Didn't argue. Rising from the bed, she approached the wardrobes lining the walls of their bedroom. Opening the furthest one to the left, she stood on her tiptoes in order to reach the highest shelf. Moving aside two shoe boxes stacked one on top of the other, she reached to the rear and retrieved another small box. This one was wrapped in purple velvet and edged with gold detailing. It was a keep-sake box. Returning to the bed, she sat down. Lifting the lid, she eyed the contents. A multicoloured bead necklace and a small ring sat atop of some photographs. Both items were costume jewellery and of no real value bar the sentiment, given to her by a foster parent years before. Pushing these aside, she took out the photographs. Most were black and white and taken in the fifties and sixties but there were others, older still. The last remaining images of her family. She passed through these quickly, images of her biological mother and grandparents, lingering for a moment on a shot of her own mother as a toddler sitting on the lap of a stern-looking lady, presumably dressed in her finest clothes, with a bearded gentleman standing behind them. She had no real memories of any of them. Some residual feelings perhaps although whether they were genuine memories or optimistic imaginings she would never truly know.

Continuing on, she reached a coloured shot. Putting the other pictures down, she held this photograph in front of her in both hands. The image was far from the highest quality, grainy and deteriorating with age. The corners were tatty and the colours faded. The memory of that day, however, was not. Posing for the shot were five children. All girls, barely into their teens, standing before a closed five-bar gate wearing summer clothes and smiling for the camera. Her fingers drifted over the image, stopping when they came to the girl on the right. She wore a red hooded rain mac, was slightly built and far shorter than the others despite being approximately the same age. She stood off to the right, a half step away from the others who were all linking arms and grinning. She appeared lost. She was. Sarah's fingers stroked the face of the child and she closed her eyes, blinking back the tears.

"Sarah!"

"I'll be right there," she called back, her voice threatening to break. Hurriedly, she put the pictures back in the box and secreted them away again. From the same wardrobe she pulled a red evening gown. It was one she knew James approved of. Coming to stand before the mirror, she held it in front of her. If she wore her hair up with this dress, she could be ready soon enough. Checking that her mascara hadn't run, she took a deep breath staring at her reflection.

"I'm sorry, Sooz," she whispered quietly.

The words sounded hollow to her even as she said them.

CHAPTER EIGHTEEN

APPROACHING THE JUNCTION, they turned left into what would have been the car park at the rear of the old pub. The building itself was fenced off with several 'for sale' signs hanging from the walls and displayed in upstairs windows. To go beyond the rear of the parking area would once have taken you into a paddock accessed from a track running adjacent to the main road. However, they were now driving through a small development of new-build homes, a mixture of completed and semi-built properties, on a road yet to receive its final layer of tarmac, all within the boundaries of Hunstanton, a popular coastal town. The car rose and fell abruptly as Tamara caught the wheels on a raised drain cover. She was grateful not to be driving her Healey down here. The designs were contemporary, styled with a mix of aluminium windows, cream render and cedar cladding. Eric referred to the choice of window frames as the curious *grey tide* in reference to the trend gradually working its way around the coastal towns of Norfolk. Tamara found herself wondering if this was a place she should be looking at for herself. On-trend house-designs with their open layouts and manageable outdoor spaces were one of the few modern approaches to living that she found appealing.

"Number fourteen," Tamara said, almost confirming it to herself.

"Yes," Eric said, his eyes scanning the houses as they drove past.

Parking was already limited with several residents pulling their vehicles part way up onto the pavement. They were here early, so no doubt the congestion would ease once everyone left for work. She pulled up outside the house just as a woman stepped out, pulling the front door closed behind her. She was dressed in a business suit with a camel overcoat thrown over one forearm, carrying a red leather shoulder bag. They were out of the car and approaching her as she unlocked her car, a sleek Audi coupe, drawing her attention.

"Tara Byrons?" Tamara asked. The woman looked up as she placed her bag and coat in the car and was about to get in herself. Turning, she eyed their approach. Tamara took a measure of her, taking out her warrant card as she did so. Tara Byrons was in her early forties, tall, slim and angular of face. Her hair was shoulder length, cut in a bob and framed her features. "DCI Greave and Detective Constable Collet. May we have a word?"

Tara eyed both of them with a surprised expression before glancing at her watch.

"I was just leaving for work," she said, not bothering to hide her irritation. "What's this about?"

"I appreciate you're heading out but it won't take long. We have a few questions," Tamara said, employing her warmest smile by way of encouragement. "We'll be quick, I assure you."

Tara closed the car door but her expression conveyed her displeasure at the delay to her commute. She came to the rear of the car where they waited.

"Okay. What is it I can do for you?"

Tamara felt dwarfed by her. Admittedly she was in heels but Tara Byrons stood in excess of six feet tall. "We're interested in your relationship with Susan Cook."

"Susan?" Tara replied with surprise, the wind disrupting her well-presented hair. She casually brushed it away from her face with her hand. "That's a name I've not heard in years."

"Maybe we could talk inside," Tamara said.

"I guess so," Tara said.

This close to the sea, the wind was whipping in off the water and being funnelled up the street by the buildings, striking them with a constant icy blast. Tara collected her bag from the passenger seat of the car and gestured for them to follow as she headed back up the drive to the house. A man appeared from the neighbouring property and Tara and he exchanged conventional greetings without any real feeling. His gaze lingered on the two police officers as he passed while Tara retrieved her house keys from her bag and unlocked the front door. Stepping through, she held the door for them as they entered.

Tamara took in the interior. It was as she expected: modern, light and airy with white painted walls and open plan to the kitchen. The picture window to the front had a view down the street. With the slight incline they were able to see the sea, visible in the distance. A number of landscape photographs were mounted on the walls. They were stylish, some in monochrome or sepia and probably taken locally. Her eyes lingered on several shots of Tara Byrons herself, presumably from her university days. One was a team shot taken at what appeared to be a rowing event with the four participants brandishing medals for the camera. Moving to read the wording of the graduation day print nearby, she saw Tara was an alumnus of Cambridge University.

"Would you like a coffee or cup of tea?" Tara asked. "I skipped my usual after getting back from my morning run because I was a little behind."

Without waiting for a response, she went to a machine on the work surface. Eric declined but Tamara welcomed a black coffee despite not being a fan of the throwaway machine pods.

"You said this is about Sooz. What could you possibly want to know from me after all these years? Have you found her?"

"What makes you ask that?" Tamara said.

Tara looked at her as if it was the most obvious question to have had asked.

"Because you're here," she replied flatly. The machine whirred as it dispensed the trickle of rich coffee into a small cup. She passed the freshly-made espresso over to Tamara, who accepted it gratefully. "Is this to do with the body you found at Thornham?"

Tamara made to sip at her coffee but it was far too hot, maintaining eye contact with their host as she did so.

"Word travels fast around here, doesn't it?"

"No one's talking about anything else," Tara said, setting about making a drink for herself. "Are you sure I can't tempt you?" she asked Eric.

He declined.

"They said on the news it was a woman's body and may have been in the water for some time. I must admit whenever I hear about an unidentified body in the news, local or national, I tend to think of Susan," Tara said with the slightest suggestion of a shrug. "Without a resolution to what happened to her, I guess it's only normal."

"You're probably right," Tamara said. "You wouldn't be surprised to hear if it was her then?"

Tara pursed her lips, her brow furrowing in concentration as she thought about it.

"Judging by where her car was found, along with what she was like as a person, no. I always thought she must have taken her own life. I guess I wouldn't be surprised at all. Is it her?"

"Enquiries are ongoing," Tamara said flatly, blowing gently on the surface of the liquid in an attempt to cool it down. Tara accepted the comment without question. "Had she exhibited any signs that she was that way inclined?"

Tara had her back to them as she prepared her coffee, answering over her shoulder.

"I think Susan struggled to cope with life. Some people manage to deal with the adversity that comes your way and others... fall by the wayside, don't they. I'd put Susan down as one of those."

"Were you also friends from Wellesley Manor, along with Sarah Caseley?"

The question appeared to throw her, for there followed a brief moment of hesitation.

"You've spoken with Sarah?"

Tamara nodded.

"Then you do think it's Susan... or you wouldn't be here."

"We've been through the records of all those present at the children's home at the same time as Susan Cook. Your name was in the file."

Tara inclined her head to one side, meeting Tamara's gaze head on. She seemed to be gauging her. After a moment, she answered.

"Yes, I met Susan there. I don't recall whether Sarah was there at the same time or if Susan introduced us later. I really can't remember."

"What do you remember about your time there?"

Tara exhaled in a short burst, lifting her cup from the machine and holding it in both hands.

"I would be lying if I said it wasn't a difficult time," she said, glancing out of the window. A cargo ship was passing on the horizon, hugging the coast as it headed north. "Wellesley was a hostile place, full of mixed-up kids. The only thing we had in common was that no one really wanted us. Everyone had a story."

"What was yours?" Tamara asked. "If you don't feel like I'm prying."

"I was a cliché," Tara said with a wry grin. "I came from a broken home, absent father and my mother couldn't cope. She had four children and we were all tearaways. Probably as a result of our mum being run ragged. In the end, it was inevitable."

"You're a teacher now?" Eric asked, glancing up from his notebook.

"Yes. I'm deputy head at a local junior school," she said. "Now I get to see it from the other side."

"I hear it's tough in the classroom these days. Is that your assessment?"

"I would say that we see children with all manner of issues these days, which does indeed make it tough. Perhaps things aren't as different from how they used to be. We tend to look back with our rose-tinted glasses on but, arguably, we're better trained to recognise particular conditions these days. Behavioural indicators that passed us by in the profession until relatively recently are now more recognisable."

"Looking back at your time at Wellesley, particularly the time spent with Susan, is there anything that stands out from then? Anything that could draw you back there?"

Tara laughed but it was without genuine humour. It seemed more edged with regret. She shook her head, biting her lower lip.

"There is much that went on back there, most of it I try not to think about. As children, you have to understand we were the unwanted. Some of the girls were lucky, only passing through until a better option could be found with family members or if their parents managed to sort themselves out. After a while…" The words tailed off, Tara seemingly struggling to articulate them in a way she liked. "Once you've been there for a certain period of time, you realise that this is your lot. There aren't any saviours coming to take you to a better place and you have to make do, just get on with it. After you'd been there a while, you are able to assess people. Pretty comprehensively too. You see those children who come in and you judge whether they'll be staying long term or moving on. Some kids were delusional about their prospects, forever talking about when their *real parents would come for them*. Then there were those of us who knew. We knew that Wellesley was as good as it was going to get." She met Tamara's eye. "That was the most crushing moment. Once you'd accepted that, then it was all right."

"How bad was it?"

"It's not that it was bad, so to speak. Things went on there, much as you would expect."

"What type of things?"

Tara sipped at her coffee, her expression was stern and yet reflective, as if she was recalling painful memories.

"Some of the staff were not what one might hope for," she said after a brief period of quiet contemplation. "Don't get me wrong, many of us were truly dreadful children to care for and often got exactly what we deserved. I don't want you to see the staff as entirely to blame, nor do I wish to fall into the realms of victim blaming but you have to realise that Wellesley wasn't a place only for local children. There were kids coming in from all over... Essex... the Midlands... the south coast. We were all damaged and vulnerable to varying degrees and it wasn't the most supportive of regimes."

"Are you saying you were mistreated?"

Tara stood with her mouth slightly open, arms folded across her chest, sporting an expression set in stone.

"Much that passed as normal back then wouldn't be acceptable now," she said. "Let me say that. Not all of the staff, mind you. Some were exasperated at their inability to control... no, that's the wrong word," she said thinking hard. "Their inability to positively influence our lives. At the other end of the spectrum, there were those who seemed to take a genuinely sadistic pleasure in controlling the lives of vulnerable children."

"Are we talking about physical abuse... sexual?" Tamara asked. Tara Byrons pulled herself upright, gently placing her cup on the work surface alongside her.

"We talked amongst ourselves. Comments were made and

fingers pointed, yes. How much truth there was behind what some girls said, I do not know."

"Your own experience?" Tamara pressed, aware that she needed to tread carefully but Tara appeared to be a woman of fortitude.

"Not me, no. I don't think I would ever have been considered as a potential candidate. I never fitted the criteria. I wasn't socially detached or malleable as abuse victims often are. That's the teacher in me speaking now, one with years of experience in safeguarding. I dare say it's not something I was aware of at the time."

"Did Susan fit the criteria?" Tamara asked.

Tara exhaled deeply, locking eyes with her.

"This wasn't the conversation I was expecting to have when I woke up this morning," she said with a brief shake of the head. Tamara waited, determined to glean as much from this conversation as she could. Often, an impromptu chat could be far more revealing than when a witness had the opportunity to think hard on the subject matter. "Susan... possibly, yes. She would speak of things that happened back at Wellesley but... she was an odd one. We were friends and everything but you never really knew with her. She was always prone to exaggeration or flat-out storytelling. Sooz was also one of the girls who would slip out of the home at all times of the day and night."

"Where would she go?"

Tara shrugged.

"She'd be picked up at the gates by her boyfriend, often more than one. That's what she used to call them, her *boyfriends*."

The disdain Tara displayed towards them was clear.

"How would you have described them?"

"They were men... Susan was maybe fourteen at the time, fifteen at the most. Some of the girls were younger still."

Tamara considered the information, feeling a deep sense of foreboding in the pit of her stomach. None of this formed part of Susan's case file with social services nor came up in any of the previous statements from friends or colleagues. The historical exploitation of children in care was well documented. Vulnerable children were open to grooming by older men who often presented themselves as loving partners, showering the girls with presents and affection only to pass them around their social circle in a systematic process of abuse. The victims would often fail to consider the perpetrators as criminals, often this interpretation could also be laid at the feet of the local police who didn't recognise these figures as abusers. To the girls, these men demonstrated love and care for them when they felt no one else was doing so.

"Were concerns raised by the staff? Was anything ever made formal?"

"Regarding the men?" She nodded.

"Not that I recall. Usually, it was the most disturbed girls who fell into that particular group. I think some of the management were quite pleased to have them out of the way for a while."

"What about the events you describe from within Wellesley?"

"Oh, yes," she replied, frowning as if it was a silly question. "I'm surprised you're not aware of the reports. It's all on the public record. A number of allegations were made but nothing ever came of it. We talked about what may or may not happen but, ultimately, the whole thing just went away. Some of the girls were moved on. Whether that was a result of the investigation or not I don't know. Things changed a bit at the home after that. For a time at least. With hindsight, I wonder if anyone really wanted to know what was going on back then. I wonder if they figured it best for everyone concerned if it all just went away. The children… well, we just got on with it. No choice really."

"Was there a particular member of staff who was implicated?" Tamara asked.

"The allegations went right to the top," Tara replied, meeting her eye.

"Was Susan one of those who made an allegation?"

"Oh, you're at the limits of my memory now. I can't really remember. I'm sorry."

"What about these men who Susan used to associate with. Do you know any of their names or where we might begin looking for them?"

"I'm sorry," Tara said. "I wouldn't know where to start. I'm not sure anyone aside from those who used to go with them would know."

"Who did go with them?" Tamara asked, glancing at Eric to make sure he was keeping track of the conversation. He stood off to her left, pocketbook in hand. Tara Byrons hesitated. "It might be important."

"I know," Tara said, sighing. "I'm just conscious that this is people's lives we are talking about and this was all such a long time ago. I wouldn't want any inaccuracy in my memory to adversely affect the present."

"We will be discreet," she said. The comment appeared to reassure Tara who took a deep breath, looking to the ceiling.

"The two names that spring to mind are Kirsty Davies and... Sarah," Tara said quietly, lowering her gaze to Tamara.

"Sarah Caseley?"

Tara bobbed her head in confirmation.

CHAPTER NINETEEN

Tara Byrons checked the time, deliberately making a show of looking at her watch. The lead detective smiled. It was polite, manufactured, probably something taught to them when learning how to put someone at ease. She knew the drill; ask open questions and maintain eye contact whilst making reassuring noises to encourage responses. It was the standard approach to dealing with people, adults or children alike.

"I think we can leave it there for now, Mrs Byrons."

"Miss," she corrected.

The need to confirm she was unmarried was an instinctive response and one she immediately regretted. Where that came from she didn't know. Maybe it was a generational thing or perhaps societal, a push back against those who still raise an eyebrow when they meet a forty-something who is neither married nor has children. The unspoken assumption there must be something wrong with her or her sexuality was non-traditional. Hers could well be the last generation who saw this as an issue. The children she taught on a daily basis seemed to have a far more fluid view about sexual orientation. How quickly the world appeared to be changing. For herself, however, the assumptions still grated.

"My apologies," the DCI said, her smile widening. "I get the same thing myself. I should know better."

Looking down at the officer's left hand she noted the absence of a ring on her finger. They were of a similar age but, in her opinion, the detective looked older. Probably because she wore so little make-up and dressed in very plain and ordinary clothing. Perhaps she had misjudged her. The sense that she'd said too much came to mind but she aggressively pushed the thought away. Nothing she had spoken of was a secret. It had all been raised before and would be on file somewhere. Any investigation into Susan's death would bring it to light, so what was the point in pretending none of this happened.

Despite this logic, there was still a sense of trepidation at the scrutiny and exposure that might be forthcoming. Her effectiveness in her role at the school as well as her standing, a position she had spent so much time and effort in cultivating, could take a turn for the worse. Events such as these were what happened to other people, dramatic and certainly heartbreaking, but almost always occurring elsewhere. This happened here, within the community, and there would be many who would not care to hear it.

The two detectives made their way to the front door and out onto the driveway. She followed, only a step behind. Locking the door behind her, she walked with them until coming to her car. The lead detective offered her hand and Tara took it.

"I'm sorry to spring all of this on you unannounced. We may need to speak with you again."

"I'd prefer not to rake over all this again but, if you need to, then please do give me a call," she replied.

The detective inclined her head in thanks, offering Tara a contact card, and turned to join her younger colleague who was waiting beside their car. She watched for a moment longer before unlocking her own car and getting in. Looking in the rear-view mirror, they moved off and she felt relief wash over her. Taking her mobile from her bag, she glanced at the clock on the dashboard and sighed. The meeting she was due to chair was scheduled to begin in a few minutes. Calling the main office of the school, she waited patiently. A voice answered within a few rings.

"Hi, Mary, it's Tara. I'm sorry for the short notice but I'm not going to be able to make it in today."

"Oh dear. Are you unwell?" Mary, the head of the school's administration team, said.

"Nothing too serious, I think," she replied, laying on a deeper tone than normal. "I was going to persevere but it's for the best if I stay home today, rest up and see it off. I wouldn't want to carry something into the school."

The voice at the other end of the line chuckled sympathetically.

"There's plenty going around already. I'll let Marcus know. You take care of yourself."

"I will, thank you."

Tara hung up on the call, touching the mobile phone to her lips as she considered her next move. Scrolling through the contacts list on her phone, she found the number she was looking for, hoping it hadn't changed. They hadn't spoken for quite some time. The call connected and she waited for an answer. Just as she figured it was about to transfer through to voicemail or she would have to give up and try again later, a gruff voice answered.

"Hello."

"Hey, it's me, Tara. Did I wake you?"

"Ah... yeah, you did."

"Late night?"

"Today's my day off, so... you know how it is. I take it you've heard?"

"Yes," she said softly, angling the mirror so she could see her reflection, checking the coverage of her lipstick. "Are you okay?"

He coughed. The type of hacking cough generated by a night on the tiles, heavy drinking, smoking and a distinct lack of sleep.

"Not the greatest."

"I thought I could come over. What do you think?" The question was tentative, she didn't want to force it. The tone of his voice became lighter, he sounded uplifted.

"Sure… I mean, yes. That'd be great!"

"You're still at the same place?"

"Yeah. I'm not going anywhere any time soon."

"I'll see you in about half an hour," she said, starting the car.

Hanging up, she placed the mobile in one of the cup holders between the seats. With one last look at her own reflection, she readjusted the mirror before reversing the car out onto the road. Turning on the stereo, she selected one of her play lists. Quietly humming along to the first track that started, she set off. The traffic she usually encountered on the morning commute had largely dissipated now and the journey was done in quick time. This being the off season, roads between Hunstanton and Fakenham that would be clogged in a few months' time were presently free flowing.

Pulling into the car park soon after, there were a handful of cars present but no one within sight. Parking near to the reception, she got out and looked around. The office was shut and she made her way to the rear. A car passed her, one of the few holidaymakers still on the site. The occupants paid her no heed. Her heels clicked on the tarmac as she made her way up the path. She saw him watching her approach through the kitchen window, moving aside the blind for a better view. She didn't need to knock on the door because it opened when she was barely three steps from it. A nervous-looking Simon Cook peered out at her before ushering her inside and looking both to the left and right of his caravan before pulling the door closed. He turned to face her. Dark patches under his eyes hung as mementos of the previous night's endeavours, his hair wild and unkempt. The smell of alcohol appeared to seep from every pore.

"I see you're taking the news well," she said, casting her eye up and down him. He absently ran one hand through the hair on the top of his head, pausing to rub it back and forth when he reached his crown. His eyes were wide and he shook his head slightly.

"Threw me a bit, you know. You?"

"Obviously, I'm shocked. That goes without saying," she replied, looking around. The previous night's meal was yet to be cleared away. A takeaway by the look of the foil trays and plastic containers. Two bottles were amongst them, one upright and the other lying flat. Both were empty, one of scotch and another of gin. The general smell in the caravan was stale and unpleasant. It must have been quite some bender he'd been on. "And Connor?"

Simon shook his head. "Not great. I sent him to school. No point in him moping around here all day. Best for him to be with his mates, I reckon."

She found herself wondering who exactly it was best for but didn't comment. Simon leaned against the kitchen units pressing thumb and forefinger against his eyes. After a moment, he dropped his hand and met her eye. His was a haunted expression. Simon looked lost. She put her bag down on one of the chairs and came over to him. Holding her arms wide, he moved towards her and she embraced him. The gesture unleashed a wave of emotion and he wept, burying his face into her chest. She slowly stroked the back of his head making soothing sounds.

"It's going to be all right, Simon. It will," she said softly, looking out of the window. Reaching over with one hand, she adjusted the blind so that no one passing would be able to see them. Easing him away from her, she held his upper arms gently with both hands. Moving them slowly towards his face, she cupped his cheeks and raised his head so that their eyes met. She smiled warmly at him. He looked likely to cry again at any moment.

"Them finding her... it's brought it all back," he whispered as tears fell once more. Slowly wiping them clear with her thumbs, she kept her hands where they were, leaning in and gently kissing his forehead. Withdrawing, she met his eye again and smiled. This time he returned it.

"I'm here for you," she said affectionately. He leaned forward and she did likewise. Their lips brushed once, then twice before coming together in a passionate embrace. Simon's arms encircled her waist and pulled her into him. She didn't resist. Within moments she could feel his arousal. Some things would never change.

CHAPTER TWENTY

TAMARA GREAVE WATCHED as Janssen walked back into the room. Reacting to the call, she saw his demeanour shift as he had left to seek some privacy. It wasn't merely the lowering of the voice when speaking to a loved one in the open-plan office, there was more to it than that. Returning to the ops room with something of a spring in his step, she wondered whether he'd had some good news from a local bookie. Not that Tom was so inclined but the call certainly marked an improvement in his mood.

"Everything okay?" she asked, as he took his seat.

Janssen glanced up at her with an enquiring expression.

"The call," she said.

He smiled.

"All good," he replied, picking up the file on his desk. "Where were we again?"

"Wellesley Manor. Tying together who was there at the same time as Susan Cook."

"That's right," he said, scanning the list of names in front of him as his eyes flitted between it and the boards on the wall. "Curious. Sarah Caseley claimed the two of them barely crossed paths at the children's home. I remember that right don't I?"

Tamara revisited her notes. "A few months was how she described it. Why?"

"Social services has them both resident for well over a year. Is it a large enough place that they could have avoided each other?"

Not in her mind. The highest number of children who were ever recorded as being present was eighteen. The notion that two girls of similar ages wouldn't cross paths was unlikely. Bearing in mind the length of time that had passed there was the possibility Sarah misremembered. Going by what they learnt from Tara Byrons, that Sarah was prone to deception, however implied Sarah Caseley was not being entirely truthful. Her desire to shield her past from her husband could extend to the police investigation as well.

"I think we will be following up with Mrs Caseley soon enough. Mind you, let's arm ourselves with as much fact as we can beforehand. No doubt our visit will have set her mind churning. It will be interesting to see what else comes from it. Any joy with deciphering those scribblings you found in the room where Susan was attacked?"

Janssen took out the photographs taken by the CSI team. With their extensive lighting equipment the inscriptions were much easier to read. The images were blown up and it was these that Janssen now crossed the floor and pinned to the white boards.

"You can see these more clearly," he said, putting up the last and stepping back.

Tamara cupped her chin with thumb and forefinger of one hand, scrutinising the images. At the top of the door someone had scratched the message *I was here*. If she had to guess she would think it had been done with a crude implement and possibly without the aid of light. The room was enclosed allowing no natural light at all and the varying size and positioning of the letters suggested the person who wrote it did so using their imagination of where they perceived the letters should be. They'd be able to determine whether the letters were scribed by different hands, the rise and fall of the styles denoting separate individuals. Beneath the sentence were close groupings of individual letters. Some overlapped one another reinforcing the theory they were made in the dark.

"What do you make of them? Initials?" she asked.

Janssen glanced at her. "That was my thinking too." He returned to his desk, picking up the list of names. Some of which he had already circled. "Let's see if we can find some likely candidates. Sarah Caseley is a good start. Her maiden name was West and we have SW on the door. No other child registered at the home carried those initials. Similarly, we have a KD. There were two who fitted that grouping. Kirsty Davies and a Karen Duncroft. The latter wasn't resident there at the same time. She left a couple of years before Susan arrived."

"Assuming the list runs from top to bottom, does KD come before or after SW?"

Janssen checked.

"After. KD is the fourth visible although it overlaps the third."

"If there was a crossover between Susan and Kirsty Davies, then it stands to reason it's her. Has she turned up elsewhere in the investigation into Susan's disappearance?"

Janssen shook his head.

"No, nothing at all."

"What's that one there, is it AV?" she said, moving closer and inclining her head to try and get a better look.

"I thought so but you can see some other scratches that don't run as deep. I think it's a W, not a V. What is interesting, though, is Abigail Thomas. Thomas is her married name; although she divorced her husband she retained the name. Presumably because she'd already established her career. Her maiden name was Winston."

Tamara chewed her lower lip, taking in the implication.

"Can we confirm whether Abigail Thomas is one and the same?"

"Hell of a coincidence if it isn't, wouldn't you say?" Janssen argued. She bobbed her head in agreement. "And what I originally thought was TD looks wrong. No one matches the joining of those initials."

"Could the D actually be a B?" Tamara said. "As in Tara Byrons? She was at great pains to convey how single she is when Eric and I spoke with her this morning."

"That follows," Janssen said, re-examining the pictures. "But there's no way to be sure."

"And Susan's maiden name?"

"Cole," Janssen confirmed. "And no, there are no related inscriptions for her."

Tamara silently cursed. That would have been neat and tidy. A way of tying everyone they spoke to together to the scene of where they thought Susan was attacked. Something took her to that particular room. The markings were too coincidental for them not to carry meaning. The desire to seek out these women and ask them the significance of the inscriptions was tempting. In reality, they would need to be patient. Whatever drew Susan to the room after all this time may well have got her killed. After Tara Byrons' candid assessment of life in Wellesley Manor they had to consider the possibility that there were those who wanted to silence Susan Cook and did so in the most brutal fashion.

"What of these allegations Tara Byrons told you about?" Janssen asked.

"I can answer that," Eric said, entering ops and animatedly brandishing a file in his hand. Both of them turned to face him. "It took a bit of digging to get this."

"What have you got?" she asked him as he sat down and opened the folder.

"The allegations Tara Byrons spoke of were made against multiple members of staff detailing incidences of both sexual and physical assault against a number of girls at Wellesley. This took place two years prior to when Susan left the home and Abigail is mentioned as well. I just checked before coming back up. She was there under the surname of Winston."

"Yeah, we wondered whether that was her," Janssen said.

Eric continued. "Now, no charges were ever brought and the investigation was dropped before it was even passed to the CPS, citing a lack of evidence due to the unreliability of the witnesses."

The last part of the analysis irked Tamara. So many times, cases were not pursued where they should have been due to the victim's perceived lack of credibility. She already knew where Eric was heading.

"The two girls who made the allegations had well-documented behavioural issues and social services reported one of them as *sexually aggressive*," Eric said, glancing up from reading.

"At what age?" she said.

Eric scoured the document.

"Thirteen."

"Labelled as sexually aggressive at the age of thirteen. She was a child," Tamara said, feeling anger rise within her. "What did the investigating officer say?"

Eric chose his words carefully. "Reading between the lines, I think he didn't believe the stories and thought they were out to make trouble for the management. The scale of the abuse allegations was such that it appeared fanciful that so many members of staff would be able to get away with it for the length of time alleged. Apparently, it was one of the girls who insisted on making a formal statement while the other retracted everything in her initial statement. It was one girl's word against the management and she was disbelieved. Faced with the prospect of testimony from a thirteen-year-old girl with an attitude problem against that of the respected management, they quietly dropped it. The investigation barely got past its initial stage."

"Attitude problem?" she asked.

"She was reported as being a runaway on multiple occasions. Uniform always found her at her boyfriend's house," Eric explained, reading from the file. "Repeated instances of being caught in possession of alcohol and drugs."

"Sounds more like she was trying to escape the home," she countered. "Or herself."

"Not necessarily as a result of her experiences at the home. She could have been seeking attention. A cry for help by delivering the most dramatic of allegations," Janssen said.

"You sound like the investigating officers of the day," Tamara said, irritated by his stance.

He shrugged off the comment.

"I can see how they came to the conclusion, that's all," Janssen said, unapologetic.

She looked to Eric, burying her annoyance. Janssen was obstinate. He was also correct.

"You said the report took some finding?"

"Yeah. It was well buried. I had to go down to the archives with one of the clerks to get it. Took ages. We only have the hard copy of the report. For some reason this file doesn't appear on the digital database. I didn't get a satisfactory answer to why that was the case either. I guess no system is perfect."

"Who made the allegation? Was it Susan by any chance?" Tamara asked.

"No, it wasn't her. She doesn't even get a mention," Eric said. Tamara felt her heart sink. Eric reread the paperwork. "The complainant was Kirsty Davies," he said triumphantly.

"What's her date of birth?" Janssen asked. Eric read it out as Janssen turned to his laptop and logged in to the police national database. Eric made to speak but for some reason didn't follow up. Entering the details, Janssen tapped return. The machine processed the request while they all waited expectantly.

"Damn," he said softly, turning to Tamara. "Kirsty Davies is deceased." He looked at the information brought up on the screen pointing to the date of her registered death. It was over three decades previously. "By my reckoning, Kirsty was fourteen when she died."

"That would still have her firmly in the system," Tamara said. "Was she still a resident at Wellesley at the time?"

"I'm way ahead of you," Eric said excitedly, reaching for his notebook.

Tamara was pleased to see the enthusiasm in the young man despite the workload he was currently under. His reluctance to stop Janssen in his tracks was quite telling. Eric was on tenterhooks around his DI.

"Kirsty Davies was suspected of running away, not for the first time as I said. Police were alerted and carried out the initial search as you would expect. Friends, known hang-outs and the like. Only this time, unlike on other occasions, no one claimed to have seen her. She was found in a river two days later. I pulled the coroner's report while I was down in the archives. Initially they suspected drowning as the cause of death. Unsurprising, seeing as she was found in the water. There was a head injury at the base of her skull where it meets the neck, likely caused by a blunt force trauma and the pathologist found striations in the tissues of her neck."

Tamara sank back into her chair, raising her eyes to the ceiling.

"So they suspected she was strangled or hanged?"

"The latter," Eric said. "The police carried out a fingertip search of the area following the line of the river which passed through open fields, marsh and woodland. They found a tree with a recently broken branch and some clothing nearby matching what Kirsty was wearing on the day she was last seen. The conclusion was that she hanged herself with a makeshift noose but the weight of her body was too much for the bough and it snapped, pitching her into the river. They concluded she must have struck her head on the rocks on her way into the water. The assumption was the attempted suicide failed but the blow to the head knocked her unconscious and she drowned. It was ruled as accidental death by misadventure rather than a suicide."

"Call me cynical for thinking this," Tamara said, folding her arms across her chest in front of her, "but that sounds convenient. Based on the previous allegations."

Janssen blew out his cheeks.

"Or, at the risk of irritating you further," Janssen said, glancing over at her, "and to play devil's advocate for a moment, it also backs up the conclusion of the initial investigation. A troubled teenager, suffering from mental health issues, takes her own life. The end result of a tragic set of conditions. You can argue it either way."

Tamara met his eye. He was right, she felt the sense of irritation swelling at his dismissal of her suggestion but it passed as soon as she recognised it. She could tell he didn't have confidence in that assessment either. However, he was right to keep them rooted to the core facts of what they knew. Conjecture was useful but wild unsubstantiated theories had no place in a murder investigation.

"Something went on in that room," she said, turning her attention back to the board and running her eye over Susan's known circle of friends and acquaintances. "And one, or all, of them knows exactly what that was," she said pointedly, gesturing towards the names of Abigail Thomas, Sarah Caseley and Tara Byrons.

"Eric, can you do me a copy of the pathologist's report?" Janssen asked. "I want to go through it again at home later. And also, find out where the members of staff are now, all those working at Wellesley at the time all of this occurred. I think we should ask them the questions that perhaps weren't asked first time around," Janssen said.

"I'll do it for you now," Eric said, scooping up the file.

"Just in case they missed something," Janssen said to Tamara as Eric left them. She was looking at him intently. "I don't wear a tin foil hat but, let's face it, it is a *remarkable* coincidence."

He glanced at the clock on the wall, lowering his voice so only she could hear him as Eric busied himself with the photocopier.

"I know it's early but I've got plans for tonight and I need to pick something up beforehand. I'll go over the paperwork at home later but do you mind if I shoot off?"

She shrugged that it was okay and he thanked her, rising from his chair and picking up his jacket. His reluctance to ask was obvious for her to see. Janssen had already taken some personal time that morning and now he wanted to leave early. Whatever it was that he was up to, he was keeping his cards close to his chest. If he needed the time then she would grant it without question. There was a change in him recently, she could see it, but as to what it meant she didn't yet know.

CHAPTER TWENTY-ONE

THE WIND COULD BE HEARD swirling around outside, buffeting the boat and contributing to a greater swell in the water. The pressure of the wind through the flue saw the flames in the wood burner depressed before springing up as they fed on the increased oxygen. Putting down the knife, Tom Janssen picked up a tea towel and dried his hands as he crossed to the burner. Picking up another log, he opened the door and added it to the fire. The air temperature was unseasonably clement for the time of year but the raised wind tore through the boat making it feel less so. Nonetheless, he'd found the time spent living on the boat these past eighteen months enjoyable. The lack of facilities was a challenge but easily overcome with a bit of an effort. What he thought would be a challenge turned out to be less so. Living without a television was far easier than anticipated, although the advent of fibre broadband to the area meant even this was accessible if desired. He used the latter for work but, more often than not, found sitting down in front of a roaring fire with a book much more agreeable.

Returning to the galley and the preparation, he set about chopping the leaf of the herbs from the stems. They would go into the pan, the contents of which were currently simmering on the stove, shortly before serving to ensure they held their form. The smell of burning came to his nose and he reduced the heat, lifting the pan for a moment. Returning it to the heat he ladled in some of the vegetable stock. The liquid hissed as it touched the metal, instantly bubbling away. He stirred the contents and added another. The rice hadn't stuck. He'd caught it in time. Glancing around, he checked his prep. The Parmesan was grated and ready, as was the fresh chervil and rocket. The table was set. A chilled half bottle of white wine, partly used for cooking, stood alongside two glasses. He didn't drink as a general rule but, on the odd occasion where it felt warranted, he would. Everything was ready aside from his coat being flung across one of the seats at the dining table. Thinking hard, there was still something missing. Whatever it was it currently escaped him. Looking at his watch, Alice would arrive soon. Provided she wasn't late. Alice was arguably the most punctual person he knew. She hated to be late. Tamara Greave was the antithesis.

Thinking of Tamara, he gave the contents of the pan a quick stir before reaching for the pathologist's report Eric furnished him with before he left the office. Putting it down beside the hob, he absently stirred the contents of the pan with one hand as he reread the document. There was something about the conclusions drawn that bothered him that afternoon when they went over the circumstances of Kirsty Davies' suicide attempt. The material evidence of the damaged tree and how she came to be in the water was conceivable but it was the omissions from the report that he expected to see which bothered him. The head wound, caused by hitting the rocks lining the riverside, was significant enough to have caused unconsciousness therefore leaving her open to drowning. In such circumstances Kirsty's lungs should have been full of water. In all likelihood there could have been air trapped as well but the levels of water didn't appear to have been measured, let alone tested to ensure it was river water. If they were then this wasn't documented in the report. Where drowning was determined as the cause of death it should not only have been noted but put under much greater scrutiny. *Why wasn't it?*

"Something burning?" Alice said, descending the steps into the interior. Such was his concentration on the file, he'd failed to notice the evaporation of the liquid.

"Damn it…" he muttered, quickly adding more stock which flash boiled sending a cloud of steam rocketing upwards. He leaned back and hurriedly set about stirring the contents of the pan with gusto, feeling resistance from within it.

"Need some help?"

Alice removed her coat and scarf, hanging both on the pegs at the foot of the steps. Crossing the galley, she placed her hands either side of his waist and lifted herself onto her tiptoes as he turned his head sideways to meet her. She kissed him on the cheek.

"Hi handsome," she said with a warm smile.

"No, it's all under control," he said returning her smile with one of his own, leaning in to her kiss. "It's going as planned." Using his elbow, he nudged the pathologist's report away from the hob. Alice glanced at it.

"Anything interesting?"

"A teenager's suicide," he said, his expression changing to reflect the tragedy of the event.

"Not good," Alice said, stepping back and casting her eye over the saucepan and the waiting ingredients. "That's not what you went to Thornham for though, was it?"

He shook his head as he stared at the rice and vegetables. Some of the chopped onion was blackened but with a bit of luck he would get away with it.

"No. This happened twenty-odd years ago but could be related."

"Really? How so?"

"I haven't got that far," he said throwing a wry grin in her direction whilst adding another ladle of stock to the pan.

"What are we having, risotto?" Alice said, moving into the seating area.

"Wild mushroom risotto to be precise," he said.

"My favourite. You seem well prepared."

"I've even grilled the mushrooms first."

"I'm a lucky woman. I remember once you saying you thought all that was a bit of a faff. What are you up to, Tom Janssen?" she replied, grinning.

He laughed, adding the grilled mushrooms, a mixture of shiitake, oyster and girolle, the latter purchased at the insistence of a friend of his who was a chef at a popular Italian restaurant in Sheringham. Looking at his progress, he figured he'd manage to pull this off after all. He was no stranger to the kitchen, being quite adept at cooking and finding it calming; risotto on the other hand was not something he cared to make. The level of attention required during the entire process annoyed him. They were easy to make and just as easy to ruin. Not great for someone who found his mind drifting between subjects for much of the time.

"Are you worried you'll wear out your generator or something?" Alice asked. He saw her gesturing to the candles he'd placed on the table.

"No. I thought it might be... you know... nice," he said trying to make light of it.

"Yes. It is. Shall I light them?"

"Sure," he said, opening the drawer to his right and taking out a box of matches. He tossed them to her and she deftly caught them.

"I'll move this first," she said, reaching for his coat which lay close to the candles. At that moment he remembered what it was that he'd forgotten, and it was the most important element of the evening. Alice slipped her forearm under his coat and lifted it. He let go of the pan handle and stepped towards her.

"That's okay, I'll—"

It was too late and the movement of his coat sent something falling from the table and clattering to the floor. Alice saw it too, reaching for the box as it fell. Lowering herself before he could close the gap, she hesitated as she reached for it. Janssen stopped, letting out a sigh as he watched his evening's plan fall apart in seconds. Alice went to pick up the blue box, velvet lined, but instinctively withdrew. She glanced up at him and then away, remaining on one knee with his coat slung over her forearm. She appeared unsure of what she should do, frozen in situ. It wasn't just her. An awkward moment passed between them before she slowly rose to her feet and he quickly retrieved the ring box. Taking a deep breath, he curled his fingers around the box nestled in his palm as he stood, feeling sheepish. Alice's expression was rigid for a second before her lips split an embarrassed half-smile. He'd caught her off guard, as planned, albeit in the most unexpected of ways. He wasn't sure what should happen next.

"Is this..." Alice said, the question tailing away as they both averted their eyes from one another.

"Er... well, yes. I mean, it's not gone quite as I'd planned. I figured dinner, candles... it's a clear night and we could go for a walk along the water's edge," he said, grimacing at the thought of his plans falling into ruin. "I know all of that wouldn't be exactly special... but it—"

"Would be perfect," Alice said, her smile widening. There was a gleam in her eyes, tying into her smile. He could see her breathing was rapid and she didn't know what to do with her hands. He realised his were shaking. Opening the box, he revealed the contents to her. A Marquise Cut solitaire diamond on white gold; simple and elegant, so the jeweller advised him. By the look on her face, he had taken great advice. The moment was punctuated by a high-pitched siren, startling both of them.

"Risotto!" they said in unison.

Janssen turned and dashed back to the hob. The pan was

smoking and there was no chance he would be able to salvage the contents on this occasion. The handle burned his fingers as he reached for it and he tried again, this time using a tea towel to protect his skin. He put it aside and then joined Alice in flapping the air around the smoke alarm in an attempt to silence it. She continued to do so as he repeatedly pressed the reset button but to no avail. In the end, he unscrewed the cover and pulled the battery out. The siren ceased immediately but the ringing in his ears persisted. Throwing the towel into the sink, he sank back against the cupboards bracing himself with both palms against the work surface. The two of them caught their breath and looked at one another.

Janssen's eyes drifted to the charred remnants of his culinary efforts and he ran his tongue across the inside of his cheek. The meal was ruined… unless he could think of something he could make out of chervil, rocket and Parmesan cheese. Alice followed his gaze.

"At least the wine isn't burned," she said, gesturing towards the bottle on the table.

"I think that's about the only thing that hasn't gone wrong," he replied with a grin, considering the irony. He chose to keep things simple in order to minimise the chances of anything going awry.

She met his eye.

"Where were we?"

Looking to his left, he stepped back to the dining table and returned with the ring box. Opening it, he looked at the ring and then at Alice. Her smile returned. Despite the abject failure of what he had planned, it didn't seem to matter to her. The realisation hit him that it didn't make any difference. They could be anywhere, doing anything, and the moment would be just as special to the two of them.

"Alice," he said, coming to stand before her and dropping to one knee. He felt a little foolish, perhaps vulnerable. The words he'd spent all afternoon rehearsing came to mind in a jumble as the nerves returned. "I know you've been thinking for some time about where we have been heading and, I'll admit, I've been slow to realise—"

There was a knock on the door from above deck. At first, Janssen ignored it thinking something had been caught by the wind but it sounded again, only this time more forcefully. He sighed, inclining his head to one side. Alice laughed.

"It's just not going your way tonight, is it, Tom," she said.

He stood up, shaking his head.

"I should have put a sign on the mooring."

"I'm closest," she said, looking over to the steps. "I'll get the door, you light the candles, and don't think you're getting out of this. We're seeing this through... unless somebody else has died!"

He turned and went over to the table, putting down the ring box and picking up the matches as Alice mounted the steps to the door. Taking one from the box, he struck it and lit both candles before blowing it out, shaking it to disperse the sulphurous fumes. Picking up the wine bottle, he poured two half glasses before placing it down again. Footsteps descending from above could be heard.

"Who was it?" he asked, turning with a wine glass in hand intending to pass it to Alice. He was stunned at who stood before him. She wore her hair differently, hanging in waves below her shoulders and highlighted with auburn tints. The camel-coloured long coat she wore was cut to just above the top of her boots, vivid red, matching her lipstick. She smiled, inclining her head to one side and flicking the hair of her fringe gently away from her eyes with a gloved hand.

"Hello, Tom. You're a tough man to find, I have to say."

Janssen found himself lost for words.

"I wasn't expecting a hug but do I at least get a *hello*?" the woman asked. The soft lyrical tone of her Irish accent was familiar and reassuring.

"Samantha... what... what are you doing here?" he managed

to say after a moment of awkward silence. Samantha glanced at Alice, standing behind and to her right, before returning her focus to him.

"Is that how a husband greets his wife here in Norfolk?"

CHAPTER TWENTY-TWO

TOM JANSSEN LOOKED past Samantha to Alice. The curiosity of her expression transformed first into surprise before her gaze narrowed and indignation followed. Samantha followed his eye to Alice and she smiled warmly although he knew better. Samantha was establishing her position in the hierarchy among the three of them, asserting her dominance as she always sought to do. Alice returned the smile but it was forced and accompanied by the folding of her arms across her chest.

"Yes, Tom," Alice said, "how do we greet our wives in Norfolk?"

He felt a stab of pain in his chest followed by a flush of embarrassment, his cheeks and the back of his neck warming as she spoke. The realisation dawned that they should have had this discussion a long time ago. He sighed, shaking his head as he sought to articulate his thoughts.

"I know. This looks bad," he said, holding his hands up in a gesture of supplication, "but it's complicated."

"Who are you talking to?" Samantha asked, her eyes flitting between the two of them. He shot a dark look in her direction but Alice had heard enough. Shaking her head, she walked back across the galley and took her coat off the hook. He followed, brushing past Samantha who turned slightly to make room, placing her hands firmly into her coat pockets and glancing to the floor as he did so.

"Alice..." Tom said. She pulled her coat on, fixing him with a stare. He knew he wanted her to stay and certainly not to leave like this. Looking over his shoulder at Samantha, now progressing around the living area of the boat and casually examining whatever took her fancy, he knew he could explain but the words wouldn't come. What could he say to rescue the moment? Instead, he stood there open mouthed.

"I think it's probably best if I leave you to it," Alice said, looping her scarf around her neck with heavy emphasis on sarcasm. She pointedly nodded at him, her eyes fixed firmly on his. He was about to apologise but she broke eye contact, leaning past him so that she had direct sight of Samantha. "It was nice to meet you, Samantha."

Samantha turned and raised her eyebrows, nodding and smiling politely.

"You too... er..." she said nonchalantly with an almost imperceptible shake of the head to signify she couldn't recall her name.

"Alice," Alice said. Samantha nodded again before turning away and leaning in to look at the photographs framed on a shelf nearby. Alice exhaled slowly, biting her lower lip as she glared at him.

"I'm sorry," he said quietly, barely audible above a whisper. "I can explain, honestly."

"I wish I could say I look forward to hearing it," Alice replied in a louder voice than usual. Clearly she wasn't bothered who heard her, tightening her scarf and turning to mount the steps. Janssen sent his eyes skyward, running the palm of his hand across his mouth and chin as Alice left. The door to the deck above slammed shut with such force that it bounced open again, the wind rushing in.

"She seems lovely," Samantha said lightly from across the room.

He looked over. She had her back to him.

"She is."

"Looked a little surprised though," Samantha said, turning with a picture frame in hand. She angled the image in his direction so he could see it. It was a shot of himself, Alice and Saffy taken on the beach last winter. They were wrapped up in all-weather gear and pulling silly faces for the shot. It was one of his favourites.

"She's not the only one," he said, walking towards her.

"Is it so odd for a wife to want to see her husband once every year or so?" she asked.

The question was facetious and he ignored it.

"Ex wife," he said flatly. "Seriously, what are you doing here, Sam?"

He was in no mood for word games.

"Not yet, Thomas," she said playfully wagging a finger in his direction. "I'm still your wife. Like it or not."

"*Not*," he replied. "And once it's rubber stamped you won't be, so why are you here?"

"When you said you needed a bit of distance to get things clear in your head... I didn't anticipate you dropping out of civilisation for the better part of two years."

"It's Norfolk, Sam. It's a couple of hours from London."

"And yet... several decades as well by the look of it."

The comment irritated him. She never enjoyed coming home with him. It was okay for a weekend but Samantha always pushed to go abroad reacting to his desire to return home as a chore. Not that she discriminated. They rarely returned to her home town of Shannon, in the west of Ireland, either. She turned to face him. The dismissive attitude softened as she spoke. "You ran away, Tom. You couldn't face up to the challenge and you ran away."

A flash of anger passed through him but he didn't reply. She was correct. He didn't want to discuss it. He didn't want to *work things through* as she desired. His eyes followed her as she circumnavigated the space, casting her eyes around his new home.

"You often talked about owning a boat," she said after a minute of silence passed between them. "Are you enjoying it? Living here, I mean."

"Yes. Most of the time anyway," he said suppressing his exasperation at her presence. She would tell him what she wanted at a moment of her choosing. That was always how she worked. *What was she hoping to achieve by coming here?*

"Sam…"

"I made mistakes, Tom," she said, interrupting and turning to face him. That was the first time she'd voluntarily made such an admission since their split. It piqued his curiosity. "I was focussed on what I could get out of life… from our marriage. It was selfish and I should have given you more of what you wanted. I see that now."

The statement threw him. He waited for the follow-up that always came whenever she surprised him with objective self-criticism. However, it didn't come. She watched him, waiting expectantly for his response. She seemed annoyed when he didn't speak, breaking eye contact and resuming her roaming navigation of the room. Gesturing to the array of photographs he'd caught her inspecting earlier, she pointed to one of Alice hugging Saffy.

"Cute little girl," she said. He nodded his agreement. "Presumably not yours?"

"No, of course not."

"Well, you can't blame me for asking…" she lowered her voice to a conspiratorial whisper, "seeing as you've become quite adept at keeping secrets."

"That's none of your concern," he said. He meant it. His life would soon be none of her business once the two-year wait was at an end.

"Perhaps. I think she was a bit annoyed though," Samantha said. Her tone was such that she didn't appear overly concerned about his relationship with Alice. At least, that was the impression she conveyed. "In all honesty, I'm not surprised you're seeing someone. You're quite a catch, Tom."

He ignored the compliment. Even if he could be sure it was heartfelt, he always found flattery or praise difficult to receive without ever understanding why.

"You always wanted children... to recreate the family life you grew up with. And here you are... back in Norfolk with an off-the-shelf package that's good to go."

"It's not like that," he said, firmly shaking his head.

"You didn't need to up sticks and come all the way back here, you know."

"It was my choice," he said with a shrug.

"Do you miss London?"

"Sometimes."

"Do you miss me?" she asked, lowering her voice and coming to stand within arm's reach of him. For the first time he felt she was asking a genuine question, one exposing her own vulnerability. Part of him wanted to verbally lash out, to hurt her in the same vein as she had him. He couldn't do so. He decided long ago that wasn't his way.

"Sometimes," he repeated.

Samantha smiled. An expression of relief and not humour.

"Like I said... I made mistakes," she said, staring straight into his eyes and insisting he did the same. He didn't feel he could look away. "What if I told you I'd been thinking about where things went wrong and what we could do about the future?"

"Ah... Sam..." he said, shaking his head.

"Hear me out, Tom. You were ahead of me in so many ways... career, children... all I could see was how great things were and saw no need to make a change. I couldn't see how passionate you were for all of that and I should have. It's not too late, you know."

Rubbing at his face with both hands, he took a step away from her. Of all possible outcomes, he hadn't ever considered this.

"I think we're a bit past that, don't you?"

"Why? You still have your career. Yes, the sale of the house is about to go through but we can start afresh," she said, her words warm and encouraging. "You were right. We should be looking to start a family."

"You would move here? Can you honestly see yourself living in Norfolk?"

She snorted with derision.

"Let's not get carried away," she said, removing her gloves and holding them in one hand. Her face was glowing. The heat from the wood burner was such that standing in her overcoat was clearly uncomfortable. "May I?" she asked, indicating her coat.

He nodded.

"Of course."

"As I said, the sale is going through but—"

"I know. My solicitor is in regular contact with yours."

"Yes," she said, tilting her head to one side, "I'm aware of that. As I was saying, we can find another place to live. Daddy has said he'd be happy to stump up again like he did last time—"

"You've already spoken to your father?" he said, failing to hide the flash of anger. The man was as domineering a personality as you could ever expect to meet, a character trait he'd managed to instil in his children as well. "That figures."

"It wasn't like that," she said, sounding frustrated herself. "Don't read too much into it."

"Maybe I'll pass."

"Come off it, Tom! You can't honestly say you prefer being here to London. Even the job must be dull in comparison."

"It suits me just fine."

"No. I'm not buying it," she said. Her casual dismissal irked him.

"How's Cory?" he asked. Samantha's face fell at mention of the name.

She shrugged.

"I haven't seen him."

"Yeah, you've probably seen enough of him already."

"That's uncalled for, Tom," she said, the words were angry but her tone lacked conviction. "I made a *mistake*."

"Yes, you did," he said.

She shook her head and turned away from him looking for somewhere to put her coat. He made no attempt to take it for her, annoyed with himself for the childish barb he'd just thrown. A former colleague or a random stranger, it didn't really matter; she looked beyond their relationship to solve a problem without consideration of the consequences and ultimately only made matters worse. She laid the coat across one of the chairs at the dining table and made to put her gloves down, hesitating for a second before doing so. She'd seen something. Reaching across she picked up one of the untouched wine glasses, sipping at the contents before turning to face him.

"It looks very much like I'm not the only one making a mistake at the moment," she said. There was a gleam in her eye and he found the response catty. She inclined her head towards the table and he saw the ring box sitting alongside her gloves. It was still open, the diamond sparkling in the reflected firelight.

"That's none of your—"

"Oh... I believe it is while I still have your ring on *my* finger!"

"And will the real Samantha Janssen please step forward!" he said, throwing his arms wide and failing to check his growing resentment. "It took a while but she's still in there. The entitled little princess who expects the world to dance to her tune. Not any more, Sam. Not now."

Samantha raised the glass again. Janssen used the time to take a couple of breaths and calm himself down. Very few people were able to get a rise from him but his wife was certainly proficient at it. Once he welcomed someone beyond his personal barriers, he struggled to maintain an emotional discipline when finding himself in an emotive situation. Despite growing up in an open family environment, he was the one his mother always held concerns over. He was quick to fall for people without ever considering their long-term compatibility.

"This isn't exactly how I planned this conversation would go," Samantha said, sounding conciliatory. "I know... I know a lot has happened and much of it is my fault," she said, placing the flat of her free hand against her chest. "And I know we would have a lot of work to do in order to put things right between us. But... and I'm aware it is a *big but*... all it takes is a willingness to try, to want it to happen. If you tell me that you can't even consider it then I'll walk away now."

She put the glass down on the table and came to stand before him, reaching out and grasping both of his hands with her own and pulling them towards her.

"You can run from things, Tom. You can hide yourself away, take a new job..." She looked around. "Even get yourself a boat if you want. But when it comes down to it you can't change who you really are... and all of this," she said, rocking her head from one side to the other, "just isn't you, Tom. You outgrew this place and everyone in it a long time ago. That's how we found each other."

Samantha moved in towards him, still holding his hands firmly in hers. In her boots she was almost equal to his height, slouching as he was against the galley work surface. She was close. So close he could smell the fragrance of her hair mixed with that of her perfume, sparking memories from happier times. Angling her face up to his she edged further; he didn't stop her until he felt the warmth of her breath on his face. He closed his eyes.

"I think you should leave now," he said quietly. Feeling an involuntary flinch in the palm of her hands as he said the words, she stopped, holding position for a moment longer before withdrawing. Opening his eyes, he saw the expression of vulnerability in her face as she released her grip. Stepping away, she raised a hand to her eye as she turned her back on him. Walking back to the dining table, she picked up her coat and put it on. All the while, he saw her staring at his photographs while she readied herself to leave. Picking up her gloves, she turned to him and he saw a black smudge at the corner of her left eye where her mascara had started to run. Coming back to him, she held her gloves in one hand. Stopping when she came alongside, she reached up and cupped his cheek with her free hand.

"It is good to see you, Tom," she said, gently withdrawing her hand from his face.

On this occasion, he was in no doubt she meant it. Walking towards the steps leading up on deck, she stopped and picked up a pen lying on the counter at the end of the galley. It lay next to several unopened envelopes. She leaned over and scribbled something on the top one, finishing her efforts with an elaborate sweep of the hand. Placing the pen back down, she rested both hands on the counter seemingly staring straight down at what she'd just written.

"I'm staying at a hotel in Wells for the next couple of days, Tom," she said without looking up. "I hope we can talk again."

Without another word, nor looking back at him, she turned and mounted the steps to leave. He watched her go. He said nothing. His inner emotions were in turmoil feeling a confusing mixture of anger, frustration, relief and… disappointment. Holding the remaining glass of wine by the stem, he twirled it in his hand. The liquid swirled within the glass. Walking over to read what Samantha left him, he noticed the mobile number first. It was new. Beneath that was written one sentence.

YOU'RE WORTH FIGHTING FOR, *Tom Janssen* x x

• • •

EXHALING DEEPLY, he reread the line, lifting the glass to his lips. He took a sip. It was dry and not to his taste. It was to Alice's, which was why he chose it. Thinking of Alice brought his sense of guilt to the fore. Tipping the contents into the sink, he set the glass down and reached for his mobile phone. Alice's number was on the home screen, itself a picture of her and Saffy set as the background. His thumb hovered over the icon but he hesitated. How could he even begin to explain his past, let alone why he didn't confide in her sooner? He needed time to think. Putting the mobile aside he gently massaged his temples.

"The best laid plans..." he said quietly to himself. "Rabbie Burns... you were bang on."

CHAPTER TWENTY-THREE

TURNING LEFT off the main road Tamara drove them onto a circular driveway that wound its way around to the main entrance of the building before looping back. It was a purpose-built structure, purely functional in its appearance. A three-storey rectangular affair with a large covered entrance flanked either side by concrete pillars inspired by classical architecture. These were painted white and looked out of place in stark contrast to the red brick of the main building that dwarfed them, it bearing not the slightest artistic merit at all.

Several of the residents were sitting outside the front door under the cover of the porch. Initially, her first thoughts were that it was far too cold for people to sit out. She got out of the car as did Tom Janssen who'd been happy for her to drive today. She glanced at him with an enquiring look.

"Are you all right?" she asked.

"I'm fine," he said wearily. "For the third time."

"Yes, that's two *fines* and a *great*, so far," she said.

He shook his head but didn't comment. Coming closer to the door, she saw two of those sitting out were in wheelchairs and the other was on a small plastic chair, obviously placed there on a temporary basis. They were all well wrapped up against the cold breeze with coats on beneath the blankets that covered their legs. All three were smoking. The no-smoking signs displayed on the windows of the entrance doors explained why they were outside. She had to admit she was impressed by their dedication to the cause.

"Good morning, gentlemen," she said as they passed. Two of the men returned the greeting while the third exhaled smoke before reaching for his oxygen mask, nestling in his lap, and took a deep breath from the canister by his side; although he still managed a nod of greeting in their direction. Stepping into the lobby, the door swung closed behind them. Tamara approached the reception desk and offered the woman sitting behind it her identification.

"DCI Greave from Norfolk Police. I called earlier."

"Yes, I was made aware you were coming," the woman said, picking up the telephone on her desk and dialling an extension. "If you would like to take a seat, Dr Bevis will be with you shortly."

Tamara thanked her and stepped away rejoining Janssen in the casual seating area. Neither of them sat down. Janssen was looking through into one of the communal rooms. Many of the residents were seated in a horseshoe arrangement chatting with one another. A television could be heard but not seen, tuned into one of the daytime channels. It was unclear what they were watching. Members of staff came and went, dressed in white tunics and trousers. Some were busy readying medication for patients whereas others were marshalling those who needed assistance with their daily exercise routine.

"Penny for them?" she asked, coming alongside him.

"Brings back a few memories."

"Your parents?"

"My mother," he said, glancing to her. "She spent her last few years in a care home. After her stroke she couldn't manage at home by herself."

"Must have been tough," Tamara said, "coming to see her in

a place like this. No matter how good the care is it still isn't home, is it?"

"I was living in London at the time," he said, there was an edge in his tone when he mentioned the capital. It was noticeable and she found it curious. "I didn't make it back as often as I should have."

She sensed he didn't want to talk more about it and conversation stopped. Both her parents, although well into their eighties, were still arguably living more energetic lives than her or her siblings. West Country air is what her father attributed it to. They were an outdoor family and her parents pushed against the creep of modern life. Despite being academics and predominantly employed in the field of social sciences to this day they didn't own a television set. The Greave family library was incredible and her mother's words echoed in her mind; *everything there was to learn could be found in a book.* During her childhood their stance was a cause of some embarrassment for her among her peer group, but now she understood and this was one of the few stipulations her parents made which she still honoured.

Looking at some of the occupants of this home, the realisation dawned on her how lucky she was that fate hadn't forced her to consider this future for her parents. They'd never discussed such eventualities. Not that they talked much these days at all; a situation she should make an effort to resolve. Although, she'd had the conversation in her mind several times before and never acted upon it.

"Inspector Greave?"

Tamara turned to see a man approaching. He was in his mid-fifties and dressed in a well-tailored suit. She could spot the difference. Her own choice of attire, predominantly a large jumper and casual trousers, belied her experience of the finer aspects of her higher than average middle-class upbringing. Dr Bevis offered his hand and she chose not to correct his mistake in her title.

"Tamara, please," she said. His rather stern expression broke into a grin revealing dazzling white teeth. All in all, she considered that private social care did pay after all.

"This is Detective Janssen," she said, introducing her colleague. Dr Bevis nodded in his direction and Janssen smiled.

"I understand from our telephone conversation earlier that you wish to speak with one of our residents."

"Yes. Mr Nicholas Levy," she said. The doctor's expression changed, his brow furrowing. "Is there a problem?"

"Not as such, no," Dr Bevis said, gesturing with his hand for them to accompany him. He guided them to the nearby staircase and began his ascent. Lowering his voice, he continued the conversation as he took the lead. "You will understand that although we are not a medical facility as such, we do care for those elderly people who have conditions requiring wraparound care. Many of these residents have acute conditions."

"Does this apply to Mr Levy?" she asked.

Dr Bevis nodded.

"Nicholas came to us some years ago now. He was diagnosed with early onset dementia. His condition rapidly deteriorated and… well… you'll no doubt see for yourself. I don't know what you expect to gain from speaking with him but, following your call, I checked in on him and he was having one of his more lucid days today, so you never know."

Tamara glanced at Janssen over her shoulder. His glum expression indicated he was as optimistic as she was.

"I'll admit I'm not an expert on Alzheimer's as a condition, doctor, but isn't it the short-term memory that is greatly affected with the older memories remaining largely intact?"

Bevis nodded enthusiastically.

"That is a reasonable assessment, yes."

"That's good news for us," she said. "We are looking to speak with him about events that happened many years ago."

"If only his case was that simple, Inspector. Although, those memories will have stronger connections allowing greater recall, the patient can struggle to differentiate between the past and the present. If you follow?"

Again, Tamara didn't correct him on the use of her title.

"So it leads to greater confusion."

"Correct. Dementia not only affects the memory but as the condition advances it leads to a further deterioration in other faculties. Sufferers often find themselves struggling to find the right words to articulate their thoughts, rapid and changeable mood swings alongside confusion or general apathy. These symptoms can manifest at any time, collectively or independent of one another. One can never be sure what you will get but you'll certainly receive one or more if you spend any significant amount of time with them."

He paused as they reached the landing, turning to face both of them. He held up one hand, palm facing them.

"All I'm saying is please don't get your hopes up... and if Nicholas reacts badly do try to be patient with him. If he senses your frustration it will only make him more agitated."

Tamara glanced at Janssen and he bobbed his head in agreement.

"We understand," she said with a smile.

Dr Bevis appeared to appreciate their assurances and resumed course. Walking them along the corridor to the third door on the right, he pulled up just short, looking to both officers in turn before rapping his knuckles on the door. Pushing it open, he stepped forward.

"Nicholas," he said, leading them in, "you have some visitors."

Tamara went through first and cast her eye around the room. Nicholas Levy was sitting in a high-backed chair by the window, overlooking the manicured grounds to the rear of the building. His palms lay flat against the arm rests of the chair and for a moment she thought he might be sleeping because there was no verbal or physical acknowledgement of their arrival. The room was decorated in neutral tones and of a decent size. A bed was set against one wall and beyond that was another door in the far corner. This was open and she could see it led to an ensuite shower room. Two chairs and a small occasional table were set beside the large floor-to-ceiling window which was south facing and flooded the interior with a tremendous amount of natural light.

Dr Bevis came to stand before Levy, angling his head as he observed his unresponsive patient staring out of the window seemingly at nothing in particular, before turning to them and smiling apologetically.

"As you can see," he said, "good days and bad."

Tamara eased past the doctor to come before Nicholas Levy, the former owner and operating manager of Wellesley Manor. Leaning forward, she put herself directly in his line of vision casting a shadow over the elderly man. She knew he was in his early eighties, having checked before they travelled. If she had to guess she would have said Nicholas Levy was at least a decade older, if not more. Even slouched in the chair as he was, she could tell he was a tall man, skeletal, with sunken eyes and greying skin. There didn't appear to be any colour in the man aside from the dark patches visible on his forehead and hands. His hair was lank and looked greasy, clinging to his scalp where he had any.

"Mr Levy," she said inclining her head to one side and smiling. "I'm DCI Greave, from Norfolk Police."

There was a brief moment where it didn't appear as if he was likely to register their presence at all but, as Tamara made to stand up, there was a brief flicker in Levy's eyes. A second later, he turned his head fractionally towards her and she saw the pupils of his eyes dilate. A brief sign of recognition.

"You might do better with the informal approach. It often bears better results."

Tamara accepted the doctor's advice.

"Nicholas," Tamara said. "My name's Tamara. I'm with the police."

"Rebecca?" Levy asked, staring directly at her. "It's a little late for you to be coming home, isn't it? You should have been back hours ago."

Tamara smiled affectionately, glancing up enquiringly to Dr Bevis who splayed his hands wide.

"As I said. You shouldn't expect too much. Rebecca was Nicholas' wife," he said lowering his voice. "I'm afraid she is no longer with us and hasn't been for some time."

Tamara nodded. Looking back to the man, she reached out and placed her left hand gently on the top of his right. He looked down at it, frowning.

"Where's your wedding ring?" he asked her accusingly.

"Nicholas," she said. "My name is Tamara. I'm from the police. We've come to speak with you about your time running Wellesley Manor. The children's home. Would that be okay?"

Levy's eyes shifted level with hers and narrowed.

"Wellesley..." he said softly, nodding slowly and bringing his left hand across to sandwich her hand between his. "We did good things at Wellesley, you and I."

"You cared for children," she said.

"We cared for lost souls... too many to count," Levy said, raising his eyebrows in a matter-of-fact way.

"Do you remember a young girl by the name of Susan? Susan Cole?" Tamara asked, referring to Susan Cook by her maiden name and watching closely for a reaction. There was none she could discern. "How about Kirsty Davies?" Levy's hand on top of hers tightened its grip slightly. Whether it was a reaction to the name she wasn't sure. "Nicholas. Do you remember Kirsty Davies?"

Levy's head dropped, pulling his chin in towards his chest as he drew a deep breath. Rolling his head to the left and bringing it up he drew level with her, withdrawing his hand from atop hers. His expression clouded and she saw an involuntary twitch from his upper lip. She waited patiently for his response, he seemed ready to speak. After a moment his eyes widened as he stared at her unblinking.

"You're not Rebecca!" he hissed. "Who the devil are you and why are you in my bedroom? My wife will have your eyes out if she finds you here."

Nicholas Levy became agitated, shifting in his seat with his arms and legs shaking in apparent fear.

"It's okay, Nicholas," Dr Bevis said, coming to stand in front of him. The elderly man looked up at him, the expression of anger morphing into a state of confusion.

"I don't understand... who are these people?" Nicholas said, eyeing both Tamara and Janssen standing behind her with his back to the window.

"They are police officers, Nicholas," Dr Bevis said, placing a reassuring hand on the man's upper arm and rubbing it gently. The doctor looked to Tamara who stood up and backed away. "Sometimes there are triggers. We try to avoid using words such as *remember*. Doing so can lead to confusion when patients struggle to do so."

"I'm sorry. I didn't know."

"Get out!" Levy shouted at Tamara, almost spitting the words. "Get out of my house, damn you. You shameless whore!"

Saliva caught at the edge of his mouth, running partially down his chin. With a newly discovered strength he lurched forward in his chair with each insult. Dr Bevis sought to keep him restrained, albeit taking great care when doing so. The doctor looked over his shoulder.

"I think it might be best if you step out now," he said.

Tamara nodded, backing further away. Janssen placed a hand on her forearm, moving sideways and protectively placing himself in between her and Levy.

"Bitch!" Levy screamed.

Dr Bevis was attempting to calm him down, uttering reassuring words in a remarkably measured tone but to no avail. Nicholas Levy was arching his back and attempting to free himself from the doctor's grasp, even though Bevis was barely applying pressure such was the old man's frailty.

Janssen ushered her from the room and once they were in the corridor the sense of relief was palpable.

"That went... well," Janssen said, stepping aside for a nurse to pass by and enter the room.

Tamara found herself breathing hard.

"I shouldn't take it personally," Janssen said, glancing past her and back into the room. They could no longer see the incumbents but Levy was still shouting.

"I won't," she said, running a hand through her hair.

"There's no way Nicholas Levy met with Susan Cook at Wellesley the other night, and if... and it's a *big if...* he had anything to do with abuses at the home then there is no way he will ever face a trial in this condition."

Tamara shook her head, following his gaze back into the room.

"There's one thing I'm confident about though, irrespective of that little performance back there."

"What's that?" he asked.

"Invoking the name of Susan Cook made no impact at all. But at the mention of Kirsty Davies, it was a different matter altogether."

"I didn't see that. Are you certain?" he asked, sounding doubtful.

"Absolutely," she said, fixing him with a resolute stare. "What I can't tell you is why? What was the name of the other one who still lives in Norfolk?"

Janssen thought hard.

"Baker. Neil Baker. He runs a water sports outfit along the coast."

"Then that's where we're going next."

CHAPTER TWENTY-FOUR

THE REGISTERED ADDRESS of Neil Baker's office in Burnham Deepdale was all shut up when they arrived. Tamara put her hand to the glass of the door to shield the reflection of the low winter sun and scanned the interior. There were no lights on and it appeared as if no one had been present all day.

"Maybe he closes up in the off season," she said, thinking aloud.

Janssen turned to her and shook his head, momentarily blinded by the sun. It was a crystal-clear day, blue skies and a gentle breeze carrying in off the sea. These were near perfect conditions for being out on the water kite surfing or paddle-boarding.

"This is an all-year-round gig," he said. "There are a number of locations to hire boards along the coast and locals keep the businesses going through the closed season. They have much more freedom when the beaches and the water are clear of tourists."

"Can I help you at all?" a voice said. They both turned to see the newcomer. He'd just stepped out of the café situated in the building next door. Janssen showed him his identification. "I'm

Terry Marchant. I run the café here. Is something wrong, it's not Neil is it?"

"We're looking to speak to Mr Baker. Have you seen him at all today?" Janssen asked.

The man shook his head.

"Sorry, can't say I have. He did say that he had things lined up over Holkham way this week and we wouldn't be likely to see much of him."

"Holkham Beach?" Tamara asked and he confirmed with a brief nod.

"Thanks," she said.

Marchant returned inside his café, keenly observing them as they headed back to the car.

"I think that'll have got the tongues wagging," she said with a wry sideways smile. Janssen didn't comment, his expression remained fixed. He looked like he hadn't slept. Janssen's mobile beeped and he took it out, glancing at the screen. It was a text message. He read it before slipping the phone back into his pocket. "Problem?" she asked.

He glanced sideways to her without breaking step.

"Why do you ask?"

"You don't seem quite yourself, that's all," she said. He didn't reply. "How did it go last night with that thing you had planned?"

He looked across at her briefly before looking to the ground.

"That badly?" she asked.

He let out a laugh but it was one without genuine humour.

"You wouldn't believe me if I told you," he said.

"Try me."

"You know how sometimes in life when you think you've almost managed to put something behind you only for it to come back and bite you, stronger and harder than you ever thought possible?" he asked.

"I might have experienced something along those lines," she said, an image of Richard coming to mind.

"Exactly that," he said as they reached the car. She unlocked it. He glanced at her across the roof opening his door, with an expression of frustration written across his face.

"Is this related to Alice by any chance?"

He got into the car without a word, forcefully shutting the door.

"Guess it is," she said under her breath and got in her side. Turning the key in the ignition, she looked over at Janssen. He was staring straight ahead. "Holkham?"

"Holkham," he agreed. She put the car in gear and set off.

THE DRIVE over to Holkham Beach didn't take long. Today was ideal for all those who wanted to get outside following the recent spell of unpredictable weather. A storm front was scheduled to roll in later that evening and so people were making the most of it. Despite this, the car park was barely half full when they pulled up. A wide range of people were out and about, families, dog walkers or those out for a daytime run. Leaving the car, they made the short walk along the wooden boardwalk through the pine trees to where the woodland opened up onto the sands. From here the beach stretched miles in both directions. It was another five-minute walk before they reached the edge of the bank of dunes standing between the trees and the sea. At the high point they looked up and down the beach. To their right they could see numerous kites on the move indicating their destination.

Further along the beach they could now see several people out on the water riding boards pulled along by the wind. The tide was coming in and the waves were such that a couple of them were able to gain a little height off the breakers. Seemingly, the remaining kite surfers were relatively inexperienced and prone to falling off. As they drew closer, they saw two figures on the shoreline offering advice and encouragement. Both were male, one in his late fifties and the other was probably in his twenties. Assuming the former was Neil Baker, Tamara indicated for them to speak with him. He was shouting instructions to a teenage girl who was struggling to stay upright on her board.

"You've got to keep your weight evenly spread between both your feet!" he called out as they came into his peripheral vision. Turning to them, he smiled a greeting. "Beautiful day, isn't it."

"Yes, it's stunning. Detective Chief Inspector Greave," she said, brandishing her warrant card. He glanced at it briefly.

"Chief Inspector?" he said with a half-smile, splitting his attention between her and the surfers a short distance away. "Who died?"

He shot her a broad grin. She didn't mirror it.

"Susan Cook," she said. "Or Cole... if you need to cast your mind back."

Baker's face dropped.

"Yes, I remember Susan," he said, turning to face her. His students forgotten. "I remember when she went missing as well. It was in all the papers."

"She was resident at Wellesley when you worked there. You remember her well?"

"Well enough," Baker said. "Poor kid. She was mixed up. I mean, most of the kids were but she was particularly difficult."

"How so?" she asked.

"Behavioural problems... self-destructive tendencies..." he said with a shrug, glancing briefly at Janssen standing alongside her before meeting Tamara's eye once again. "A very damaged young lady."

Tamara found the phrasing interesting. That was similar to how Tara Byrons described Susan.

"What did you make of her disappearance at the time?"

"I figured..." his eyes flitted between them again, "that she'd done herself in. From what I heard she went totally off the rails after leaving Wellesley, mixing with all sorts of shady characters.

She was prone to that when she was with us. I dread to think what happened after she left."

"She got married and had a child," Janssen said, his eyes drifting out to those in the water. Baker shrugged defensively.

"Yeah, well... I'm pleased she did. Pity it didn't work out."

"Yes, a pity," Tamara said. "We found her body earlier this week, in the water over at Old Thornham Harbour. She was murdered."

Baker frowned.

"That's... terrible news. Her poor kid," he said, pursing his lips.

"Everything all right, Dad?"

Baker turned to the other instructor on the beach who was looking over with a concerned expression. He had collar-length hair that was being buffeted by the breeze and he kept having to push it aside, attempting to tuck it behind his ears and away from his face.

"It's all good, Kyle," he replied with an accompanying thumbs-up gesture. Kyle returned his attention to those in the water. "That's my youngest. He's come on the payroll as I'm looking at scaling back my workload."

Tamara was surprised. Neil Baker seemed in good health and couldn't be needing to retire just yet. He wasn't old enough. Unless he wanted to. He seemed to notice her assessing him and answered the unasked question.

"Don't let my outward appearance fool you, detective. My time is growing more limited by the day. I am in dire need of a new kidney," he said flatly, glancing briefly towards her before turning back to watch his son issuing instructions.

"Are you on the transplant list?"

"For the past year or so, yes. My consultant tells me my age is not an issue but an underlying heart complaint is. Even if a match became available, the chances of surviving an operation would be slim. Regretfully, the bell tolls for me."

"I'm sorry," Tamara said.

Baker shrugged.

"That's life, I'm afraid. One day you're chugging along quite nicely taking whatever's thrown at you and then out of the blue everything changes. Forgive me for being blunt but what has all of this got to do with me?"

"We're investigating another angle to the case," she explained. "Think back to your time at Wellesley, some allegations of mistreatment were made against the staff. Do you remember?"

"Hah!" he retorted. "Of course I do... but not by Susan."

"No, by Kirsty Davies."

"So what?" Baker said emphatically. "Still nothing to do with me."

"We have strong reason to believe that Susan Cook returned to Wellesley on or around the evening of her murder, last weekend," she said, fixing him with a stare. "Any idea why she would do that, Mr Baker?"

Neil Baker held her gaze for a moment, his expression stern and uncompromising.

"I have no idea why she would do that, nor why you think I would know."

"We are working with a theory that something she experienced during her time at Wellesley brought her back to Norfolk. Susan met someone at Wellesley, or was followed there, and whoever that person was killed her. She broke into the building and found her way to an interior room that clearly held some significance to her. Does this ring any bells with you, Mr Baker?"

Neil Baker looked away, staring out towards those among the breakers. She had the impression he wasn't really observing them, merely taking the time to arrange his thoughts and she couldn't help but wonder why that was.

"When Susan disappeared... I read about it in the paper. A big thing was made of it when they found her car, I recall."

"You really do remember her," Tamara said.

"Yeah. At the time, I wondered if... if she took her own life. I'll level with you, Detective," he said, glancing away to his right where Kyle was keeping half an eye on proceedings. Turning towards her, his face was contorted. "Things were going on at Wellesley, back then. I knew it. Many of the staff knew it."

"What sort of things?"

"Sexual, physical abuse..." he said drawing breath and bringing himself upright. "Those kids... some of them were so messed up they didn't know what to believe or who to trust. Sometimes it felt like we were running a borstal rather than trying to recreate a supportive environment for them. These kids barely knew what a positive role model should look like let alone know how to benefit from it."

"Are you looking to blame the children?" she asked, feeling her anger rise.

"No, no. Of course not," he replied, waving the comment away with a hand gesture. "That's not what I'm saying. My point is they were left vulnerable to those both inside and outside of Wellesley. You have to put it in a wider context. Hardly anyone cared about those kids, not their families, if they had any, not the state or some of my colleagues who should have known better."

"You make it sound like you were detached from all of this, as if you were watching from a distant vantage point," Tamara said. "Did you not think to report it?"

"There was nothing that I could do!" Baker said flatly, becoming agitated. "Just remember I was a junior staffer at that point and these kids... and no one was looking out for most of these kids. We felt we were constantly losing a battle with them. The kids themselves fought us, the management... even the police saw them as a waste of their time," he said wagging his finger accusingly in her direction. "These kids were the unwanted. The unclean." He glared at her but she remained unmoved by his argument. "Who was going to believe someone like me?"

"It isn't my place to judge—"

"But you are judging me, aren't you?" Baker snapped.

"You were in a position of responsibility. Children in these situations rely on people like you when no one else is looking out for them. That was part of your job after all."

"Which is why I got into it in the first place!" Baker hissed. "After all of that... along with everything that surrounded Kirsty Davies... I stayed put doing what I could. For a while anyway, but I couldn't even keep the children on side. They were climbing out of the windows at night and willingly running off to be with..." The words tailed off and he reached up with a hand, running the flat of his palm from his eyes down across his face. He took the pause to gather himself. They waited for him to continue. "Who the hell cared? I felt like it was me standing at the centre of a perfect storm. The darkness swirling around me, out of control. And yes... before you ask... I've felt the guilt over my inaction every single day. What if I had spoken out... backed Kirsty when she called for help? What then? Could I have changed things?"

"Why didn't you?" she asked.

"I was scared for one thing," he said with a dismissive shake of the head. "Who was I to challenge anyone of that stature?"

"There's more though, isn't there?"

"Yes," he said, averting his eyes from her gaze. "Even with everything I knew... everything I *thought* I knew, I still couldn't quite believe her."

"Kirsty?"

He nodded.

"One hell of a messed-up kid, that one."

"Who was it?" Tamara asked. Baker looked at her, expressionless. "Who was it abusing the girls within Wellesley Manor?"

Neil Baker looked at his son, currently knee deep in the breakwater instructing a teenager in the correct positioning of her feet on the board. Exhaling deeply, Baker shook his head.

"I guess it doesn't make any difference now… not the way he is these days." Holding her gaze, he spoke through gritted teeth, "Nicholas. It was Nicholas Levy. Now… don't bother asking me to testify about it. You and I both know that with his health and his family ties, he will never see the inside of a courtroom."

CHAPTER TWENTY-FIVE

"Now, if you'll excuse me, I have work to do," Neil Baker said, glancing at both detectives. The quiet one, the giant mute standing next to his boss didn't utter a sound. He just stood there like he had throughout the entire conversation, watching, listening. The woman on the other hand stared at him. He felt she was trying to see beyond his words, through his facial expressions. That was her job after all, but there was more to it than that. She was looking for someone to blame. He knew her sort. If there was the chance to lay it at his feet then she would take it. That wasn't going to happen. Even in what precious time he had left, there was still much to lose.

"You can go," Tamara said to him.

He nodded his thanks and walked away, feeling her eyes burning into the back of his head as he headed towards Kyle. The big one's gaze followed him too but he ignored the attention, crossing the sand to join his son at the water's edge, taking care not to let the sea water swamp his boots.

"What did they want, Dad?"

He looked back over his shoulder at the retreating forms of the two detectives.

"They were police, looking to rake over some old ghosts, son. We'll see if anything comes of it but I doubt it."

"Did you do something wrong?"

"No. Nothing to worry about."

At that moment, one of the new starters fell from their board crashing face first into the water. She managed to right herself and came up for air just as the next wave struck, swamping her and carrying her closer to the shore.

"I think you're needed," he said, gesturing for Kyle to go to her aid.

"You sure?"

"Yeah, yeah. You go," he said, pushing Kyle towards the stricken girl. Kyle broke into a run and splashed through the knee-high water with speed to come to her aid. Putting his back to the wind, he looked down the beach. The police officers were almost out of sight now having climbed the dunes heading back to the path. Unzipping his jacket pocket, he took out his mobile. Scrolling through his contacts, he found the number and dialled it. The call was answered within a couple of rings.

"I had a feeling you would be calling sooner or later," the voice said by way of greeting.

"You already knew?" he asked, annoyed.

"Yes, of course."

"I don't suppose it crossed your mind to give me the heads up," he said bitterly.

"Forewarned is forearmed and all of that?"

"Exactly," he said, with no attempt at masking his frustration. "What are you playing at?"

"How was I to know they would start putting things together so soon?"

The voice was confident, perhaps overly so. This wasn't unusual.

"Is that what you think... that they are putting it together?"

He was worried now. Based on the conversation he'd just had, he figured they were only fishing. What little he gave them was nothing more than they could easily obtain through multiple other sources. That was always his intended course of action should questions ever be asked. He couldn't issue a flat-out denial, that would only imply his guilt. And a scandal such as this, even from a historical viewpoint, could still cause immense damage to his present-day life. And he was well aware of the capacity for that to happen if he wasn't proactive.

"They were bound to ask questions once Susan's body was found. It stands to reason."

Neil Baker's gaze carried to where his son stood with the student. They were both laughing, she had her arm around Kyle's shoulder and he was helping to stabilise her position on the board.

"I think we need to meet, discuss things," he said. There was a moment of silence at the other end of the line. He checked the handset in case the call had dropped. The connection remained active. "Did you hear me?"

"I'm not sure that's a good idea. Particularly with the police hovering around."

"Exactly why we need to. The less said over the phone the better. Listen, we have a lot to lose if this all goes south on us and—"

"Okay, okay… we should meet. When?"

Neil thought about it. The police were clearly doing the rounds, asking questions of those who were present at the time. If they were diligent, and he had to believe they were, the woman in particular, then the scrutiny would only increase as time passed.

"Tonight, before they get any closer. Can you do that?"

He waited for a response, listening to the steady breathing down the line despite the sound of the advancing waves in the background.

"I have a few things I need to take care of first but… I can do that."

"Good. I think we should meet somewhere out of the way, just in case. How about you?"

"Agreed. I know just the place."

Kyle came bounding back to him through the water, grinning as he reached the shoreline. His hair was soaked, as were his clothes from his chest downward. He must have gone over in the surf whilst helping the girl.

"I'll have to go now. Text me a time and the whereabouts later," he said, hanging up without saying goodbye.

"Who was that?" Kyle asked.

"Just talking to a man about a dog. Is she all right?" he asked, inclining his head towards the student who was now back up on her board.

Kyle looked over to see his charge whooping with delight as she caught the wind and started to pick up speed. She waved in their direction. Kyle applauded and waved back.

"I think I might be in there," Kyle said, forming a broad smile.

Neil clapped his son on the back and returned the smile with one of his own. He felt a sense of relief having made the phone call. There was no reason for this to go bad. All they needed to do was manage the situation. Much as they had done before.

CHAPTER TWENTY-SIX

TAMARA GREAVE CAST a sideways glance at Janssen as she pulled into the car park of the station. He'd barely said a word since they left Holkham. He contributed sparingly to their brief discussion of Neil Baker's memory of events, a damning indictment of the management at Wellesley Manor, but even that was broadly him agreeing with her assessment. Janssen always held his own opinion and willingly offered it, to her at least. *What was going on with him?*

Parking near to the main entrance, she switched off the engine. The secure yard at the rear had limited space and, besides, she was not permanently based here. The nature of her role, overseeing a widespread semi-rural community, had her travelling between many locations of the north coast. The roving brief she'd been given gave her licence to be where she was most needed. The team here, under Janssen's stewardship, was always thought of as the least of her concerns. However, it was obvious to her that his mind was elsewhere and not focused on where she felt it should be.

He turned to her. It must have been his sixth sense, that feeling you get drawing you to look at someone when you realise they are watching you.

"What?" he asked.

The tone was hostile. It really wasn't like him.

"Nothing," she said. "Just thinking."

"Right," he said, clambering out of the car without seeking clarification. She chose to ignore the reaction, still looking in his direction as he closed the door. If he was unwilling to open up then there was little she could do about it. Her gaze followed beyond him towards the main entrance. At the corner of the building, hovering there, and looking decidedly awkward she saw a woman. Even from this distance she knew it was Sarah Caseley.

Opening her door, she caught Janssen's attention indicating towards the entrance with a flick of her head. He looked across, taking care to appear casual.

"I wonder what she's doing here," he said.

"We're shaking the tree. Maybe she's the first to lose her grip," she said.

He nodded.

"I'll head in through the back. If she hasn't made it into the station yet, then she's unsure. Probably best if you go alone for now," he said. "Kid gloves."

"Agreed."

Janssen headed off to their left and the rear of the station while Tamara walked towards the public entrance. Sarah Caseley remained where she was, lingering at the corner of the building out of view of the interior of the station. As Tamara drew nearer, Sarah made a beeline for her. It was as if she was waiting for her to arrive. How long must she have been loitering for?

"DCI Greave," Sarah said, forcing a smile. She was clearly agitated. If not for the body language and anxious expression, Tamara would have been forgiven for thinking Sarah was in her usual routine. She was immaculately presented, dressed in high-end clothing and perfectly made up. She imagined her being rarely ever seen in public, or at home for that matter, without this level of effort. For Tamara's personal taste the make-up was over the top, albeit expertly applied, and far better suited for a photo shoot than for day-to-day wear. To Sarah Caseley, this was her personal standard. Tamara wondered whether it was akin to putting on a suit of armour.

"Tamara, please," she replied. "Are you here to see me?"

Sarah nodded, looking past her, seemingly checking that no one else was within earshot. Tamara did likewise. There wasn't another soul in sight.

"It's cold out here, would you like to come inside where–"

"No!" Sarah said. The aggression in her tone took her aback. It must have been apparent. "Could we walk for a bit?" Sarah asked, her tone softening.

Tamara agreed. Doing up her coat, she looked around. There was a path leading away from the station that took them in a circuitous route along the edge of the surrounding fields. Gesturing for Sarah to walk alongside they set off.

"What brings you here?" Tamara asked after a few moments. Sarah had something to say but obviously found it difficult to talk about it. "I'm presuming this is off the record... but it must be important for you to make the effort."

Sarah took a deep breath, her body language relaxing a little as they navigated the neutral space. Tamara understood. Police stations were intimidating places for those unfamiliar to them.

"I wasn't entirely honest with you the other night," Sarah said at last. "At my home."

Tamara nodded but didn't speak, conscious of not filling the space with her own thoughts. She allowed Sarah to set the pace, both in their movement and the developing conversation.

"It is true that I am worried about James. He really doesn't know about my background before I was adopted," Sarah said. Even now, she was still struggling.

"It's more than just home though, isn't it?"

Sarah looked sideways, bobbing her head in confirmation.

"I was a difficult teenager, Tamara. Believe me, I do know

where it all came from but that doesn't really help. Wellesley was a truly awful experience on so many levels and… I didn't want to be there. I did whatever it took to get out as often as I could. As did some of the others."

"Kirsty Davies and Susan, by any chance?"

"Yes."

The answer was simple and offered without emotion.

"Where did you go?" Tamara asked. "Did you stay together?"

"Mostly," Sarah said. "It depended on whether we could all get out at the same time. Sometimes we would distract attention to allow one another the freedom to get clear. It was kind of fun sometimes." She laughed, the tension in her face dispersing a little. "To get one over on the staff."

The narrative ceased for a moment and the atmosphere changed a little as Sarah thought on her next words.

"I don't really want to go into the details," Sarah said a moment later, glancing nervously across at her. "That's not what I came to talk about."

"But it is one reason why you haven't spoken to your husband, though. What you got up to and who with, when you ran away from Wellesley. It's not so much that you came out of a children's home that concerns you, is it?"

"I see you've been doing your job well," Sarah said, apparently resigned to the fact that her past was better known than she hoped.

"Do you know who these men are, where they can be found now?"

Sarah shook her head.

"No, and I've no desire to revisit that period of my life. We were all looking for something back then. At the time they gave us what we thought we needed. Material things, attention… love," she said, turning melancholy. "The things they used to get us to…" She didn't allow herself to finish the comment.

"You told us that your time at Wellesley with Susan was

brief," Tamara said. "But the records show you were there at the same time for well over a year."

"I know. I lied," Sarah said. "I panicked. James was due home and I didn't want all of this coming out. I still don't."

"That might not be within your control. Mine neither, come to think of it."

Again, Sarah nodded before turning her eyes to the sky. Gulls called overhead, their appearance inland indicated the coming storm forecast for that evening.

"You asked about Wellesley."

Tamara nodded.

"Yes, I did."

"I think I know why Susan went back there," she said, slowing their pace and coming to a stop. She turned to face her, meeting Tamara's eye. "There was a room... on the ground floor." Her expression took on a faraway look, her eyes closed, as if she was recollecting something painful to remember. "We... the girls... used to refer to it as *the hole*. It's where they took us to separate us from the others when we misbehaved. At least, that's what they used to say. Once you crossed some arbitrary line, sometimes even if you hadn't, you'd end up there... for days on end on occasion although it was often hard to tell. Believe me, when you're isolated and alone in the dark you soon lose track of time. You relied on the others to tell you how long you were down there for."

"There was more to it than that."

"Oh... much more," Sarah said, sniffing loudly, her voice cracking as she looked across the fields towards the sea visible in the distance. "At first I thought it was where they intended to break us. To force us to conform. There were no windows, no light... one bulb hanging from the ceiling and sometimes they would even remove that so you couldn't see anything at all. All you had was what you could hear, feel... smell," the words came with venom, her face contorted in anguish as she vocalised her experience. "The smell of cigarettes... I used to smoke myself but these were different, distinctive. Menthol." A tear ran from the corner of her eye and she ignored it as it broke free, running the length of her cheek.

"I know the room you are talking about," Tamara said. Sarah looked to her, pain etched in her expression. "Susan went there. I believe that was where she was attacked."

"Poor Susan," Sarah said, taking out a tissue from her coat pocket and gently touching it to her face in an attempt to preserve her make-up.

"It's not too late, Sarah. You can still—"

"No, no," Sarah replied, shaking her head and dismissing the suggestion outright. "There's no way I'm ever going public with all of this... and not only because of how my husband will definitely react. No. There are others."

"Others?"

"Do you think anyone wants to hear from someone like me? Do you think my opinion counts... that I count?"

"I think you count, yes. You'd be surprised how supportive people will be if this comes to light. Things are different now. Past events are seen through a different lens than they used to be."

Sarah shook her head emphatically.

"Then you are either delusional or in the minority. Maybe both. People didn't want to know about girls like us at the time and they damn sure won't want it put before them now." The weight and emotion carried within those words were significant. "When you hold up a mirror to society, it doesn't want to see its reflection. They'll blame me, Susan... anyone but not their own complicity. Our abusers weren't just the staff or the sick bastards who picked us up at the gates but all those who turned their backs on us, shunting us away where we couldn't be seen. Leaving us to the mercy of people like..." She caught herself, pulling up at the last moment. Resuming their walk, she set off, catching Tamara off guard.

"People like who?" Tamara asked, hurrying to come alongside.

"People who should have known better," Sarah said.

The barrier that Tamara felt had almost fallen was raised again in its entirety. Perhaps stronger than before. Sarah Caseley was about to mount a resolute defence from behind it.

"Why did you come to see me if not to bring all this to light?"

Sarah Caseley turned to face her, a look of determination on her face.

"To ask you to let it go. There's nothing to gain from dragging all of this up again. All it will do is ruin more lives... that some of us have spent years trying to carve something positive from after what we went through. You'll destroy it all. Susan is dead, Kirsty... took her own life and Wellesley closed long ago. If they don't bulldoze the place it will probably fall down eventually of its own accord. *Nothing good* will come from this. Don't you see?"

"You said it yourself, Susan is dead. There's no way I can *let it go*, as you ask," Tamara said. "It's my job to get to the truth."

Sarah shook her head.

"No, of course you can't. It was foolish of me to ask. But all this... raking over old ground is nothing to do with it. Susan had her demons but what happened to us there is not what this is about. I'm certain of it."

"If so, then it won't feature in the inquiry," Tamara stated. "No one who is investigating this case is out to ruin lives. We're looking for the truth."

Sarah stared at her, hard.

"And you should know this," Tamara said, matching Sarah's steely determination with an expression of her own. "I always get to the truth."

"In that case you should also consider what life at Wellesley was like for us... is it any wonder we did everything we could to get away? Sometimes, even running into the arms of anyone who would take us."

Tamara sensed there was something significant contained within those words, an implicit statement beyond the obvious, but before she could press the thought home Sarah turned and walked away. She was left to ponder the meaning alone, watching Sarah Caseley's retreating form as she strode purposefully away from her.

CHAPTER TWENTY-SEVEN

TAMARA UNLOCKED the front door to her guest house as quietly as she could, hoping not to give away her arrival. She'd been here for a month now and the couple who owned the house were pleasant, more than pleasant, she liked them but tonight she wanted to head straight to her room without interaction. There were four rooms to the house that they let out through an internet site. The husband worked seasonally, running a small charter boat taking tourists out to observe the wild birds and the seal population in their natural habitat.

This being the quieter period of the year, she was currently the only guest. Added to this, they had recently had their first child and more often than not she found herself dragged into conversations about babies and what was and wasn't happening for them as they expected. Bearing in mind one of the primary reasons for the breakdown of her engagement to Richard was her lack of desire to have children, she felt even less inclined to be reminded of exactly why her personal life was in tatters.

Mounting the stairs, they creaked under her weight but no one appeared and so she hurriedly made her way up to her room. Stepping into her personal space, she closed the door behind her and exhaled deeply. It was a large room, furnished in a modern style belying the age of the building which she thought must be centuries old. There was an ensuite bathroom and a small kitchenette that she could use to prepare the basics but she had full use of the downstairs facilities if required.

She really needed to get her own place but, until she and Richard were able to resolve their differences, she was stuck at something of an impasse. If she made a purchase, then she would need her share of their property near Norwich. To ask Richard for this would no doubt set him off. Taking the open bottle of white wine from the fridge, she poured herself a glass and crossed to the sofa set beneath the window, sinking down onto it and casting her eye over the harbour outside. The thunderous clouds were rolling in, just as the forecast predicted. Squally rain showers, heralding the storm front, were visible in the lights ringing the quayside along with the vessels at anchor rising and falling with the sway. Gusts of wind slammed against her window. She was grateful to be inside.

Her thoughts turned to Richard. He still harboured desires of the two of them coming back together. This was partially due to her reluctance to pull the trigger completely and partly, she thought, down to his stubbornness. Richard was a man used to getting what he wanted, whatever it was he'd set his sights on; and for her to call time on their relationship without his consent was something he was unlikely to accept, irrespective of whether it was right for both of them. There was more to it though. She wasn't leading him on with false hope; at least, this wasn't her intention. All of her friends and acquaintances were married now, starting or growing their families. For a time there didn't seem to be a weekend between spring and late summer where she wasn't summoned to attend a wedding or christening of one friend or another. Those invitations were becoming fewer as she approached her forties. Thankfully, so had the questions from her friends regarding her own plans. That might change when news leaked about the latest relationship collapse. Not her mother, though. Richard was always one of the first subjects raised whenever they spoke. Regrettably, that wasn't often at the moment.

Shifting her thoughts to Janssen, she wondered what was troubling him. She'd never seen him like this. He was a good man and a thoroughly decent detective. Beyond that, she had an urge to be closer to him, an instinct she'd curbed since taking up this promotion. Her emotions were all over the place and despite having a professional reputation in her work life, she was well aware of her failings in her personal. The last thing she needed was a rebound affair with someone who worked with her. Even if the desire kept rearing itself inside of her. Besides, maybe she was flattering herself somewhat. Whenever she thought he might share similar feelings to hers, something would be said to make her believe the connection was in her imagination.

Sipping at her wine, she thought about eating. Reluctant to brave the inevitable interaction in the kitchen downstairs she glanced towards the clock at her bedside and realised the likelihood was that she wouldn't eat tonight. She'd stayed at work later than intended, packing Eric and Tom off early whereas she remained. She was still amazed at how the restaurants closed so early in this town. Aside from the sparse fast food outlets, unless you went to a hotel you'd struggle to get a meal after eight o'clock, particularly at this time of year, and the convenience stores were anything but.

Standing up, she went over and put another bottle of wine in the mini fridge to chill. If she couldn't be bothered to sort out dinner then the least she could do was unwind properly.

SHE WOKE WITH A START. For a moment she couldn't remember where she was. Her back ached and she realised she'd been lying awkwardly on the sofa. The rain was driving in sheets against the window in front of her as the wind howled outside. Was it this that had awakened her? The wall lights of her bedroom offered a soft glow illuminating the room. The sound came again, a knocking at her door, only this time more impatient. Easing herself upright and off the sofa, she stretched feeling the twinge once again in her lower back. Regretting having fallen asleep, she eyed the clock on her bedside table as she crossed the room, seeing it was almost one in the morning.

Brushing the hair away from her eyes, she cracked her bedroom door open to find Tom Janssen standing before her. Opening it further, she failed to hide her surprise.

"Tom. What are you doing here?"

She pushed the door wide and beckoned him in.

"I tried to call but you're not answering your phone," he said, following her into the room.

"Yes, I'm sorry. I turned it off," she said, embarrassed as she saw Janssen cast an eye around the room. The bed was unmade from the previous day and dirty laundry was piled on an occasional chair alongside it. On the table next to the sofa stood a glass alongside two empty wine bottles, side by side. He didn't comment. "What's going on?"

"Uniform responded to a 999 call earlier this evening, from the Caseley residence. It sounds like we need to head over there."

"Right, okay," she said, rubbing at her cheeks and trying to wake herself up. Her head was foggy, her mouth dry. "What do we know?"

"There seems to have been an altercation. James Caseley called it in. Eric's already out there."

"He was quick off the mark," she said, hunting for her keys.

"He's on call tonight, remember?"

"Oh yes, of course," she said, scooping up her keys and indicating they should go.

Stepping out into the corridor the sound of a crying baby could be heard downstairs. Wailing was probably more apt. Janssen shot her a sheepish look.

"I think I woke the baby. I imagine I'm not popular with your landlady tonight."

Tamara led the way downstairs. Connie was in the kitchen, bobbing her daughter up and down in her arms as she tried to settle her. Upon seeing them appear at the foot of the stairs she turned away from them in an obvious affront. Passing out through the door, Janssen took care to close it softly and minimise the noise. It was a little late for that.

"I'll have to look at moving sooner rather than later, at any rate," she said to him, hurriedly fastening up her coat as they scurried to the car through the driving rain. "You can drive."

He would have to. She was well over the limit. Coming to his car, they got in. As she was putting on her seatbelt, Janssen reached past her into the glove box and came out with a packet of breath mints. Handing them to her without a word, he started the car and the wipers immediately kicked in to clear the water from the screen. She nodded her thanks and put two of them in her mouth. It wouldn't do for her to arrive at the scene smelling of alcohol. Examining her reflection in the vanity mirror of the visor, she realised there was nothing she could do about the rest of her appearance which had taken on a somewhat dishevelled look.

In the driveway of the Caseley's home they found three liveried police vehicles parked behind James Caseley's brand new Range Rover. One of the police vehicles was a canine unit and the handler was already scouring the substantial grounds surrounding the property. The front door was open and they shook off their coats before entering. Greeted by a uniformed constable, she directed them towards the kitchen where Eric was sitting with James Caseley. The detective constable saw their approach and rose to meet them at the threshold with a concerned expression.

"Sarah Caseley has gone missing," he said.

James looked up from his seat at the dining table where his hands were clasped firmly together, fingers interlocked. The bombastic character they'd met previously was now a shadow of himself. The man looked shell shocked. Eric lowered his voice.

"Mr Caseley arrived home from London tonight, sometime after ten o'clock to find his wife missing and the house in disarray," Eric said, glancing over his shoulder at James. He remained where he was, staring straight ahead. "The living room has been turned over. It looks to me as if there was some kind of a fight rather than it being a burglary."

Janssen turned and cast a look in the direction of the room in question. There were double doors off the hallway leading into it and even from this vantage point debris from an overturned table was visible. Eric answered the unasked question.

"Forensics are on their way, so I've kept everyone out of there for now. There is blood on the carpet but not enough to be anything more than a superficial wound."

"Is anything missing?" Tamara asked. Eric looked her way, hesitating as his expression changed. She inclined her head, speaking barely above a whisper. "Yes, Eric. The boss is hammered. Do try not to cause a scene."

"Right... no, of course not," he said, clearly unsure of how serious he should take the comment.

"Is anything missing?" she asked.

Eric looked to his pocket book.

"Nothing obvious that we would expect to see from a robbery but..."

"But?" she asked, concerned by the edge to his tone.

"They've been into Mr Caseley's gun cabinet."

Eric guided them back into the hall, walking them to the far end where they came to another door. It was cracked open and Eric eased it inward using the tip of his boot. Tamara leaned in, reluctant to enter and risk contaminating any potential trace evidence. The study was large, originally it was most likely the drawing room before the house was extended at some point in the past.

A large desk stood near the centre of the room, adjacent to a period fireplace. A chesterfield sofa and two matching club chairs were at the far end. The walls were adorned with portraits, presumably depicting prominent family members from previous generations. The desk was clear, with whatever had been atop it now strewn across the floor including the lamp. Several of the drawers were open and they too had been emptied on to the floor. To the left of the sofa was a locked gun cabinet. The glass set within the doors was smashed, as was the lock.

Tamara immediately considered that this wasn't the approach of a targeted professional. The county was predominantly an agricultural area and therefore awash with shotguns. There were regular weekend shoots and many of those who attended didn't work the land but they liked their guns. As a matter of course, the police were hot on maintaining security for those with firearms but it wasn't unusual for the weapons to be targeted for robbery. In this case she doubted it. Aside from one missing slot in the rack, the others still had their weapons in situ.

"What were they looking for do you think?" Eric asked.

"The key to the chain," a voice said. It was James Caseley, he'd come to stand a few feet behind them. "I keep the cabinet locked and the guns chained."

"Besides you, who knows where the keys are kept."

Caseley thought about it.

"Just Sarah, I should think," he said, his response was monotone, staring at them with a blank expression. He shook his head. "I didn't believe her. I thought she was cracking up."

"What do you mean by that, Mr Caseley," Tamara said, coming back to stand with him. He stood there, arms by his side, slowly shaking his head.

"She told me she was in danger… that she felt threatened and I dismissed her," he said, looking to the floor. "All this time she was going on and on… and I ignored her for the most part."

"What did Sarah say?" she pressed him. He raised his head, meeting her eye.

"That… they might come for her."

"Who might come for her?"

He shook his head, becoming agitated and confused. Putting his hands to his face he covered both his nose and mouth with his palms.

"What have I done? I should never have left her alone."

"Mr Caseley," Tamara said, trying to get him to focus on her. "Who was your wife afraid of?"

"She wouldn't say. That's why I thought it was all in her head… people watching her, following her… but it wasn't, was it? Please find her."

James Caseley reached out and clasped her right hand with both of his, his eyes imploring her to help him.

"We will do our best, James," she said, seeking to reassure him. He released his grip and she withdrew her hand while at the same time observing his. There were no marks or abrasions that she could see. Nor were there any on his face. The collar of his white shirt had a layer of dirt at the edge, common if worn for a full day. It was unlikely he had showered and changed this evening. Confident that his present state of mind would have garnered an Oscar nomination if faked, she pretty much ruled him out as being a part of whatever this incident was.

"Does Sarah have her own car?" she asked.

Caseley nodded.

"Yes, she has a Mercedes… C class."

"Is it here?"

"It would be in the garage if it is," he said.

"I'll check," Eric said, hurrying past them to get outside. "If not I'll put the description out there."

Tamara thought hard.

"Mr Caseley, you invested in the lights and cameras in order to increase security at your wife's request. Is that correct?"

"Yes. I do listen to Sarah… I just didn't realise—"

"Were the gates open when you returned home this evening?"

"Yes, I believe they were," Caseley said, his brow furrowing in concentration.

"May we see the footage?"

"Of course," he said. "We can view the feed from my laptop in the kitchen."

He set off with purpose, evidently pleased to be doing something constructive, and the two detectives followed. The laptop was at the end of the dining table and he powered it up. They waited patiently while he double-clicked the icon and loaded the software. Then, he cursed softly.

"Damn."

"What is it?" she asked, coming to look over his shoulder. The screen was blank aside from an error message.

"It can't connect to the hard drive... where the footage is relayed from," he said, glancing up at her. "The drive is in... my study."

The three of them headed back to his study. This time, Tamara entered and Janssen placed a gentle restraining hand on Caseley's forearm as he made to follow.

"It's in the corner unit, behind my desk," Caseley said, guiding her with an outstretched hand.

She took great care to open the unit without leaving prints of her own. Inside, towards the rear of the first shelf she found an array of cables. There was no sign of the hard-drive unit. Looking back at the two men standing in the doorway, she shook her head.

"It's gone. Maybe it wasn't the keys to the gun cabinet they were looking for after all."

James Caseley visually deflated. The excitement of a breakthrough destroyed in moments.

"I didn't realise she was in danger... I really didn't," he said, looking to Janssen.

"I don't think any of us did, Mr Caseley. The empty slot in the rack," Janssen said, pointing towards the smashed cabinet, "are you missing a firearm?"

Caseley looked across, Tamara followed his gaze spying the shotgun cartridges scattered over the floor at the base of the unit. The ammunition was supposed to be stored separate to the weapons but this wasn't the time to pull the man up for a violation.

"Yes," Caseley said. "It's missing my P and V."

"P and V?" Tamara asked.

"Perugini and Visini, custom made and inscribed for me in Italy."

"Is there anything distinctive about it?"

Caseley considered the question, his expression one of deep-rooted concentration.

"Oh, most certainly. It's a twelve bore, over and under barrel... weighted for game shooting which makes it lighter and easier to wield. The stock is trimmed to suit me and..."

Tamara sensed there was more he could add but the description tailed off. It was a momentary distraction for him which didn't last.

"We'll do our best to find her," she said, returning to stand with them outside the office. Touching Janssen by the forearm, she casually led him away from Caseley. Once happy they were out of earshot, she turned to him.

"We have to work on the possibility that Sarah has been kidnapped and more than likely by someone who is now armed."

"Agreed," Janssen said. "Where do we start looking though? I'm assuming this has to do with Susan and therefore it logically follows that it revolves around Wellesley. Shall we look there?"

"Not a bad call," she agreed.

At that moment, Eric appeared bracing himself against the jamb of the front door with an excited look on his face.

"A member of the public has called in a report about a white Mercedes being driven erratically. They thought the driver was drunk. It's too coincidental not to be Sarah's car."

James Caseley appeared behind them, very animated.

"Is it her? Have you found Sarah?" he asked.

"Please leave this to us, Mr Caseley. Uniformed officers will remain here with you while we look into this."

She signalled to a constable waiting at the front door who came forward and guided the stricken man back towards the kitchen. He appeared lost and confused by the events of the evening.

"Where was the car seen?" she asked.

"Heading towards the harbour," Eric said.

"The Old Harbour?" she asked.

Eric nodded.

"Let's head over," she said, looking to Janssen. "Have an armed response unit meet us there and bring the canine unit we have here with us. When was the report called in to us?"

"An hour ago," Eric said.

"Then they have an hour's head start."

CHAPTER TWENTY-EIGHT

THE HEADLIGHT BEAM from Janssen's car illuminated the police car parked across Staithe Lane, the access road that skirted the edge of Thornham and led to the old harbour. A constable stood alongside the car in a high-visibility jacket flagging them down. Janssen pulled up, lowering his window. Rain carried in through the gap on the wind. The officer bent down to address them, placing a gloved-hand on the windscreen pillar to not only steady himself against the strength of the wind but also protect his face from the driving rain. The officer grimaced, water streaming from the rim of his cap as he spoke.

"We can't go any further than here, sir," he said. "The storm has brought a larger than expected tidal surge. The water has breached the banks and flooded the track alongside the old harbour. The forecast says it'll get worse over the next few hours."

Janssen looked ahead, straining to see for himself. The night was the blackest he'd seen in a long time and all he could see was the horizontal rain cutting across the beams of his headlights.

"What of the Mercedes?" Tamara asked from the passenger seat.

The constable lowered himself further so he could address her directly.

"It's up there, ma'am but we couldn't see any of the occupants."

"The ARV?"

"On its way," Janssen replied.

The dog unit arrived, pulling up behind them. The officer got out and went to the rear to let the German Shepherd out.

"Your call," Janssen said, looking to Tamara. "The track floods around here, that's not unusual but…" He left the thought unfinished.

Tamara looked around, staring into the inky blackness that refused to offer them any detail of what they faced.

"The canine unit will be useless if the area is underwater," she said, disappointed. "There are numerous tracks leading off from here, aren't there?"

"Yes," he said. "It's a popular walking route into the wetlands."

"We can't go blundering around in the dark, particularly if the suspect is potentially armed. Can we gain access to the area somewhere else? Do the tracks come out elsewhere?"

Janssen thought about it. He could see what she was thinking. The choice of a location was important in understanding the motivation of their suspect, to get a steer on what they hoped to achieve. Sometimes though, the locations that were dismissed could be equally as important.

"Yes, it's wide open. If you're keen to, you can walk out of here at several points. There's a wildlife reserve as well as a number of tracks into the dunes giving access to the shoreline and another comes out in Brancaster. It's still pretty remote and a strange place to come?"

"On a night like this… absolutely. This is where we found Susan. It isn't random," Tamara said. "This is a specific choice that's been made to come here."

The temptation to see this as the killer striking again was

strong, but at the same time, it was too neat for him. There must be something else at play here.

"If Sarah has been brought here by the killer then we can't afford to wait," he said.

"We're not following them into the marshes, Tom," Tamara said. "We'll draw in some numbers and put a cordon around the area, close off routes in and out—"

"Are you kidding?" He squeezed the steering wheel with both hands. "We can't seal off an area of this size. We'd need an army."

"It's the best we can do until daybreak," Tamara said. "If the conditions were better then we could deploy search teams, but like this…" she indicated the exterior, the wind slammed against the car, gently rocking it, as if to prove her point, "it would be irresponsible."

"If Sarah is with Susan's killer then she's as good as dead if we leave it until dawn!"

"Tom," she said turning in her seat to face him, "I know it's a shitty thing to do but we can't offer up any more casualties out there. In these conditions, flooding… we can't take that risk. We'll organise a search team, draft in as many uniforms as we can but we will wait until morning and go out at first light."

Janssen met her eye. She was right. But that didn't mean he had to like it. Without another word, he got out of the car and slammed the door. He began issuing instructions to the waiting officers. Glancing back into the car he saw Tamara watching him. He was unable to interpret her expression. After a moment, she took out her mobile and made a call. It was going to be a long night.

As THE DARKNESS receded their surroundings came into focus. Janssen surveyed the team they'd managed to assemble in the early hours. With himself and Tamara Greave were fifteen others. A mixture of uniformed officers, two canine units and several volunteers from the local swift-river rescue team who were knowledgeable about the waterways and how they behaved in these conditions.

The storm front passed over by four o'clock in the morning, thankfully taking the rain with it. The heavy wind remained, most likely hampering their efforts by prolonging the level where the water would remain high. The coastal cloud was disappearing and soon the sun would rise. In the meantime, they would proceed under the slate grey of the pre-dawn light. The search team moved forward as Tamara came to join him, thanking someone on her mobile before hanging up and slipping the handset into her pocket. He gave her an enquiring look. She shook her head.

"There have been no sightings at any of the choke points of the cordon," she said. "It looks like all the sensible people stayed at home last night."

He assessed her. She looked tired. Unsurprising as they spent the night in the car waiting for the onset of dawn. Neither of them managed any meaningful sleep. He was confident they'd done everything they could to put a presence at the ends of any pedestrian access to the marshes, known routes in or out, but he also knew that to seal the area off was an impossible task. A knowledgeable local could easily slip past them in this terrain, particularly during a night such as this.

They joined the search team, armed with probes to test the ground ahead of them, advancing along Staithe Lane. The old coal shed came into view as the sun crested the horizon. The building was submerged beneath flood water, a newly created island with a handful of boats floating nearby. Janssen glanced to his left at the two armed response officers who'd joined them as a precaution. In all likelihood whoever attacked and abducted Sarah Caseley would be long gone by now, but they provided reassurance nonetheless.

The water ran halfway up his shin and the group waded

onwards, keeping to the known path. Once beyond the coal shed they would split and head into the marshes along the walking routes guided by those with knowledge. The raised path, leading towards the beach via the bird-watching hides, was above the water line. To the left lay the wetlands and the wildlife nature reserve. To the right were the tidal creeks with the sand dunes in the distance.

Even in daylight there were risks and the going was slow. It didn't take long to come across the white Mercedes. It was sitting out of the water at an awkward angle, the nearside front elevated. It looked like it was parked on the track running alongside the main access point to the harbour. Either the driver misjudged where they were or the flow of the water carried it towards deeper water because Janssen figured it had come to rest on the edge of the riverbank, teetering on the edge.

He warily approached with two others, one a canine unit officer, tentatively stabbing at the ground in front of them as they walked. He thought he knew where the ground should be but, until he could see it, it was best to be cautious. The interior of the car had not escaped the onset of the flood. The level of dark brown water in the cabin reached the height of the front seats, higher in the rear. Peering in through the glass, he saw it was empty. The rear of the car was precariously hanging over the bank and inaccessible until they could pull the car further away from the deeper water. This wouldn't happen until the tide went out.

The canine unit officer indicated that there was no suggestion of a human presence within the car and he shook his head at Tamara who acknowledged the information with a raised hand. Janssen was relieved, fearing that Sarah may have been transported to the harbour much as Susan had only days before.

He stopped to look around. The rising sun bathed them in light, reflecting off the still water all around them. They would find Sarah today, he was sure. One person could have left the area on foot during the night but to do so with a captive in tow was unlikely. The question on his mind was what state would she be in when they did?

The landscape was flat in every direction with the nature reserve to one side and the open sea visible beyond the dunes to their right. Between that point and this one, brush rose out of the water. Any of it could easily screen a human being from view. The receding flow of flood water could conceivably carry someone out to a deeper place or deposit them in one of the hidden tidal creeks if the topography of where they lay was conducive to doing so. Perhaps his notion that they'd find Sarah quickly was optimistic.

The search team needed to fan out to either side of the raised path with a second team heading along a separate track through the marshland towards Thornham itself. Using his probe as a pole, he moved back to where the search party was preparing to set out to find Sarah Caseley.

Janssen was pleased to find their assumptions were correct. Although precarious, the water levels were passable closer to the established walking routes. During the darkness of the previous night it was unlikely anyone walking through would deviate much from these routes. The water level could well have been lower when they did so, therefore making it easier still. The choice to come here pushed home in his mind the conclusion they were dealing with a local. No stranger would make the choice.

The search moved slowly but with purpose. They were looking for anything that didn't belong, items of clothing, footwear or personal effects that wouldn't be readily discarded as a matter of course. Janssen found time to think as they progressed, his mind sifting the possibilities. Was Tamara right? Had they already spoken to their killer? If so, they were missing the link, the one piece of information or mistake that would pull it together. Assuming Sarah Caseley was another victim, targeted much as Susan Cook had been, then what tied them together was their time at Wellesley. Working on the most plausible theory that Susan knew something that got her killed, it was conceivable that Sarah was a party to the same knowledge, making her a potential target.

The obvious suspects would be the staff at the children's home which brought the allegations made by Kirsty Davies into the mix. The accidental death of Kirsty didn't sit well with him. Investigated at the time and dismissed, he was reluctant to pour scorn on his fellow officers for running a flawed inquiry but it didn't feel right. Reviewing the documentary evidence taken at the time, it read as a cold investigation, unfeeling and dismissive.

Investigations were supposed to deal in the facts but in this case the approach spoke to him of seeking a swift resolution. When cases were shut down with speed, things were inherently missed. The same was true now just as it was back then. The thought occurred to check on Kirsty Davies' known biological family, if she had any. Perhaps someone else thought there was more to this and Susan's reappearance triggered a catastrophic response. A shout went up off to his right. Everyone stopped and all eyes turned in that direction to the one officer with his arm raised. Tamara, acting as coordinator, would assess the finding before redirecting the search. No one was to move unless she gave the word. The last thing they needed was for people to deviate from their location, thereby breaking the methodical approach to the search pattern. By the look of the reaction, their search for Sarah Caseley was over. Tamara beckoned him over before kneeling down into the water.

Setting off to cover the ground as quickly as he dared, he heard the call go out over the radio for an ambulance and a flutter of excitement and relief passed through him. Potentially, she was still alive. Coming alongside Tamara he found her kneeling in the water, ignoring the fact the water was seeping over the rim of her waders and soaking her clothes. Gently cradling Sarah Caseley's battered head, ensuring her airways were clear, Tamara looked up at him anxiously. Sarah's prospects appeared bleak. Unsurprising based on her spending the night out here. Casting an eye back towards the starting point of the search where paramedics were on standby, he could see two of them making their way towards them.

"They're coming," he said.

Sarah moaned. It was a low, guttural sound and barely audible. Her face contorted in an involuntary spasm. He was amazed she was still alive. Lying with much of her body submerged in cold water, her skin colour was beyond pale taking on a grey hue. She must be suffering from hypothermia as a minimum. Sarah sported a head wound slightly above her right temple, the blood having ceased flowing and congealed. Her left eye was visibly swollen, as was her cheek below it. Having seen enough beatings over the years, he knew someone had set about her.

"Help is on its way, Sarah," Tamara whispered leaning in to her ear.

Sarah mumbled something. Her lips barely moving, she was incoherent. Her eyelids fluttered momentarily and for a brief moment Janssen wondered if she was coming round.

"What was that, Sarah?" Tamara asked.

Her breathing became shallower still and her lips, tinged blue from the cold, moved slightly as she attempted to form words. Only one part of what she said was recognisable.

"Abi—" she repeated quietly before drifting into unconsciousness. Tamara glanced up at him.

CHAPTER TWENTY-NINE

JANSSEN RANG the bell for a second time, stepping back from the door and looking at the front of the house. The curtains were open on the ground floor as well as in the upstairs rooms. He glanced at his watch. It was eight-thirty. Still early. Tamara travelled with Sarah Caseley to the hospital in the ambulance, keen to be alongside her should she regain consciousness. He was about to head around to the rear of the property when he heard a sliding bolt disengage from the other side of the door and a key turning within a lock. A figure could be seen through the sliver of frosted glass set into the door. Moments later, the door cracked open. Abigail Thomas eyed him warily. He doubted he'd woken her. She was fully dressed and appeared ready for the day ahead.

"Inspector," she said with a welcoming smile. "Whatever can I do for you at this time?"

"Mrs Thomas. Would you mind if we had a chat? It's regarding an acquaintance of yours, Sarah Caseley."

"Sarah? Yes, of course. Please come in," she said, pulling the door wide and beckoning him forward.

She was already setting off back into the house as he entered, wiping his feet on the mat. Despite changing out of the all-weather kit and waders he wore in the search for Sarah, his shoes still carried mud from the waterlogged area where they'd left the car. Watching Abigail, he noticed her movement was stiff and this piqued his curiosity.

Hurrying to catch up with her, he followed as she led them into her living room. A mug of steaming coffee sat on a small table next to an armchair beside the open fireplace. A fire was set but not yet lit, kindling stacked neatly with a small log of silver birch resting on the top. A box of matches was open on the hearth and several of the sticks were loose on the slate alongside it as if they'd fallen from the box.

She noticed him looking.

"Would you mind doing the honours, Inspector?" she asked, pointing to the fire. "I find the winter hard enough but when it is also damp I truly suffer. I'll make you a coffee while you do that. You look like you can do with one. How do you take it?"

"Black, no sugar please."

She was right. He was feeling the effects of having no sleep overnight. Undoing his coat, he knelt down and picked up the matchbox watching over his shoulder as Abigail gingerly wandered away into the nearby kitchen. Striking a match, he was irritated as it flickered into life only to expire before he could extend his hand to the firelighter at the base of the stack. The next fared better and he leaned in, holding the flame against the block and it caught immediately.

Sitting back on his haunches, he waited patiently for the kindling to catch. Once confident the flames were taking hold, he gathered up the loose matches and put them back in the box before lifting the guard into place. Abigail returned with another mug, passing it to him as he stood.

"Thank you," she said, gesturing toward the fire. "You're very kind. I am struggling at the moment."

"What with?" he asked.

"Blasted Rheumatoid Arthritis," she said, holding out her hand in front of her and staring at it. The joints of her fingers were swollen and several of them appeared hooked, reminiscent of a claw. "It gets worse every year, particularly in the winter."

"And it's not just your hands, is it?"

She let out a laugh of derision.

"Certainly not! You're good at this. You must be quite the detective," she said with a wry grin. He returned it. "It's targeting all of my joints. I've never been one to do anything by halves, you know. In for a penny, in for a pound as they say."

"Forgive me," he said, "but you don't seem old enough."

"Oh, if only that were true, Inspector," she said dryly, offering him a seat while she eased herself into her own beside the fire. He sat down on the sofa, cupping his mug with both hands and appreciating the warmth it generated.

"I thought that at the time when the doctor diagnosed it. Thirty-eight. That's how old I was. Apparently, it's common from forty onwards. Particularly in women. Who knew? I guess I was just lucky to be ahead of my time." She sipped at her drink, casting a glance to the fire before continuing. "My hands were deteriorating at quite an alarming rate, particularly when bearing in mind my choice of career. I figured I'd been overdoing it, what with getting the gallery up and running plus I had a full order book... several exhibitions to gear up for as well. Everything was going at a fantastic pace. The most successful period of my life bar none. And then this."

Her expression turned glum as she examined her right hand in front of her.

"You're still painting though," he said.

She nodded.

"Of course. And some days are better than others. I'm sure I will always paint in some capacity," she said with a sigh. "Unfortunately, my recent works are not considered as catching as those produced in my heyday. That makes me sound so old, Inspector. It was barely six years ago. Anyway, enough of my moaning. You said you needed to speak with me about Sarah."

"Yes. I take it you know her?"

"Of course I do, yes. We are friends," she said. "We go back a long way."

"Back to your time together at Wellesley?"

"Yes."

Abigail didn't elaborate further. Again, he found it odd how Sarah Caseley didn't confirm the friendship when they first spoke rather than pretend she'd only heard of Abigail by way of her local fame.

"Can you tell me when you last saw her or spoke with her?"

Abigail paused for a moment, raising her mug once again but her eyes never left his.

"Yesterday. I saw her yesterday. She came here to the house. Why do you ask?"

"Sarah was attacked last night," he said. Abigail's mouth fell open.

"My word. How awful. Is she okay?"

"She was abducted from her home, seemingly beaten and left in the marshes. We found her early this morning. I'm afraid her condition isn't good."

Abigail raised a hand to her mouth, her eyes scanning the room. He found himself assessing her. Not only her responses to the information but also her physical condition. There was no way this woman could have trashed the Caseley's home, let alone overpowered Sarah and dragged her into the marshes. She wasn't physically capable.

"That's... just awful," she said, looking to the floor. "I can't find the words."

The fire was burning well and he got up to place a larger log on the fire before setting the guard in place and returning to his seat.

"Abigail, do you know anyone who would wish harm upon Sarah?"

She shook her head emphatically.

"What was it she came to see you about?"

"Sooz," she said, momentarily looking at him before averting her gaze from his. "She was struggling with finding out about her. Susan, I mean. A terrible business what has happened to her. To think when you first visited me that it was Susan you were referring to."

One hand still held her mug and the other was absently fiddling with the pendant of her necklace.

"Why come to you?"

The question drew a dark look from her which dissipated almost immediately. He sensed her reticence.

"We are aware of the allegations surrounding your time spent at Wellesley. Several people have confirmed what they thought was going on, some of it rumour and some as close to confirmation as we are likely to get after this many years."

"In which case, Inspector," she said, "you will understand the level of trust that exists between those of us who experienced that place. The type of bond you only get when forged in adversity. Sarah needed to talk to someone and she doesn't have anyone else."

"She has her husband. He cares for her. I witnessed that last night."

"Hah!" she said, throwing her head back as she derided the notion. "James Caseley is a well-known chauvinist and philanderer. He's not interested in anything but himself."

"Sarah did say she was concerned about him learning of her past."

"Whatever nonsense was she talking about?"

Janssen was taken aback but took care not to show it.

"James knew everything there was to know about his wife," Abigail said, shaking her head.

"So, she wasn't keeping her time at Wellesley from him?"

Abigail exhaled deeply.

"I love Sarah like one of the sisters I never had, Inspector, but she is quite the mixed-up woman. One never really knows with her, so prone to… well, it doesn't seem right to belittle her under the circumstances, but she does struggle to tell the truth."

"Her husband… knows everything, you said. Can you elaborate for me?"

"Sarah struggled at Wellesley. Some of us found depths of resilience we never knew existed whereas others… it nearly broke them. It was a long time before Sarah was able to put it behind her. She mixed with the wrong crowd, whilst at Wellesley and beyond it. Nasty people who exploited her vulnerabilities. I didn't see her for several years… she fell into routines that, well… let us just say may have brought her across your path. Living off immoral earnings."

"Are you saying she prostituted herself?"

"Developed a career as a sex worker, I think the modern term is, isn't it?" she said, inclining her head to one side and lowering her voice despite them being the only two present. Placing her mug back onto the table, she put her hands together in her lap. "Not walking the streets, I should say, but she'd seen what effect she had on men from a very early age and… sought to exploit that. To turn the tables so to speak. Exploit the foolishness of men much as they had her from the age of thirteen."

Janssen sat forward, resting his elbows on his knees as he processed the information.

"And her husband, James. He knew what exactly?"

"How on earth do you think they met?" Abigail said, splaying her hands wide. "She was perfect for him. James is quite a few years older than her, so he got his younger, trophy wife to show off to his friends. She knew the score. She knew how to keep him happy and, likewise, so he did her. It was a nigh-on perfect match. Plus, he gets to dominate her much of the time and she's conditioned to take it."

Janssen felt like concurring with her conclusion but held himself back. It wasn't his place to pass judgement.

"All we managed to get out of Sarah this morning after we

found her was your name. It was all she could say before she was taken to the hospital. Why do you think that was?"

Abigail Thomas took in a deep breath, raising her eyebrows as the corners of her mouth turned downward. She shrugged.

"I'm afraid I have no idea. I'm sorry."

He felt his mobile vibrate in his pocket. Withdrawing it in case it was Tamara, he saw it was a text notification. Tapping on it without looking at who the sender was, he read it.

I HAVEN'T HEARD from you, Tom. I need to know what's going on x x

HE CLOSED THE MESSAGE, slipping the handset back into his pocket.

"That didn't appear to be good news," Abigail said, reading his expression. Her own turned to concern. "Is it Sarah?"

He shook his head.

"It's unrelated. No news on Sarah as yet. Tell me, why did you pretend not to know Susan Cook?"

"I wasn't aware that I did any such thing."

"When we visited you before, it was Susan that we'd found at Thornham."

"And I seem to recall you were unaware of who she was at the time, Inspector."

"So, she hadn't paid you a visit prior to her death?"

Abigail shook her head, her eyes never left his.

"No. Susan did not make contact with me prior to her death. If she had done so, I would have told you. I haven't seen her in decades, Inspector. Have you made any strides into finding out how she died? Do you believe her murder is connected to what happened to Sarah last night?"

"Do you?"

Again, she shrugged.

"I wouldn't know. I wish I did."

He decided to take a different track.

"Can you think back to your time at Wellesley, for me. We are aware of the allegations made against Nicholas Levy—"

"Nicholas!" she said, sitting forward and shaking her head. "Who on earth is pointing the finger at Nicholas? He was a lovely man. Such rubbish."

"We understood Nicholas Levy used to isolate the girls in what you referred to as—"

"*The hole*," she finished for him. "Yes, but that wasn't Nicholas. He was so rarely at Wellesley, what with all of his other business interests. No, it was Neil Baker who ran the place. He was the wolf in sheep's clothing. A truly evil little man."

The look on his face, usually so well concealed, must have been obvious to read.

"You didn't know, did you? You thought it was Nicholas who… did those things to us."

"Baker isn't mentioned in the files I've read. The allegations from Kirsty Davies cited Levy."

"Kirsty had many problems but she was bright. She felt the best thing for her was to get away from there and thought throwing as much mud at Nicholas was the way to do it. No matter what it did to the poor man's reputation."

"But she could have nailed Baker. You all could."

"Inspector, you make it sound so simple," she said, shaking her head. "As much as I admire what Nicholas Levy gave to us all… a home when no one else wanted us, he still sought to protect the reputation of Wellesley above all else. Above even our welfare. The scandal would have brought the whole thing to a close. Don't you see, Neil Baker was sidelined and quietly moved on. That was how it was dealt with. No one wanted the truth at the time and I doubt now will be any different."

Janssen stood, taking out his mobile.

"Excuse me a moment," he said, heading out into the hall. Looking up Eric's number, he called him.

"Eric, where are you at the moment?"

"I've just dropped James Caseley at the hospital, didn't want him driving in the state he's in. I reckon he hit the bottle last night. Can't blame him I guess."

"How's she doing, Sarah?"

"No change. Still unconscious. Suffering from acute hypothermia. It's a good job we got to her when we did. It's touch and go, but any more time out there and she'd definitely be a goner for sure."

"Okay. Listen, I want you to swing by and pick up Neil Baker. You know where to find him?"

"Yes… erm…" Eric said, sounding confused. "What for?"

"Tell him I need a word," he said. "And if he doesn't want to come in for a voluntary chat… nick him."

"What for?" Eric repeated.

"Start off with abduction if you need to and then we'll go from there."

"Ab…" Eric said, stopping himself. He knew better than to argue. "Do you think he attacked Sarah Caseley?"

"At this point I'm not sure," he said, lowering his voice to make certain he wasn't overheard by Abigail.

"Will do."

"And, Eric…"

"Yes?"

"Have some uniform meet you there just in case… and be careful."

Janssen hung up, touching the mobile to his lips.

"Neil Baker," he said quietly to himself.

Returning to where Abigail sat in front of the fire, he started looking through his contacts as he spoke to her.

"Under the circumstances, I think it would be sensible for me to have a car stationed outside your house—"

"You will do no such thing, Inspector," she said.

"It would only be as a precaution. Bearing in mind what has happened to two of your friends I think you need—"

"I'll not hear of it," she said, waving away the offer.

"Honestly. If I was in danger then I'd be the easiest target there is. But I'm still here. No, whatever you are dealing with, please feel free to get on with it. In the meantime, I'll crack on as usual."

Janssen dropped it. He wasn't going to be able to get her agreement.

CHAPTER THIRTY

JANSSEN STARED at the whiteboards on the wall of the ops room, scanning the spider's web of friendships, acquaintances and potential abusers that tied everyone to Susan Cook. It struck him how delving deeper into what was a relatively simple missing person's case could unravel such intrigue.

"Where are we with Neil Baker?" he asked.

Eric, beavering away at his computer with a telephone clamped between ear and shoulder, glanced up at him. Eric was on hold with the service provider of Baker's mobile.

"Friends and family haven't seen or heard from him since you saw him at Holkham. Later that day he sent his son a text to say he was taking himself off for a few days but didn't say where."

"Is that unusual?"

Eric shook his head.

"Apparently not, no. He's prone to impulsive actions by all accounts. Kyle, his son, said he called him last night after the hospital got in touch because he'd missed his dialysis appointment. He goes three times per week, every week and was booked in the same day you spoke with him. To miss one is unusual. The call dropped to voicemail and Neil hasn't returned it."

"Bank accounts, credit cards?"

"Nothing. If he's spending then it's with cash," Eric said. "Unless we're too late and he's already skipped the country." Eric frowned. "Do you think that's likely?"

Janssen didn't answer. He was still trying to comprehend how Baker managed to pull the wool over his eyes so easily. Naturally suspicious, a required trait in a successful detective, Baker didn't trigger his senses as he would usually expect. Maybe Tamara was right. He was off his game. The turmoil in his personal life was affecting his work. Once this case was resolved he had some decisions to make.

"Yes, I'm still here," Eric said despondently. Seemingly placed back on hold, he sighed and returned to his screen.

Without any hits at petrol stations, shops or ATMs, they were running short of leads as to where Neil Baker may have gone. Baker's description and vehicle details were already in circulation and if he tried to board a flight out of the country he would be detained. Janssen was confident Baker hadn't left the country. There was no evidence of an online purchase with airlines or ferry companies. Should he attempt to do so with cash, then his passport would flag up their interest. No. Neil Baker was still in the UK and he would hazard a guess he remained in the area.

"Yes. Brilliant. Thank you," Eric said, suddenly animated and sitting forward in his chair. Moving his mouse, he clicked on something on the screen "Yes, I have it, thanks."

Eric replaced the receiver, looking up with a broad smile on his face. Janssen was already coming to stand behind him.

"What have you got?"

"Every data point relating to Neil Baker's movements in the past week. Well, his phone's anyway."

"And by data points you mean—"

"Connections to cell towers. That means we can plot—"

"Where he's been. Yes, I get it. Start with the most recent, would you."

Eric opened the spreadsheet on his computer. They watched the circle spinning on the screen for an agonising few seconds, as the machine processed the request. The screen flashed into life with data. Eric immediately sorted the information, applying timeline filters.

"Where's he been?" Janssen asked.

"Just a sec—" Eric said, looking closer at the screen. Copying the information in one cell, he carried it to another screen, inputting it there. A new tab opened with a map. Janssen recognised the topography. It was still in north Norfolk. Eric zoomed in and the image generated a shaded circle, at the centre point was the last cell tower Baker's phone was connected to. The remainder of the circle was the area covered by that particular tower. It was extensive.

"Is there any crossover?" he asked.

"Between towers?" Eric asked.

Janssen nodded.

"There is but," he said pointing at the screen, "but this is live data. His mobile is connected to this tower right now."

Eric broadened the map, bringing the area into sharp focus. It was predominantly rural as much of north Norfolk was.

"What on earth do you think he's doing there?" Eric asked.

Janssen knew where to find him.

"Come on, Eric," he said, clapping the constable on the shoulder. "Let's be going."

"Going? Going where?"

THE RED LANDROVER was parked before the main entrance to Wellesley Manor. The anticipation of getting a result, growing since they left the station, was immediately dashed. Janssen switched off the engine and glanced across at Eric before getting out. By the look on his face, Eric was in no rush to do so either. The running lights of the Landrover were on. The engine wasn't. It must have run out of fuel. The cabin of the vehicle was shrouded in grey, masking the interior from view.

As they walked closer, Janssen could make out the still form of a figure in the driver's seat. Wisps of smoke drifted into the air via the crack in the window, lowered just enough to fit the hosepipe through. Not wishing to disturb the hosepipe, he walked around to the passenger side of the car. Pulling his sleeve down over his outstretched hand, he carefully pulled the handle and opened the door whilst stepping back to allow the cloud of exhaust fumes pass him by. He shielded his mouth and nose with his free hand. After a few moments, the cabin cleared and he was able to come closer to examine the body. It was definitely Neil Baker. He was in the driver's seat, slumped forward towards the steering wheel, head bowed. Janssen crouched down, changing the angle so that he could look up at Baker's face from below.

"Should I call an ambulance?" Eric asked, although in a half-hearted tone.

Janssen reached over and gently searched for a pulse. The body was stone cold. He already knew but had to be certain.

"A bit late for that, I'm afraid," he said, glancing back at Eric.

Turning his attention to the deceased, he could find no indication of bodily trauma. Inspecting the backs of his hands, he could see that Baker didn't appear to have been involved in a fight of any description. Aside from the cherry-red lividity under the skin of every exposed part of his body, he looked unharmed. Baker's nose was almost black, probably due to the blood pooling there as his head slumped forward after death.

"Do they always look like that?" Eric asked.

Janssen replied over his shoulder. "Depends on the length of time and the volume of exposure to the carbon monoxide," he said quietly. "It diffuses across the alveoli, binds to the haemoglobin of the blood which generates that red or bright pink colour after death."

He looked at the dashboard. It was still illuminated. He was right, the engine cut out after the car ran out of fuel. The smell of the interior was oppressive and he could feel his head already starting to pound. Withdrawing from the car, he took in a lungful of fresh air. Eric looked nauseous. Perhaps this was his first experience of seeing a suicide like this. There would be more in his career.

"Call it in, would you," he said. "I'm going to take a look inside."

Crossing the short distance to the front door, he found the crime scene tape hanging to one side. The building was sealed by the CSI team following the discovery of the location where Susan Cook was attacked. On this occasion, the door opened far more easily. The day outside was overcast but not necessarily dark but had no effect on the gloomy interior. Using the light on his mobile, he moved deeper into the building. Someone had been in here since they taped it off and he was pretty sure where they'd headed.

He was confident no one else was present in the building but he still proceeded with caution. The advanced state of decay of the property meant he had to be wary particularly in light of the fierce storm they'd just had. Coming to the room the girls referred to as *the hole*, he found the door open. Again, the crime scene tape had been removed. It lay at his feet by the entrance to the room.

Entering the room, nothing appeared to have changed. It had been meticulously examined by the crime scene technicians, every inch catalogued and photographed. Standing in the centre of the room, he angled the light from his mobile around looking for anything that caught his attention. There was nothing. *He must have come in here for a reason.* That is, unless he was reliving past events... past glories as abusers often liked to do. Maybe it was one last experience to stimulate the memory before taking his own life.

Abandoning his search, he returned outside. Eric was on his haunches next to the driver's side door. It was open which irritated him. The lad should know better than to do that until CSI arrived. Eric must have read his expression as he approached, rising and offering an explanation as he did so. Janssen had been set to give him a ticking off.

"There's something in the foot well," Eric said, pointing towards Baker's feet.

Janssen set his anger aside, coming to see for himself. A piece of paper, torn from a notebook, lay between the deceased man's feet in front of the pedals. It wasn't folded and angling his head to one side he was able to read it.

I'M SORRY. *None of them deserved it.*
   They didn't deserve me

THE NOTE WAS unsigned and the wording shaky and erratic.

"What do you make of it?" Eric asked.

Janssen didn't reply. Instead, he examined Baker's footwear as well as the carpet mat lining the floor beneath them. His eyes followed up the back of the man's legs. Retreating from the cabin, he scanned the ground around the car. Moving to the back of the vehicle, he gave the rear seats a cursory glance before coming to the boot. Careful not to disturb the hose protruding from the exhaust pipe, he donned a pair of latex gloves and tested the rear door of the Landrover, finding it unlocked.

"Suicide," Eric said to him. "The pressure of realising the truth was about to come out, do you think?"

Opening the door at the rear, he stepped aside, allowing it to swing past him before inspecting the interior. It was empty. Closing the door again, Janssen looked around. His eyes tracked across the building and then the surrounding countryside. A place where such unspeakable evil could happen in such a beautiful location. Meeting Eric's eye, he shook his head.

"Only if he was able to slide himself backwards to get into the car."

"What's that?" Eric asked.

"The heels of his shoes. There's mud up the back of the shoe and it's spread to the base of his trousers."

"Someone dragged him to the car?" Eric said, shocked.

"That'd be my guess. I don't doubt the fumes killed him but I reckon he didn't know anything about it. Take a look for yourself and read the note again."

Janssen stood aside as Eric swapped places with him, moving closer and rereading the handwritten note before moving to the shoes.

"The writing is shaky, I'll grant you," Eric said. "Couldn't that be down to emotion... the hysteria surrounding what he was about to do?"

"Or an indication of coercion. Looking down the barrel of a loaded shotgun would strike the fear of God into you and deliver a similar effect," he said. "Besides, working on the assumption Baker assaulted Sarah Caseley... where's the shotgun?"

Eric shrugged.

"Could have discarded it somewhere."

"Why bother if you're coming here to kill yourself?"

Eric couldn't argue. On an entirely superficial level, suicide ticked every box but scratch the surface and the truth was there to see.

"The only way this gets better for us is if Neil Baker came with a ribbon and a bow," he said. "Someone wants us to shut the investigation down, laying it at Baker's door."

"Neat and tidy," Eric said. "But who?"

Janssen took a deep breath, running a hand through his hair. Nobody they'd come in contact with in this case appeared capable of telling the truth. Everyone seemed to be lying. The one thing he could be certain about was that no one could be trusted. His phone rang. Answering the call, he saw it originated from the station.

"Sir, there is someone waiting to see you at the station."

He recognised the voice of Gavin, the civilian desk clerk who manned the front desk throughout the week.

"I'm not going to be back there any time soon, I'm afraid," he said. "Can you take some details and I'll get back to them."

"I am afraid she is quite insistent, sir."

For a moment he feared Samantha was back in the station and he pictured her haranguing the desk clerk, demanding to see him but he pushed the thought aside. Not even she would be that daft.

"Who is it, do you know?" he asked.

"A lady by the name of Gretta Mulholland. She wants to speak with you, she claims, on a matter of urgency. I explained you were out in the field but..." He lowered his voice. Presumably she was nearby and within earshot. "But she won't say what it's about. She'll only speak with you or DCI Greave and I don't know when the DCI will—"

"Tell her I'll be there shortly," he said, hanging up. Turning back to Eric, he indicated towards the Landrover. "You'll have to hang on here for forensics to arrive. I'll have someone in uniform swing by and pick you up. I've got to get back to the station."

Striding back to his car, he was more than curious to know what brought Gretta all this way to see them.

CHAPTER THIRTY-ONE

JANSSEN OPENED the door to the interview room and entered. Gretta Mulholland, the leader of the community of Brethren where Susan Cook lived for the years of her disappearance, sat alone behind a solitary table. An empty plastic cup was the only thing visible in front of her, a vending machine coffee provided by one of the uniforms for her while she waited. She momentarily looked up as he walked in, but her gaze soon dropped to the table before her. On their previous meeting she seemed so in control, authoritative. Now, seated in the interview room, wrapped in a grey overcoat and scarf, she appeared far older than her years, somewhat frail and diminutive.

"Gretta," he said, closing the door behind him and taking a seat opposite her. "I must say I was a little surprised to get the call."

She looked up, meeting his curious gaze. Bobbing her head, she signalled she understood.

"It is not a journey I made lightly, Inspector."

He could see the lines on her face along with the darkness in the skin surrounding her eyes. She was deeply troubled, appearing not to have slept well for days.

"The news you brought us about Susan... about her death threw me greatly."

He had the impression at the time this wasn't the case, but he didn't comment.

"And I am afraid I wasn't entirely honest with you," she said, her eyes flicking up to meet his eye before quickly averting them again.

"How so?"

"I knew Susan was coming back here and I knew why. What happened to her here many years ago motivated her to come in search of us, the Brethren... nearly ten years ago now."

"She sought out your community?"

She shook her head.

"No. She was seeking her mother," Gretta said flatly. "She sought me."

Janssen felt his shoulders drop. He hadn't seen that coming. Susan Cook was abandoned by her mother as a child, but he didn't know of a connection to Gretta. She read the surprise in his expression.

"Gretta is a chosen name, Inspector, and I subsequently married. I feared you would find the link between us from the moment you arrived at Bluebelle. In time, I'm sure you would."

"Why didn't you just tell us—?"

"I have a great deal to lose, Inspector. The community that Jefferson, my late husband, and I strived so hard to build relies on trust and togetherness. How could I destroy that? Tiffany Cole was a young girl, struggling to make her way in the world, when she fell pregnant. She made many mistakes, lived a life of abject sin. I laid her to rest twenty-five years ago. Her time had passed."

"No one knew?"

"No," she said, shaking her head. "They didn't. Not even my husband knew of Susan. My past, yes. He was a decent and loving man who forgave the sins of my former life. You see, Bluebelle was his ancestral home and together we built our community, looking to make a difference with the glory of God. When Susan arrived, I'd recently lost Jefferson. He passed away suddenly from a heart attack and I'll admit I was floundering in my grief. It was the strength of the community alongside my faith that got me through. I took my daughter's reappearance as a blessing, another opportunity at redemption. I ensured Susan knew that our past would always remain between the two of us from the moment she came to my door. She accepted that, making her a far better person than I will ever be. I could never have blamed her for the anger and resentment she carried but this wasn't the case. She needed someone. She needed her mother."

"How did she find you?"

Gretta rolled her eyes, her mouth falling open.

"To this day I do not know. Susan was an intelligent and resourceful young woman… far more so than her mother at the same age I can assure you. I left… when I left her, I did so outside of a hospice. I knew it was church run… that they would look after her far better than I could. See her go to a good home. I tucked a couple of photographs I had inside her coat pocket. They were of me and her, taken as a child. These must have been kept somewhere, I don't know. All of this goes to show you how young a girl I was. The hospice contacted the authorities and I was tracked down by the police and arrested. That was the best thing that ever happened to me. I was forced to face my demons, the alcohol and the drugs. I found solace in His presence. My child was being cared for better than I ever could… and I left. I didn't expect to see Susan ever again. In any event, she tracked me down. As I say, a resourceful girl. I was as impressed as I was surprised."

"Why come forward with this now?" he asked.

Gretta sighed.

"Several reasons, if I am honest. Despite what you might think, my conscience has troubled me since the day I left her. Susan was in my thoughts and prayers every day since and if I was unfit or unable to do right by her in life then, perhaps, I should do so in death."

Janssen sat back, folding his arms across his chest and thinking through her words.

"And do you not fear a backlash from your community, should your secret come out?"

She fixed him with a stare.

"It is out already, Inspector. I summoned the group and spoke with everyone before I came here. No doubt, they will be making their assessment of my future as we speak. I will place myself in their hands and whatever they decide, punishment or forgiveness, it will be as nothing compared to what I will live with until my dying day. I should have stopped Susan, protected her as it is a mother's duty."

"You couldn't have known what would happen."

"Be that as it may. The time for secrets is at an end. The day comes to us all when we must face judgement having passed through the gates of heaven, and I intend to do so with a clear conscience."

She reached down beside her, coming back up with a folded plastic carrier bag which she set upon the table. There was a brief moment of hesitation before she pushed it across towards him. His eyes narrowed, unsure of what he was looking at. Turning the bag over, he unfurled it and inspected the contents. There were a bunch of envelopes inside, all open and held together with an elastic band.

"What am I looking at?" he asked. Gretta raised herself upright.

"These are personal letters," she said. He raised an enquiring eyebrow towards her. "Personal to Susan. I took them from her accommodation prior to your arrival."

"Why would you do that?"

"I was terrified, Inspector."

The tone of her voice and the despairing look in her eyes told him her answer was genuine.

"Terrified of what I might lose if everyone came to know the truth of my past." She fiddled with her hands, turning them over and over within themselves. "There are many things I regret in life, Inspector Janssen. Having my daughter was not one of them. I see that now. I cannot and will not speak her father's name... I can barely look at myself in the mirror when I think of him. I was frank with Susan. I would not discuss her father no matter how much she pressed... and believe me, she did press hard, but I shall carry that to my grave. It is time for people to hear about my wonderful child who I am proud to have known."

"Her personal effects. A diary?" Janssen asked, peering into the bag.

"I burned it."

"You did what?" Janssen felt a surge of anger which he quickly quelled.

"I'm sorry. I shouldn't have done so but after your visit... I tried to bury everything, conceal the past as best I could. Susan spoke of me, her childhood and her feelings about our relationship now. At that moment, I couldn't allow that to be seen."

"There would have been information in there potentially vital to finding her killer."

"I know," Gretta said. Her tone belied the sense of gravity in her actions. "But it is done and cannot be reversed."

"You said you knew why she returned to Norfolk," he said, splaying his hands wide. "Care to enlighten me?"

"To confront her demons while there was still time, Inspector. To make amends for an injustice."

"You make it sound like she was against the clock."

"Oh, very much so. My daughter was suffering from cancer, Inspector."

"We know. The pathologist noted that."

"Were you aware her last bout of chemo had failed? That there was little more that could be done for her?"

Janssen shook his head. "No. I didn't. I'm sorry. How long did she have?"

"Months, years… who really knows?"

"What was the injustice you mentioned?"

Gretta sat forward, calmly placing her own hands on the table, palms down, she gestured towards the bag in front of him. "You need to read the letters."

"Have you?"

Gretta inclined her head to one side.

"Some of them, yes. At times the tone is friendly, at others… less so."

"Who are they from?"

"People who Susan loved, Inspector Janssen, and apparently keeping secrets runs in our family."

———

JANSSEN SAT ALONE in the ops room, sifting through the handwritten letters sent to Susan Cook. Rarely did he ever feel as caught off guard as he was in this very moment. Tamara wasn't answering her mobile with each call passing to voicemail. Placing the letter in his hand down on the desk, he rubbed vigorously at his face in an effort to shake off the fatigue. He needed a clear head. The sound of someone entering ops came from behind him. Turning, he saw Eric entering.

"Good timing, Eric. Get your coat, I need you to run an errand."

Eric stopped where he was. His finger and thumb had barely touched the zipper of his coat. Eric looked at him and then the clock on the wall. Janssen read his mind.

"You can grab some lunch on your way out."

"Where am I going?" Eric asked with a hint of frustration.

"I need you to catch up with Tara Byrons."

Eric glanced at the clock again.

"At this time, she'll be in school. Do you want me to pick her up?"

"No," Janssen said, shaking his head. "I want you to keep tabs on her. See where she goes and who she talks to. Nothing more. Don't let her out of your sight and report back to me with every move she makes."

Eric frowned.

"Why are we interested in her?"

Janssen stood, picking up the letter in front of him and offering it to Eric.

"Because she's known where Susan Cook has been for some time."

Eric scanned the page, his eyes darting up to meet Janssen's.

"How long?" Eric asked.

"I don't know for certain, but they've been exchanging correspondence for the last couple of years at least."

"Why is she lying to us?"

"That is the question, Eric. Why, indeed?"

CHAPTER THIRTY-TWO

ERIC COLLET STIFLED A YAWN. His back ached from being in the car and he was in desperate need of a toilet. Glancing at the clock on the dashboard he sought to calculate how long it'd been since he last slept, giving up after a few moments. It was too taxing. The temptation to close his eyes was growing. Looking up and down the street, which was quiet, he considered going for a walk. *Would he stand out if he did?* There wasn't a great deal of passing traffic, so the answer was probably yes, he would.

Tara Byrons' Audi was parked on her drive. It was a nice-looking car and he found himself wondering how much it would cost to run. Would it suit him? It was a bit flash. *Becca might like it.* He dismissed the thought. She wouldn't. She wasn't into cars or material things in general. She was all about people. He loved that about her. He figured it came from having a large extended family with many nieces and nephews. This was probably why she was always talking about the future and asking him what his thoughts were regarding children. Planning. That's what she enjoyed.

A man came out of a neighbouring property to Tara's carrying a white bin bag. He glanced up the street, his gaze lingering on Eric who found himself involuntarily shrinking into his seat, trying to remain unobserved. *Was he looking at him?* Walking to the end of his drive where the bins were set out awaiting collection, the man dropped the bag in before closing the lid and returning inside the house without another glance in his direction. Eric relaxed.

There were so few of the houses with cars outside. Most people were presumably at work. He was sitting in his unmarked car up the street from Tara's, as close as he dared but far enough away not to be conspicuous should she glance out of her window. Having first gone to the school he failed to see her car among the others in the staff parking zone. Casually ringing the school on a false pretence, he was advised Tara Byrons was unavailable. A brief conversation followed and he left the call having learned that she was off work due to illness. They couldn't offer him an expected return date. This intrigued him as she seemed quite well when he and Tamara spoke with her.

Had she gone off sick following their visit? She didn't strike him as the fragile type. In fact, quite the opposite, his impression of her was athletic and supremely fit. His eyes felt heavy and he adjusted the heating dial in the car, reducing it to sixteen degrees and turning the blowers up. The blast of cold air on his face and particularly his feet was unpleasant but he needed to remain alert. For what, he didn't know. Deciding it was no use, he would need to stretch his legs if for no other reason than to ward off his recurring thoughts about sanitation, he switched off the engine and reached for the door handle.

Barely had he set one foot onto the pavement when the door to Tara's house opened and she emerged. Cursing under his breath, he couldn't dive back into the car. That would be suspicious and probably attract attention. He closed the car door, leaving it unlocked in case he needed to move quickly. Setting off up the path to the nearest house, he stopped to tie his shoelace and chanced a look in her direction. She was casually dressed and definitely not heading into work. Even from this distance, he thought she looked well enough and certainly not bedridden which was the impression given to him earlier by the school.

She glanced up the street towards him as she opened her car door but there was no indication of her recognising him. He rose and resumed his course just as Tara reversed her car out onto the road. He dared not look at her again as he made his way up the path to the front door. Pressing the door bell, he heard it ring inside as Tara's car passed by behind him. Once she was clear, he turned his head and saw her reach the end of the road, indicating right as she approached the junction. The door before him opened and a woman stood there, an expectant look on her face. He cracked a smile.

"Yes. Can I help you?" she asked.

Eric shook his head, embarrassed.

"No, sorry. Wrong number."

Hurrying back to his car, he jumped in. The tyres protested with a squeal as he turned the car around and set off at pace. With a bit of luck, he could make up the distance. Explaining how he'd lost his quarry while sitting outside her house was not a conversation he wanted to have with his boss.

A break in the traffic meant he could pull out of the development without delay and headed in the same direction as Tara. Within moments, he hit a queue of traffic lined up behind a tractor making its way along the carriageway. Fortunately for him, Tara's Audi was visible near to the front of the very same line of cars. Familiar with the local roads as he was, Eric knew no one was getting past the hold up any time soon. They snaked their way along the coast road for another couple of miles before he noticed Tara indicating to turn across the oncoming traffic.

By the time he reached the junction, she was some distance away and he followed. Pleased to be out of the slow-moving traffic and onto an open road, he accelerated. Tara Byrons must have responded the same way, utilising the pace and power of her car because he was unable to close the gap. However, the roads here were long and despite a few twists and turns, the opportunities to diverge onto different routes were few and far between. Eric was able to keep track of Tara's car with relative ease.

Only when she appeared near to her destination did Eric come close enough for him to feel the need to slow down in order to avoid raising her suspicions. Tara turned left and into a caravan park. Eric did likewise. Just beyond the entrance, the road split with one route leading to the facilities block and a small car park while the other headed directly onto the site and the caravans. It was the latter route that Tara followed. Eric pulled into the car park. It was the less risky option and he was confident he'd be able to keep an eye on her from this vantage point.

The site itself was quiet with barely anyone around. Eric was able to bring his car to a stop directly in front of the gap between the building housing the office and convenience store and what he thought was a laundry block. This offered him a decent view, if slightly impaired, of the permanent static homes and the access road leading to them. He watched as Tara parked her car on the other side of the building to him. She casually surveyed the area before heading to her right and out of his field of vision.

Hurriedly clambering out of his own car, Eric quickly covered the ground between his car and the convenience store using it to shield his approach. The shop was closed, the window shutters pulled down. Peering around the corner, he caught sight of Tara walking purposefully towards one of the caravans. Reaching it, she rapped her knuckles on the door. Seconds later it opened outward with Simon Cook holding it clear. He was evidently pleased to see her. As Tara stepped up, she leaned into him and they shared a brief but passionate welcome kiss. As she passed by him, his eyes followed her in and his hand drifted from the door frame to her lower back. With a last lingering glance around the exterior, Simon returned inside pulling the door closed.

"Well, well, well," Eric whispered to himself, glancing at the screen of his mobile as he brought up the short burst of pictures he'd just taken. Despite the distance, the quality was good. Zooming in and checking the first image, he saw the two of them were easily identifiable.

Selecting Janssen's mobile number, he pressed the handset to his ear whilst walking back to the car.

"I didn't have any joy with Tara at work, she's called in sick this week," he said, skipping the formalities so keen was he to share what he'd learned. "I managed to pick her up at her house though. She just left and I've followed her to the caravan site where Simon Cook lives."

"I sense there's more," Janssen said.

"By the look of how they greeted one another, they're closer than just good friends," Eric said, adjusting his mobile. "I'm sending you some pictures."

There was silence as Janssen placed him on hold and presumably viewed the attachments. Shortly afterwards, his voice came back on the call.

"I'm far from an expert when it comes to what women find appealing in a man but I'd suggest Simon is punching way above his weight with someone like Tara Byrons."

"I was thinking the same," Eric said. "It's a match that doesn't make any sense at all to me."

Eric reached his car. Casting his eye back towards the static caravans, he was pleased to be able to see Simon's caravan from where he stood. "At least, not from Tara's point of view. I can see the appeal for him." Suddenly struck by the potential to misconstrue the last comment, he sought to clarify. "I mean, you know. He doesn't have much going for him—"

"Don't worry, Eric. I'm thinking the same."

"What do you want me to do?"

"Stay with them for now. I'm on my way to pick up Tamara

from the hospital," Janssen said. "Sarah Caseley is classified as in a critical but stable condition. It's unlikely we'll get to speak with her any time soon. I'll fill Tamara in and we can go from there."

Eric said his goodbyes and hung up, putting the mobile down on the passenger seat. Taking the wallet from his back pocket because sitting on it was uncomfortable, he tossed it down alongside his phone and thrust his hands into his coat pockets. It was chilly today and feeling tired only made it seem colder still. Letting out a sigh of resentment for his lot, he considered that at this moment in time Tara and Simon were enjoying the afternoon far more than he was.

ERIC WOKE WITH A START. For a moment he'd lost his bearings and couldn't remember where he was. He was cold, his body stiff. The windows of the car were steamed up. A figure stood alongside the driver's door. Whoever it was rapped their knuckles on the window again. Eric's head was pounding. His entire body felt heavy. He must have been wrenched from deep sleep. Turning the key to the standby position to activate the electrics, he dropped the window. Simon Cook bent over, peering into the interior at him and shaking his hand vigorously at his side. His right hand was bandaged across the knuckles and banging on the car window appeared to have aggravated the injury.

"Is there something I can help you with?" Cook asked.

Eric shook his head, momentarily at a loss for words. It was dark outside. The overhead lights lit up the car park with an artificial orange glow. *How long had he been asleep?*

"You've been parked here for hours. This isn't a truck stop," Cook continued, inspecting the back of his hand. "This is a car park for a private business."

"I know... I know," Eric said, looking at the clock. It was gone six o'clock. "Hurt your hand?"

Simon Cook stared at him, his brow furrowing.

"I work here. Raked my knuckles on the linchpin hitching up a caravan to a truck." He glanced around the interior of the car. "What are you doing here?" His inspection of the interior paused as his eyes fell on the passenger seat.

"I was just… erm…" Eric mumbled.

"Are you a policeman?" Simon Cook said, surprised. His expression clouded.

Eric suddenly felt defensive. *How could he possibly know that?* They had never met. He followed Cook's gaze to the seat beside him, where he'd thrown his wallet. It lay open, his warrant card and constabulary crest visible for anyone to see. Silently cursing, he shook his head.

"What are you doing here? Are you following me?" Cook said. His tone was tinged with fear or anger, perhaps both, Eric couldn't tell.

"No, no. Not at all," Eric said, feeling a surge of panic from within. "Where's Tara?" He blurted out the words without thinking. Cook was taken aback.

"Tara… I… I don't know what… I…" he said, looking confused. Eric was stern, waiting for an answer. Cook shrugged apologetically. "I don't know. She went home, I think. Why, what do you want with her?"

Eric was in a mess. What mattered now was to locate her. Scooping up his mobile, he saw three unread text messages and several missed calls from both Janssen and the DCI. He was going to be in real trouble. Ignoring Cook's question, he turned the key in the ignition and started the car. Leaning forward and wiping the inside of the windscreen so he could see out of it, he then hurriedly fastened his seatbelt.

"Hey!" Cook said in protest as Eric put the car in gear. "Answer me, damn it! What do you want with Tara?"

Eric glanced at the man and away again, the urge to leave screaming at him internally. Flicking the switch, the window automatically rose as he moved off. Simon Cook was still audible, haranguing him as he sped away across the car park.

"Shit! Shit! Shit!" Eric barked at himself, looking in the rear-view mirror at the animated form of Simon Cook.

There was no way he would be able to explain this one away. Before calling in, he had to find Tara Byrons otherwise it would hit the fan. The return drive to Tara's address was stressful. Every car Eric came to was sworn at, every intersection and subsequent delay only contributed to his growing anxiety. He was relieved to find her Audi parked in the driveway when he pulled up in the street outside her house. Lights were on indoors and Eric breathed easier as he parked in a similar spot to when he was there earlier. This evening, the street was lined with parked cars and he was lucky to find space.

Picking up his mobile, he arranged his thoughts before calling the station. Reading the text messages first, his chest tightened as he saw the demands for him to call in alongside questions as to where he was. Aside from the missed calls, there was a voicemail notification from Tamara. Listening to Tamara's voice, she sounded annoyed.

"Eric, if you get this message before speaking with either Tom or myself, we want you to bring Tara Byrons in for interview."

There was a pause and he thought she was speaking to someone in the background, the conversation was muffled. Then her voice returned.

"Call me when you get this, Eric."

Unsure of which instruction to follow first. He got out, forced to wait for another car to pass before he could cross the road, he felt panic rising. He'd screwed up but if he could bring Tara in without any complication then it was salvageable. Seconds later, he was standing at her door. He pressed the doorbell button and waited, fiercely rubbing his hands together to warm them up. There was no answer, so he rang the bell again only this time for twice as long. Lowering himself onto his haunches, he lifted the letterbox flap but the view was blocked by the draught-excluding brushes. Growing concerned, he stood up and gave the bell three more short bursts before hammering his fist against the door. The front door to the adjoining property opened and a man's head poked out, looking around the corner directly at him. It was the same man he'd observed earlier putting out the rubbish.

"Back again?" he asked.

Eric was unsure what to say, merely nodding in reply.

"You're police, aren't you? I saw you here a couple of days ago talking to Tara."

"You have a good memory," Eric said, adding silently in his mind – *great hearing as well.*

"If you're expecting Tara, she's not in," the man said.

Eric frowned, stepping back and casting an eye over the front of the house. The downstairs was lit up, as were the landing and at least one of the upstairs bedrooms.

"She went out. I saw her leave."

"But her car's here," Eric protested.

"There's a rear gate from her garden. All of us on this side of the street have one. They open onto the bridleway running alongside the field at the back. That's Tara's preferred route for her morning run every day."

Eric found the man's knowledge of her routine creepy, albeit useful on this occasion.

"Is that what she was doing, going for a run?" he asked.

The man shrugged.

"How should I know? I'm just her neighbour."

"When was this?"

"About an hour ago, I should think."

Eric swore.

"Thank you," he said, turning and retreating from the front door. Taking out his mobile, he hesitated with his thumb hovering over the green call button. He was certain Janssen would tear strips off of him but he was more fearful of Tamara's reaction. Taking a deep breath, he pressed the button and waited. Moments later, Janssen answered.

"Eric. Where have you be—"

"Sir, I'm sorry," he said, interrupting as soon as he'd plucked up the courage. "I've really messed up. She's not here. Tara's gone."

CHAPTER THIRTY-THREE

TOM JANSSEN SLAMMED the receiver down drawing Tamara's attention.

"Damn it," he said, looking over to her as she approached. "Eric's only gone and lost Tara."

"How did that happen? Was she aware he was following her?"

Janssen shook his head.

"No idea. She's on foot, so can't have gone far. The next-door neighbour says she went out the back way but not dressed for a run."

"Nosy neighbours have their uses," Tamara said. "Where's she off to, do you think?"

Janssen rubbed at his temples, thinking hard. Both he and Tamara spent the late afternoon scouring the correspondence Gretta provided. Tara Byrons and Susan Cook were in contact repeatedly over the past three years, elevating Tara to a person of significant interest. The apparent relationship between her and Simon Cook was an unexpected angle they'd not seen coming. He struggled to comprehend how that worked. Simon could never be described as a catch.

"The letters allude to a past neither of them was prepared to write about," Janssen said. "At least, Tara wasn't. Maybe Susan did from her end but Tara only ever hinted at it."

"Okay," Tamara said, perching herself on the edge of the desk next to him. "Let's go back a bit. Susan disappears. We're unsure of whether she was running from something, or someone, but she seeks sanctuary with her biological mother."

"And for whatever reason," Janssen continued the narrative, "after nine years she concludes she has to come back in order to put something right. The fact she went to Wellesley leads us to think it's something that went on there, arguably involving other girls or members of staff. Perhaps both, who knows? Seemingly that takes us to Neil Baker, although I find it hard to believe Nicholas Levy wasn't involved—"

"Perhaps unaware would fit with Levy," Tamara suggested. "If he wasn't actively involved in the abuse, having found out he may well have sought to cover up what was going on after the fact."

"If he didn't know, and he was such a decent man as Abigail Thomas insists, why would he do that?" Janssen said, glancing up at her, tapping the end of his pen against his lower lip.

"If we can put aside the potential damage to his family name and reputation, the scandal would have undoubtedly forced Wellesley's closure," Tamara countered. "All the good work and positivity he could bring to those children's lives would have been lost. The same approach has arguably been seen in other widespread scandals. The historic abuses in the Catholic Church for example."

"It wasn't right in those circumstances either," Janssen shot back. "Baker was moved on. Who knows who else he's had access to in the last couple of decades. Giving them a free pass only emboldens abusers like him."

Tamara held her hands up.

"I agree. I'm not condoning it. I can just see how it came about."

"So what of Neil Baker?" Janssen said, rising from his seat

and crossing to examine Baker's entry on the information board. "Murdered and disguised as a suicide. The way it was done was too obvious. Amateurish. It was never going to pass us by."

"Strikes me as an idea made up on the fly," Tamara said. "A quick solution to the problem he'd become."

"Which was?" Janssen said without taking his eyes off the board, standing with hands on his hips. Tamara came alongside him.

"Our conversation with him... it must have rattled him somehow," she said, tapping an entry on the board next to his name. "He was prepared. I'm not saying he was necessarily expecting us specifically but the police, or a journalist maybe, one day. That's why he threw us Levy."

"Knowing he was unfit to face questioning or a trial?"

Tamara nodded.

"Accusations are thrown at Levy..." Janssen thought aloud. "If he has to testify then Baker confirms Levy's involvement. The man himself cannot be cross examined due to his medical condition, never facing trial because he's unable to understand the charges levelled against him."

"The case is made public and Levy is convicted in the eyes of the general public who want someone to blame," Tamara concluded. "Baker gets a bit of stick for not coming forward sooner but, and this is the important bit, he is only ever considered a witness rather than a perpetrator."

"So who killed him?" Janssen asked. "Another unidentified abuser we are unaware of? There were other staff we have been unable to track down."

"It's a possibility," Tamara agreed.

"But you're not convinced of that, are you?"

"No. I'm not. Baker was killed in a hurry. It wasn't given a great deal of forethought. Whether he was coerced into writing his suicide note or it was added as an afterthought, I don't know, but I do get the impression it was a rush job. If not, the killer would have thought it through more. Wiped the back of the shoes clean. Had him sign the note. Little details that can make or break the deception."

"But Baker felt comfortable enough to meet them at an isolated spot," Janssen argued. "Leans towards a co-conspirator for me."

"Co-conspirator, yes," Tamara said, turning to him and raising a finger pointedly. "But that doesn't necessarily mean a co-abuser."

"Okay. You've got me there. What are you thinking?"

"Something Sarah Caseley said to me the other day, you remember, when she was waiting outside the station for us?"

Janssen nodded.

"Something about how we shouldn't be surprised how the abused children living at Wellesley behaved," she said, her brow furrowing as she clearly struggled to recollect the exact words. "How they would do anything to get away... even running into the arms of anyone who would take them. At the time, I took it as a reference to the men outside seeking to exploit the girls, effectively running them as underage prostitutes in their social circles but now... maybe she meant something else entirely."

"You think she meant Neil Baker?" Janssen said.

Tamara nodded and he considered it. Stockholm Syndrome was a proven condition. The captive or the abused, which in this case was tantamount to the same thing, developed feelings for the abuser and were capable of forming strong emotional connections with them. Even seeking to defend or excuse their abusive behaviours.

"Stands to reason," Tamara said. "We're asking questions. He needed to ensure his past actions were going to be kept secret. Bonds like that become ingrained, almost habitual, but he will have needed to be sure."

"Looks like he got more than he bargained for," Janssen said. "Assuming you're right, and it's a strong theory, why does Baker get killed? The victim kills the abuser... why? They must also be fearful of retribution for their own behaviour."

"Complicity?" Tamara theorised. Janssen found that particular notion flimsy at best. His expression must have conveyed the thought and she conceded the point inclining her head to one side. "However, I'll bet every set of initials we found scratched into the door of *the hole* at Wellesley belong to Neil Baker's victims."

"And we know from the pathologist's initial examination of Neil Baker that he was dead well before Sarah Caseley was attacked, so that rules him out of that."

"Are we working on Baker's murderer and Susan's being one and the same person?" Janssen asked.

"We've no way to say either way at this point but it is conceivable," Tamara said, looking back to the information boards.

"Then does that also apply to Sarah Caseley?" Janssen said. "After all, if someone killed Susan Cook to stop her from revealing what happened at Wellesley, then they went on to kill Baker for the same reason... does it not follow that Sarah could also have been aware and they were seeking to silence her?"

"And failed," Tamara added.

Sarah Caseley was still in the hospital, a uniformed presence outside her room in the intensive care unit until such time as they could be sure of her safety.

"If we assume our killer is one of Baker's victims, who does that leave us with locally?" Janssen asked. "Sarah Caseley herself, Abigail Thomas and Tara Byrons."

"Tara's initials weren't recovered from the door though," Tamara said.

"She was well aware of what was going on," he said. "And Abigail Thomas' arthritis makes the idea of her overpowering Neil Baker, or Sarah Caseley for that matter, fanciful. You've met her. Is Tara physically capable?"

"Very fit, tall. Athletic," Tamara said, staring at Tara's picture on the board. "Successful in her university rowing team, judging by the memorabilia she has at her home. It's certainly possible.

262 J M DALGLIESH

So where is Tara heading tonight? She can't know Sarah Caseley is still alive, can she?"

"Even if she does, there's no way she could get close to her. Sarah's too well protected. What if she's trying to silence anyone who has knowledge of whatever she's trying to keep secret?"

"Following that logic, it would take her straight to Abigail, wouldn't it? Who else is there? We found Abigail's business card on Susan's body. Either Susan Cook was planning to speak with Abigail or had already done so," Tamara said.

"Yes, I get the feeling Abigail is holding back with us. She knows more than she's saying but she's not feeling threatened."

"I still don't see where Simon Cook fits into this scenario," Tamara said.

Janssen had to agree. There was always the possibility of a physical attraction. Simon Cook wasn't appealing financially nor did he give off any of the traits he would consider as attractive to women. But then again, other factors could drive them together. There were numerous psychological studies concluding that people who experienced certain types of upbringing were often subconsciously drawn to similar characters in their adult lives. Rather than seeking to replace what was missing from their childhood, the patterns of behaviour were so ingrained and habitual that they looked to repeat them. Scientific confirmation of why some men or women were attracted to people reminiscent of their parental figures.

Knowing Simon Cook's background as well as Tara's, was she attracted to his lack of emotional availability? It was possible that he was another target but somehow, he doubted it. Tara had been with Cook earlier that day. If she was going to act against him then she would already have done so.

"We should check in on Abigail," he said. "Maybe put some of this to her and see how she responds."

"Agreed," Tamara said, glancing at her watch. "We should also put Tara's description out. If anyone sees her, have her picked up."

"What about Eric?" he asked, remembering he'd hung up on him without offering instruction.

"Let him stew on it for a while," she said. "He made a mistake. Let's see what he does with it. I imagine he'll stay outside her house until we say otherwise. That's not a bad place for him to be. Call him back and tell him to be careful. If we're right, then Tara is dangerous as well as deeply unpredictable when it comes to how she'll respond when challenged."

THEY DROVE OUT TO ABIGAIL THOMAS' house in silence. For his part, Tom Janssen was running their theory over and over in his mind. Everything they considered was conceivable and yet he still couldn't find it within himself to wholeheartedly back it. Something was missing and the fact he couldn't pinpoint what troubled him was frustrating. Turning into Abigail's driveway, he saw a white van parked to the side of the house. On his previous visits he didn't remember seeing a vehicle but living this far out, Abigail needed transport. A van made sense with the added requirement of transporting her artworks. Several lights were on inside the house and the curtains remained open even though the sun had long since set. They pulled up in front of the house and he switched off the engine.

They both got out and approached the front door. Ringing the bell, they waited but there was no movement from inside. Janssen leaned over and peered through the front window into the living room. The lights were on here, as they were in the kitchen beyond. The fire was set but not lit. Remembering the struggles Abigail was having with her joints, he figured she wouldn't be present in the house if the fire wasn't lit.

"Let's try the studio," he said, inclining his head towards the side of the house. Tamara agreed and they made their way around to the rear.

Abigail's studio was illuminated with light emanating

through the door to the exterior and via the one window located three-quarters of the way down the western face. Being a former agricultural building, the window was small and the glass was clouded through age and dirt. A shape moved inside, a shadow passing across the window.

"At least she's home," Tamara said. They reached the entrance and she was about to announce their arrival with a knock on the door but hesitated as the sound of raised voices carried to them. She glanced at Janssen and he gestured for her to wait.

Moving closer, he saw the door was fractionally ajar. Remembering how it opened into a small anteroom, where Abigail kept coats, boots and clutter out of the way, he gestured for them to enter. Taking a deep breath, he carefully eased the door wider hoping not to give away their presence. The two of them managed to slip into the small room without drawing attention to themselves. Two distinct voices could be heard, one was Abigail's. The discussion between the two women was heated.

"You're a fool!" Abigail said. "How could you be *so rash*?"

"It wasn't rash. It was proactive."

He looked to Tamara for confirmation as to who the other voice belonged to. She silently mouthed *Tara*, in his direction. Where Abigail spoke with a degree of stress in her voice, Tara Byrons was calm and measured.

"You're far too passive, Abi. Always have been."

"Passive? Rather that than reckless."

"I did what needed to be done..." Tara said. "For all our sakes."

Janssen edged toward the door, looking to get a glimpse of the interior through the gap between hinge and door frame. He scuffed his heel on the uneven flag stones. That very moment coincided with a pause in the conversation and he feared he'd given them away. He held his breath, as did Tamara. The misstep went unnoticed and he edged closer to the point where he could see into the studio beyond.

The two women faced each other, a few feet apart. Tara looked as calm as she sounded whereas Abigail was tense, her arms folded defensively across her chest. The studio lighting was bright and where previously he had a sea view, via the curtain wall of glass at the gable end, tonight all that could be seen was the reflection of the interior. The studio was an island of light in the darkness enveloping it. The two women argued in what they thought was perfect isolation.

"And where do you think you've brought us?" Abigail asked, accusingly. "Do you think this is some kind of a masterstroke? You've just brought the whole sorry mess back to the present."

"Like you've put it all behind you," Tara scoffed.

"Yes, I have," Abigail replied. She sounded indignant.

"Really? Like it's not present in every piece of work you've ever painted," Tara said, rolling her arm in a sweeping gesture and indicating the works of art stacked all around them. "Every canvas is a snapshot of what makes you, Abi. Dark, bitter... the misery that sits at the centre of your heart is obvious. You're a sad, depressing bitch."

Abigail snorted with derision.

"At least I've been able to use it for something positive. What have you done with it? You're almost as bad as Sarah, hiding behind your fashion and fancy cars. You know, I'm not even sure who you are anymore... if I ever did."

"You'll see," Tara said, defiantly pointing a finger in Abigail's direction. "Sooz coming back would have brought all of this out again. She should have listened to me but she wouldn't. If she had then *none* of this would have been necessary."

"You're not half as clever as you think, T," Abigail said. "We could have convinced Sooz but you had to go off half-cocked as usual."

"*You weren't there*, remember? You flat out refused to come—"

"Why on earth would I want to go back there... why would any of us?"

"My point exactly! Sooz insisted. She wanted some morbid trip down memory lane. To stand in *that room* again, going on and on about how everything started there. I'm telling you, she'd lost the plot!"

"What about Sarah? Putting her in the hospital... what was that for?"

"Sarah?" Tara said, her show of bravado falling away. "What are you talking—"

There was an almighty crash. Both Tara and Abigail were startled, the latter emitting a scream in shock. Janssen sensed Tamara jump at the sound. His eyes captured the moment the metal patio chair smashed through the wall of glass, clattering to the stone floor of the studio interior amongst a shower of glass fragments. The central pane splintered and the glass which didn't initially follow the chair's trajectory hung in place for a brief moment before it, too, separated and began falling to the floor in pieces. A figure emerged from the darkness striding through the opening, his boots crunching with each step as he passed over the broken glass.

Simon Cook glared at each of the women in turn, his expression one of barely controlled rage. Within his hands was a double-barrelled shotgun, the stock wedged tightly against his side, the barrels trained on Tara. Instinctively, without hesitation, Janssen moved for the door. Feeling Tamara reach for his forearm, he brushed her off and advanced into the studio.

CHAPTER THIRTY-FOUR

THE APPEARANCE of Tom Janssen bursting through the door caught everyone by surprise, not least Simon Cook who, eyes wide, turned the gun on him. Janssen pulled up, extending his hands out before him in a non-threatening gesture.

"Easy does it, Simon," he said in as measured a tone as he could muster. "Let's not do anything rash, okay."

In the corner of his eye, he caught Tara glance at him and then Abigail, no doubt wondering how long he'd been present and listening to their conversation. Meanwhile, Cook's eyes danced between the three people in front of him. Both Abigail and Tara stood stock still and it was only Janssen who eased himself forward, coming to stand between the two women whilst maintaining his gaze on Cook. The barrels of the gun remained pointing at him.

In Janssen's mind, his presence changed Cook's plans. The rage initially exhibited was now replaced by uncertainty. Janssen assessed the man. His face was flushed, but well beyond that one might expect to generate from anger alone. He was sweating, his brow covered in a sheen reflecting the light from above and his hair was damp from perspiration. Cook edged closer. Janssen saw his pupils were dilated. The smell of alcohol carried to him on the wind which was now howling through the smashed window. What he was capable of would be harder to determine, his movements erratic and unpredictable when emboldened by alcohol.

"Simon," Janssen said, taking care to remain calm and reassuring in tone. "This isn't going to help. There's no need for this to escalate—"

"What the hell would you know about it?" Cook barked at him, his expression pained as he jabbed the shotgun towards him to emphasise his point.

"I know you're hurting," he said, unfazed by the outburst. "And you've been hurting for a long time."

"Simon, what are you doing?" Tara asked. Her intrusion angered Janssen. His attempt to de-escalate the situation required her to remain silent. Abigail's description of her was proving accurate. She was rash.

"Shut up!" Cook yelled.

"Yes, do be quiet, T," Abigail whispered. Cook shot her a dark look and Abigail bowed her head, averting herself from his gaze.

"Simon," Janssen said, trying to assert himself as the focus point. "This doesn't need to get any worse, no one else need be hurt. Everyone can walk away from this... if you just... lower the gun."

He gestured with a flat palm, slowly demonstrating the action.

"Like they did?" Cook said, inclining his head towards Tara and then Abigail. "They get to walk away, just like before. As if nothing happened."

"What do you mean?" Janssen asked.

"*Them,*" Cook stated, gesturing with the point of the barrels. "And Sarah... Susan. After what they did to that other girl."

"I don't understand," Janssen countered.

"He's lost his mind," Tara said, dismissing him.

"You... shut up!" Cook yelled again, taking another step

forward and pointing the shotgun towards her. "Don't lie to me, not again. That's what you are to me... *lies on top of lies*. Susan told me what you did. I didn't believe her. I should have." He took one hand from supporting the gun, furiously rubbing at his forehead. His eyes were wild and brimming with tears. "She was drunk and crying... it wasn't possible. Not for Susan... not my Susan. She would never be a part of something like that."

"What did they do, Simon?" Janssen asked, flitting his eyes between Cook and the women.

"He's stark raving mad, that's what he is," Tara said. This time, Simon Cook didn't rise to it, merely shifting his gaze onto her.

"Kirsty. That was her name."

"Kirsty Davies?" Janssen asked.

"Yeah. That was it," Cook said. "Susan told me... told me how you got her up that tree–"

"Shut up, you idiot!" Tara barked. For a moment it looked as if Simon would do just that. Her chastisement threw him. Janssen knew at that moment how much of an influence she held over him, realising what their relationship was all about after all. Power and control.

"And that's why the two of you came together," Janssen said, looking between them, eventually focussing on Tara. "You needed to know what was going on with Susan. You figured Simon would be closer to the case than you, so you inserted yourself into his life."

"Yeah," Cook said, nodding enthusiastically, "just like before. I wondered why you came back to me so soon after they found Susan. I couldn't understand. Just like I couldn't years ago when she went missing."

He fixed her with a stare. Janssen read it as affectionate, as if he was remembering a kindness done to him years previously.

"But that was a lie, too, wasn't it?" Cook said, the tenderness dissipating to be replaced by a growing hostility. "You had her dancing to your tune... you all did." He said the last to Abigail who still refused to meet his eye. Turning the gun on Tara, he continued, "I thought you cared about me... *really cared*... but you just wanted to know where she was. Where Susan had gone, so you could control her. So you could control everything. You would do anything for that."

"Used what few talents she was bestowed with," Abigail said.

"Fuck you, Abi!" Tara said quietly.

"Me... Simon, Neil... whoever," Abigail replied. "If it fits, wear it. That's you."

"Bitch," Tara muttered under her breath with an accompanying shake of the head.

It was as if the two of them didn't have a shotgun levelled at them from three feet away. Janssen found the exchange surreal under the circumstances.

"And what was it with Kirsty?" Janssen said, floating the question to the room and at no one in particular.

"It was a *bloody accident*," Tara said, dismissing the question only for Abigail to offer more.

"We were just kids, messing around," she said through gritted teeth. "Kirsty was... new... different to the rest of us."

"How so?" he asked her.

"Stronger, perhaps. I don't know but certainly less inclined to do as she was told. Not by Neil Baker, Nicholas... nor any of us, for that matter."

"She wanted the abuse to stop?" he asked.

Abigail nodded.

"Didn't you all?" he pressed. Abigail refused to meet his eye, but he noted a moment pass between her and Tara. "I'll take that as a no, then."

"Don't judge us, Inspector," Abigail said. "It wasn't abuse like you probably think. It's not like we were raped."

"If you were thirteen or fourteen, I'm afraid that's exactly how the law would see it."

"The law," Tara scoffed. "Most of us knew what we were

doing. We wanted the attention just as much as they wanted to offer it."

"You were children," Janssen said.

Tara shook her head, cutting a wry smile.

"Passed from pillar to post," she said. Abigail nodded her agreement. "No one gave a shit about us. Even when Kirsty was... died, no one came looking. Everything was glossed over and it was business as usual."

"Did you kill her: Kirsty?" he asked.

"No! Of course not," Tara said defiantly. "We had to teach her a lesson, that's all."

"To stop her from rocking the boat?"

"It was Neil's idea," Abigail said. "Get Kirsty to retract the allegations. If she wouldn't... then we would all have to leave. We'd be broken up and moved on. That's not what we wanted, what any of us wanted."

"Except for Kirsty, maybe?" he said. Again, Abigail looked away. Turning back to Tara, he asked, "And what was it about the tree?"

Tara shook her head. It was a weary action.

"We roughed her up, at Neil's behest, it's true. She ran from us and... like a pack of hunting dogs we gave chase."

"Looking back, it's like we were different people," Abigail said, picking up the narrative. "We were running, shouting... laughing even. If I could go back and speak to those girls then, I'd tell them to stop. To think about what they were doing... to realise."

Both women fell silent. Even Simon Cook appeared lost in the story as they waited for the conclusion.

"The tree?" Janssen pressed.

"She must have been tired... couldn't get away from us," Tara said. "She climbed the tree thinking she'd be safe and she was right, for a while."

"Then what?"

Neither woman spoke. They stared at the floor in an awkward silence.

"You threw rocks at her," Simon Cook said flatly. All eyes turned to him. "That's what Susan told me. You threw rocks and stones at her. She screamed at you to stop... begged... but you didn't. You kept on."

Janssen looked between the two women. All pretence at bravado or justification of what they did was gone. Both of them stared at the floor in shame.

"No. We didn't stop," Abigail said quietly, lifting her head and looking to Janssen. "And to this day, I don't understand why."

"We weren't trying to kill her," Tara said, the defiance returning in her tone. "It *was* an accident that she fell."

"Because you were pelting her with rocks," Janssen said.

"It was still an accident," Tara repeated.

"And she fell from the tree... into the water or was that afterwards?" he asked.

"That was Neil's idea," Abigail said. "When we realised... when we saw she was dead, we panicked. I mean, you can see that right? We were kids, feral and out of control but still kids. We ran back to Wellesley, thinking the worst. Tara spoke with Neil and... they came up with the idea of the suicide."

"It was Neil's idea. I had nothing to do with it," Tara said.

Her denial didn't surprise him at all. Whether she was being truthful or not, he couldn't know. Everything Tara Byrons had done thus far indicated her credibility was weak.

"It was your idea to kill Sooz, though," Abigail said. "And that was on you. I had nothing to do with it."

The accusation was stinging and poorly timed. Simon Cook snapped out of his reverie, his eyes narrowing as he lifted the gun and trained it on Tara. She took in a sharp intake of breath. Janssen sidestepped to his left, placing himself directly in between Tara and Cook, the gun now levelled at his chest. Cook remained as he was, looking beyond Janssen to Tara behind him.

"Why? Why did you have to kill her?" Cook asked, his eyes glazing over with emotion as he spoke. Internally, Janssen hoped Tara wouldn't respond. They had the answers, there was no more narrative to be heard. Nothing spoken now could take away from what they did. What Simon Cook would now choose to do with the knowledge, he couldn't know. They needed to avoid pushing any more of his buttons.

In the back of his mind, Tamara must have slipped out and called for assistance. That was his hope. He either had to talk Simon down or play this out long enough for the armed response unit to arrive. Even then, this situation was so volatile he had no idea how it would play out. One person, perhaps more, would end up dead and he wanted to avoid that if at all possible.

"*Why?*" Cook repeated, through gritted teeth.

"Because Sooz wouldn't listen to reason," Tara replied, clearly frustrated at his lack of understanding. "Nothing good would come from us telling the truth. No one cared then and no one would care now."

"Then why not speak about it?" Cook countered. "If no one cares, why not?"

"Because it would ruin us. All of us," Tara said, shooting a dark look towards Abigail. "And for what, to salve the conscience of a teenage tearaway? It's our sin and we have to live with it," she snapped.

"Except Sooz can't live with it, can she? Nor can Neil," Abigail said, regret in her tone.

"Great, Abi. What a time to get sentimental on me," Tara said, by way of belittling her.

Janssen angled his head to one side, seeking to draw Cook's attention away from Tara and onto him. He met his eye, maintaining the contact as he spoke.

"Simon, can you listen to me for a moment." Cook stared at him, unmoving. "I need you to think about this. Susan's gone. You know that. I'm here. I've heard every word that's been said.

Neither of them is going to walk away from this. Not from Kirsty, Neil Baker and definitely not from Susan. This can end now."

"She lied to me," Cook whispered.

"Yes, she did. Many times. But that's not important now. What's important is you… and your son. Think about Connor."

At mention of the teenager, Cook's expression shifted slightly but he remained fixated on Tara, the shotgun shaking in his trembling hands.

"How old is Connor? Fourteen. Fifteen," Janssen said. Cook didn't reply. "Not much older than his mum must have been when she went through all of this. Just imagine him, like her, living without parents and having to make his own way in the world at this age. What do you think about that?"

He chanced a step forward. The shaking in Cook's body appeared to be spreading. His expression was anguished, his eyes welling with tears.

"Think about Connor, Simon. Think about your son and how much he needs you. You're the one constant in his life. The one person who will always be there for him…"

He reached out slowly with a flat hand, extending it towards the barrel of the gun. He watched as Simon Cook's eyes followed the advance of the hand. The barrel wobbled more violently the closer he came to it. Janssen's hand, in comparison, was steady belying the surge of adrenalin coursing through him.

"You can't do this to Connor," he said softly, holding his breath as he curled his fingers gently around the barrel. Cook tensed. *Had he gone too far?*

Janssen stopped, resisting the urge to press home his position, not knowing whether the hesitation would be the death of him. Cook's gaze carried upwards, meeting his eye. There was a brief flicker of understanding between the two men and Janssen saw his shoulders drop. Stepping forward, he lifted the barrel away from his chest and up towards the vaulted ceiling. Cook's grip on the weapon relaxed and Janssen relieved him of it, stepping away with the shotgun in hand and drawing a relieved breath.

Simon Cook broke down, weeping openly. Throwing his hands up against his face he sank to the floor, the tears turning to sobs as the pent-up emotion tore free. The sense of relief within the studio was palpable. The tension released from both Abigail and Tara was clear to see. Abigail sought out a nearby stool, bracing herself against a work bench as she lowered herself onto it. Tara sank back against the wall, casting her eyes to the ceiling and swearing softly under her breath with relief.

"Is she okay?" Cook said quietly, looking up at Janssen. "Sarah… is she okay?"

"We don't know yet," he replied flatly, inspecting the weapon in his hands.

"I hurt her, didn't I? I didn't mean to… I just wanted the truth."

"And did she tell you?"

"She told me it was Baker," Cook said slowly, clearly despondent. "It wasn't until that detective told me he was following Tara… then I realised she was lying to me. So was Sarah."

Janssen followed his eye towards Tara who looked away, taking a deep breath as Tamara appeared from the anteroom behind her. Tara didn't protest as Tamara turned her to face the wall, pulling her arms behind her back. Placing her in handcuffs, she then forcefully pushed her against the wall. The action was done more forcefully than Janssen felt necessary.

Once Tara was secure, Tamara turned her around again easing her to the floor with her back against the wall. Coming to stand before Janssen, she glared at him but said nothing. He was surprised by her attitude. Examining the shotgun, he found there was no manual safety on this particular model. Ensuring the muzzles were pointed towards the floor, he broke the barrel. Neither chamber was primed with a cartridge. The gun was empty.

He blew out his cheeks, angling the weapon so that Tamara could see. She glanced at it. Leaning into him, she spoke in a low voice so that only he could hear.

"Looked deadly enough when I saw it pointed at you," she said aggressively. "I don't know what's going on with you at the moment, Tom, but *don't you dare* do anything so cavalier again, do you understand? Get yourself together."

Whether the question was meant as rhetorical or not, he didn't know. In any event, she didn't wait for a response. Her gaze lingered on him for a second while she turned away as the sound of approaching sirens came to ear. He watched her back as she left the studio. A flash of anger passed through him only to be immediately replaced by a sense of guilt. He didn't know where it came from. His decision to intervene as he had was instinctive, not conscious.

For some reason, he couldn't fathom why, images of both Alice and Samantha came to mind. Within moments, uniformed police officers flooded the studio under Tamara's guidance. Abigail was arrested, as was Simon Cook. Neither of them offered any resistance. With confidence that the new arrivals had the scene under control, Janssen walked to the end of the room and stepped out through the shattered window, taking care not to catch himself on any remaining shards. The wind coming in off the sea was strong and a break in the rolling clouds cast the coastline in a passing silvery light.

Taking out his mobile, he thought about what he was going to say. He'd been putting this off for days, using the case as a justification for having done so. Tamara was right. This had become all consuming, confusing… an unwelcome distraction from what he should have been concentrating on. Would this have still played out as it had if he'd been more focussed? One way or another, he had to resolve it. Pressing the handset to his ear, he turned away from the wind to ensure his voice would be heard.

"Hello."

"Hi. It's me," he said softly. "I'm sorry I haven't called but... listen, I've been thinking a lot about what you said. Can we talk? Not over the phone, at my place?"

"When?"

He looked back into the studio. Only officers in high-visibility jackets were in view. Flashing blue-lights pulsed beyond the house, illuminating the trees bordering the property.

"Tonight."

CHAPTER THIRTY-FIVE

THERE WAS something about the short time following a highly intense incident that made Tom Janssen cast a light upon himself. In the past, he'd seen others react in one way or another. Some would take time for themselves, stepping away from colleagues and family alike. He often suspected they were hitting the bottle in private. Others would congregate in a pub somewhere, settling nerves and residual anxiety by drinking together.

In the past, he may well have joined in with this. It was, after all, the done thing. Certainly by the old guard. Not by him. Not anymore. The general impression people had of him was his ability to cope, to take events in his stride. To be reliable, dependable. The reputation was reasonable and one he saw no need to challenge. He was never one to make a fuss or openly share his feelings, no matter the circumstance. In retrospect, what he was guilty of was his willingness to hide after the event. Not in his professional life but certainly in his private one. It wasn't healthy and it was a characteristic he'd recognised in himself over the years, knew he needed to work on, but always ducked out. In his mind he was powerless to affect it. In reality, it was a choice.

That was how he ended up back home, in Norfolk. Samantha and he wanted different things from their marriage. He remained unaware of this until the moment he found her in bed with one of his closest friends and colleagues. The shock, pain and humiliation were too much to bear and so he withdrew. Now, Samantha was back in his life. If he was honest, she'd never left him. Her presence was always there in the background, watching him from afar. Despite the hurt, all of the pain, the feelings remained. If anything, they only intensified. Do you cease to love someone because they hurt you or does the rejection only reinforce those ties? After all, to pledge a future to someone was not an undertaking he took lightly. It was for life. That was the commitment, the expectation.

And yet, here he was doubting those choices. For the better part of the last two years he'd moved forward as if that commitment was no longer viable, considering the intensity of those feelings as echoes of what he thought he'd lost rather than what he needed. When Samantha cast her eye around his home, this boat, she told him this wasn't for him. Being in Norfolk wasn't for him either. She was right in that he'd left here and headed to London because that was where he wanted to be. That was what he thought he needed. Sam was wrong. They both were.

Footsteps up on deck announced her arrival. Janssen felt his chest tighten in a way it hadn't when he stepped in front of what he thought was a loaded shotgun, which struck him as peculiar. She knocked on the door and he called up inviting her down. Descending the steps, he caught sight of her and took a deep breath.

Alice smiled. It was forced. She was nervous. As was he.

"Hey," she said, hovering in the middle of the galley, hands in her coat pockets.

"How have you been?" he asked. The question sounded hollow and Alice gave a cursory shrug, belying her feelings. "Can I get you something? A glass of wine or tea?"

She shook her head.

"Saffy is with Mum," she said, glancing around the living space at nothing in particular. "I'll need to pick her up in a little while but... you sounded..." The words tailed off as her gaze came back to him. "Like it was important. Are you okay?" she asked, her eyes narrowing.

"Yeah, I'm well," he said, brushing aside the question.

They were dancing around each other. The last time she was here he had practised the words, planned the evening like he would an operation. It all went horribly wrong, but he had a plan. On this occasion, there was no polish. It just had to be said.

"Listen... the other night," he said, wincing at the memory. "You shouldn't have found out that way. I kept things from you and—"

"Tom," she said, interrupting him with the gesture of a raised hand, "you don't need to explain. I mean, you do... obviously, but not like this. When you're ready to talk about it, I'll be here to listen but it has to be when you're ready. Not because you feel you owe me."

"I owe you an explanation," he protested. "And at the very least a damn good apology. I screwed up... massively."

She laughed.

"That's putting it mildly. Yes, you did," she said, the smile fading. "Asking someone to marry you when you're already married... and," she inclined her head to one side, "your current wife arrives as you do it. It's certainly a proposal that will live long in the memory."

It was his turn to laugh but in a gallows sense of dark humour.

"Definitely memorable," he agreed.

Alice's expression turned melancholy as she sought the right words.

"We all have baggage, Tom. There are things we hide from loved ones... even from ourselves. What I need to know is where you see us heading. In the light of current events," she said with a flick of the eyebrows, "are we heading anywhere?"

"Samantha," he began, looking into her eyes to gauge the reaction at the mention of his wife, "told me that all of this..." he made a sweeping gesture around the boat, "...wasn't me. Not the boat, not living back here in Norfolk... you and Saffy. She thinks I belong in London. That was why I headed there, why I married her."

"Is she right?" Alice asked, seemingly fearful of the answer.

"No. It suited her, us being there. It suited our lifestyle. But that was all her, not me," he said. Alice took a breath and she seemed to rise in stature, her shoulders pressing back as he said the words. "This is where I belong. *This is me.*"

He moved towards her, pleased to see she didn't back away from him. Reaching into his pocket, he took out the ring box. Meeting her eye, he held it in the palm of one hand and went to open it with the other but she reached out quickly and smothered the box with her hand, stopping him from doing so.

"Believe me when I say this would go down as the second worst proposal in history, Tom. I do hope this isn't how you resolve every difficult moment in your personal life?"

He smiled, feeling a mixture of nervousness and embarrassment.

"I'm not going to marry you, Tom Janssen," she said, the words stinging him as soon as they left her mouth. She cut a half-smile, holding her eyes on his. "But... I also don't want you to take the ring back for a refund. Perhaps you should hold onto it for a while."

He looked at her hand, clasped on top of his. She tightened her grip, pressing down on his hand affectionately.

"I can do that," he all but whispered.

Alice's smile broadened and she lifted herself onto tiptoes, still holding her hands in his, and kissed him on the lips. He didn't respond, somehow understanding that he wasn't meant to. She withdrew, patting the back of his hand as she did so.

"I need to get back to Saffy," Alice said softly, retreating through the galley towards the steps to the deck above. Pausing as she mounted the first tread, she looked in his direction. "I mean it, Tom. Only when you're ready."

He nodded and she continued on. Once she disappeared from view, he let out a deep sigh and glanced at the box in his hand. What on earth made him think this was a good idea? His thoughts turned to Samantha, picturing her as she got into the taxi outside her hotel. Despite everything, he owed her an explanation too. She accepted his decision without argument. A first for her but then again, he'd steeled himself for the conversation. Something in his expression made her realise he meant what he said. They were over and it was best for the both of them that it was. Even if it didn't necessarily appear that way right now. They could easily have lost another decade before that particular realisation struck home.

Opening the nearest drawer, he placed the box inside and pushed it to. His mobile beeped and he saw it was a text message from Tamara.

JOIN ME FOR A DRINK?

HE CALLED her back and she answered immediately. By the sound of it, she was already in her new-found favourite haunt with shouts and laughter audible in the background.

"I thought you were annoyed with me?" he said.

"Oh, I am. You're an infuriating man at the best of times, Tom. Are you coming?" she asked, raising her voice to be heard.

"I only drink on special occasions, remember," he advised her. "But I'll happily buy you one and sit there watching you drink it."

"Perfect date," she replied. "You know where to find me?"

"I do," Janssen said, hanging up. Casting an eye towards the drawer, the ring box was still visible. He reached for the drawer handle, hesitating at the last moment before pushing it fully closed. "When I'm ready," he told himself, pulling on his coat and collecting his keys before heading out.

TAMARA BROUGHT the car to a stop and switched off the engine. Janssen got out and opened the rear passenger door, offering Gretta his hand in assistance. She gratefully accepted and the two of them set off up the path to the front door. Tamara remained where she was. Looking through the bay window into the sitting room as they passed, he glanced inside. There were two occupants, a woman who noted their approach with a smile and a gentle wave, easing herself from her chair and heading out of the room to meet them, and another, a teenage boy. Gretta's gaze lingered on the boy. All of a sudden she seemed nervous, more so than she'd been since they picked her up from her hotel. She caught him watching her, her expression apologetic.

"I really don't know what I am to do here," she said.

He doubted that. Gretta was an intelligent woman. For the last thirty years, her life had been steeped in secrecy and dominated by a sense of shame she'd yet to come to terms with. It would take time to overcome. Forging a meaningful bond with a perfect stranger, even one with a strong blood tie, perhaps longer still. Awkward conversations lay ahead. That prospect would be enough to unsettle anyone.

"You told me you regret not being there for your daughter," he said, indicating towards Connor who sat with his back to the window, unaware of their presence.

"More than you could possibly know, Inspector."

"You have the opportunity to be there for her son."

Gretta met his eye. "Susan never told me she had a child. Probably thought I'd push to see him."

"Now's your chance."

"And what would you have me say to him?"

There was no right answer. No script to follow that would smooth the process. He tilted his head to one side.

"The boy's lost his mother... for the second time. Whatever happens in the coming months, he's also lost his father for the foreseeable future. He's got no one else. *Only you*. Be there for him."

The sound of a key turning came to them, followed by the door opening. A kindly lady greeted them with a warm smile.

"Gretta?" she said. "My name is Marjorie. Welcome. Please do come in."

Marjorie Esher was the foster parent who had taken Connor in when Simon Cook was arrested the previous night. Janssen smiled as Gretta was ushered in. She offered him a nervous smile, one borne from gratitude he believed. He didn't follow, merely acknowledged Marjorie with a brief smile of his own as he left Gretta in her company. She was far better placed to handle it from this point. Turning away as the door closed, he walked back down the path. Tamara was waiting for him beside the car, leaning her back against it and talking on her mobile phone. She hung up as he reached her, returning the mobile to her pocket.

"What do you reckon?"

He glanced back at the house. He could see three figures now standing in the sitting room. Turning back to Tamara, he bit his lower lip with his teeth.

"They've got some tough times ahead but," he said, pausing briefly to articulate his thoughts, "they have one another. A bond forged in adversity such as this can be very powerful. Any word on Simon Cook?"

"I just heard. He's been held over until trial. What with the seriousness of the assault on Sarah Caseley, and his chequered record, he was never likely to get bail."

"And Sarah?"

"Better news," Tamara said. "She's off the critical list. Looks like she'll pull through. That's good news for Simon. It'll mean the difference between a few years and a life sentence. According to Eric, James Caseley is back to his overbearing best."

Janssen cut a wry smile.

"Let's see how long that lasts when the circumstances surrounding Kirsty Davies' death are reopened."

"Speaking of which," Tamara said. "We have a meeting with the CPS on that very subject this afternoon."

"So soon?"

"Yes. I think the Chief Constable is keen for us to get to the bottom of all this sooner rather than later. An historic child abuse scandal is not something that the top brass wants on their doorstep."

"Well that's going to depend on what Abigail and Tara are willing to offer, isn't it?" he said. "Not to mention Sarah when she recovers. And they're all going to have questions to answer regarding Kirsty's death. Judging from what was said yesterday between Abi and Tara, the finger pointing is going to get messy."

"True enough," Tamara said. "Neil Baker is dead and we've no idea whether Nicholas Levy was a party to the abuse or its cover up. His medical condition will see he never enters a courtroom either way. Baker was right about that. I'm just pleased it's the Crown Prosecution Service who will need to figure out who gets charged with what. It's all such a mess."

Janssen laughed. She looked to him with an inquisitive expression.

"And here we were thinking a coastal assignment would be a peaceful one."

"There are bad people everywhere, Tom. At least the sun shines here more than most. Everything okay with you?"

The question was tentative and he found her gauging his reaction intently. An image of Alice came to mind and he smiled.

"Yes. I'm sure everything is going to turn out just fine."

Tamara's gaze lingered on him for a moment, searching his expression for any hidden meaning. Then, she smiled.

"Come on. Let's get back to the station. Paperwork awaits."

Turn the page for a preview of the next book in the series;
Tell No Tales
Hidden Norfolk - Book 4

FREE BOOK GIVEAWAY

Visit the author's website at **www.jmdalgliesh.com** and sign up to the VIP Club and be first to receive news and previews of forthcoming works.

Here you can download a FREE eBook novella exclusive to club members;

Life & Death - A Hidden Norfolk novella

Never miss a new release.

No spam, ever, guaranteed. You can unsubscribe at any time.

Enjoy this book? You could make a real difference.

Because reviews are critical to the success of an author's career, if you have enjoyed this novel, please do me a massive favour by entering one onto Amazon.

———

Type the following link into your internet search bar to go to the Amazon page and leave a review;

http://mybook.to/Kill_Our_Sins

———

If you prefer not to follow the link please visit the Amazon sales page where you purchased the title in order to leave a review.

Reviews increase visibility. Your help in leaving one would make a massive difference to this author.
Thank you for taking the time to read my work.

TELL NO TALES PREVIEW
HIDDEN NORFOLK - BOOK 4

THIS TOWN WAS SO different to what she'd thought it would be when it was first spoken of. On the coast, with a beach running as far as the eye could see and bathed in sunshine… most of the time, at any rate, it was just like home. But it wasn't home and now it never could be. The beach was predominantly made up of stone and shingle and while the skies were powder blue and the sun shone, the warmth upon her skin was negligible. Even the wind coming in off the sea, more of a gentle breeze today, was bitter and cold rather than warm and inviting as was her experience back home.

The cold cut to her core and she shivered. Drawing her coat ever more tightly around her she hunkered into it, casting a glance up the street. A few people were visible, milling about around the greengrocer and getting ahead with their plans for the day. They paid her no heed as she sat on the bench in silence. Her coat was thick, heavy, but still she felt the chill. Apparently, it was expected at this time of year albeit a little on the cold side. The winter seems to last so long here, feeling as if it would never end. A song was playing through the radio inside the Butcher's nearby. She'd heard it many times recently, performed by two brothers who sang about losing the feeling of love. It was popular and struck a nerve with her.

Just a short while ago there seemed to be immense hope for the future, such promise of better days to come.

A fresh start.

But that was then. For a brief moment she contemplated how her life had changed in such a short period. How it came to pass was clear. However, what the future would hold, she didn't know and dared not think about. The low rumble of an approaching bus rounding the corner came to ear and a quick glance at the town clock saw it was right on time, as she was told it would be. Standing up, she reached down and looped her fingers around the handle of the weathered, brown leather suitcase at her feet containing all that she owned in the world.

The bus came to a stop alongside her, the noise from the engine growling as the door flipped open. She cast a glance to either side of her up and down the street before hefting the suitcase onto the bus and clambering aboard. The case was small but so was she, slight and reserved. Several of the passengers eyed her as she took her seat but no one spoke. Placing the case at her feet, she slid across to sit beside the window. The bus pulled away from the kerbside, jolting her backwards in her seat.

The conductor came to her, bracing himself against the seat in front as the bus lurched forward, and she purchased her ticket. His gaze lingered on her, longer than she felt necessary, as he handed over the slip of coloured paper and she averted her eyes from his. For a moment she thought he knew. *They all knew.* But he walked away without a word. The bus took the next turn and the sea came into view. The white caps of the breakers stood out in the bright sunshine, the light shimmering on the water. It was magical, bringing forth memories from her childhood just a few short years ago.

This place wasn't magical.

She felt her eyes beginning to water and she steeled herself, fighting back against the tide of emotion. This was the way it had to be. There was no other choice, that was clear. A lady, sitting across the aisle caught her eye. She was elderly with a kindly face. She smiled and it was returned. Rummaging through her handbag, the passenger produced a handkerchief and offered it across the aisle.

"Don't worry. It's clean," she said.

Accepting the cotton square with a brief smile and a nod, she then recoiled and looked away, fearful of drawing attention to herself. Wiping her eyes, she made to return the fabric but the lady was already out of her seat and moving to the door as the bus arrived at the next stop.

Soon enough, they were on the move again and the town was rapidly disappearing from view behind them. She felt a flutter of fear in her chest and reached into her coat pocket, her fingers curling around the tight bundle of notes within.

Where she went from here would be God's will... if not His judgement.

<hr />

Tell No Tales
Hidden Norfolk - Book 4

<hr />

ALSO BY J M DALGLIESH

The Hidden Norfolk Series

One Lost Soul

Bury Your Past

Kill Our Sins

Tell No Tales

Hear No Evil

Life and Death*

*FREE eBook - A Hidden Norfolk novella - visit jmdalgliesh.com

---

The Dark Yorkshire Series

Divided House

Blacklight

The Dogs in the Street

Blood Money

Fear the Past

The Sixth Precept

Box Sets

Dark Yorkshire Books 1-3

Dark Yorkshire Books 4-6

Audiobooks

The entire Dark Yorkshire series is available in audio format, read by the award-winning Greg Patmore.

Divided House

Blacklight

The Dogs in the street

Blood Money

Fear the Past

The Sixth Precept

Audiobook Box Sets

Dark Yorkshire Books 1-3

Dark Yorkshire Books 4-6

*Hidden Norfolk audiobooks arriving 2020